ASSASSIN IN MY BED

GABRIOLA, BC CANADA V0R 1X4

Copyright © 2022, H.B. Dumont.
All rights reserved.

WITHOUT LIMITING THE RIGHTS UNDER copyright reserved above, no part of this publication may be reproduced, stored in or introduced into a retrieval system, or transmitted, in any form or by any means (electronic, mechanical, photocopying, recording or otherwise), without the prior written permission of both the copyright owner and the publisher of this book.

ASSASSIN IN MY BED
ISBN 978-1-990335-05-1 (PAPERBACK)
ISBN 978-1-990335-06-8 (CASEBOUND)
ISBN 978-1-990335-07-5 (EBOOK)

PRINTED ON ACID-FREE PAPER THAT includes no fibre from endangered forests. Agio Publishing House is a socially and environmentally responsible company, measuring success on a triple-bottom-line basis.

10 9 8 7 6 5 4 3 2 1

DEDICATED TO JUDY

Noir Intelligence Series

The Black Hat
Spine of the Antiquarian
Kiss of the Death Adder
Assassin in My Bed

ASSASSIN IN MY BED

A Noir Intelligence Novel

H.B. Dumont

CHAPTER 1

Alicia Dupuis looked out of the kitchen window of her Victoria home as she pressed the remote control to start the SUV parked in her driveway. The defroster would chase away the early morning Pacific Ocean mist that had condensed on the windshield overnight. The radiating heat from the seat would replace the ambient chill.

An explosion rocked the house. Alicia dove to the floor in disciplined reaction. Shards of glass from shattered panes and arrowed splinters of wood from the window frames shot through the kitchen piercing everything along their trajectory. The explosion hurled her back into the perilous life she had cast off if only fleetingly and to a mirage of not so distant recollections. Memories and emotions could not be easily dismissed with the nonchalant flick of a wrist.

Alicia was acutely aware that in the duplicitous currency of security and intelligence, nothing exists without context. More importantly, intelligence and context were askew on the periphery of espionage where there were truths, partial truths and make-believe truths. Such were the defining characteristics of the arcane game with its intoxicating charm and deceptive addiction.

"Marc, Sophia, Camilla," she yelled. There was no answer. She dashed to her bedroom. Marc was not there. She pushed open the bedroom doors looking for Camilla and Sophia. They were also absent. Rightly or wrongly, she assumed that her stepdaughters were with their father, somewhere. She had been away all of yesterday and came home late last night. Not wanting to disturb anyone, she had slept in the spare room.

Wary of any possible view from outside, she cautiously returned to the kitchen where she located her cellphone amidst the choking debris. She gingerly crouch-crawled through the minefield of jagged rubble to the staircase and hurried down to the basement. She tore cardboard boxes full of family memorabilia away from a wall and opened a miniature door that exposed an underground passage to the garden shed hidden in a hedgerow at the back of the old Pemberton Estate. Her father had had the clandestine tunnel built "in case of a rainy day," he had explained with a cautioning nod that Alicia had affirmed. A career with MI6, British Secret Intelligence Service, had taught him to always anticipate what your opponent would be thinking tomorrow and not what they had been contemplating yesterday. A Berlin Wall-esque tunnel would provide an escape route from the ghosts of yesterday's missions to tomorrow's strategic contingencies, which had become today's stark reality for Alicia.

She had maneuvered the length of the passageway before, but never with such determination and haste to reach the hatch which opened beneath the work bench in the garden shed cluttered with its camouflage of rusty tools. She left through the back door of the shed and crept along the edge of the English Laurel hedgerow until she reached the adjacent street. A second explosion broke the neighbourhood silence but in the opposite direction from which she was now sprinting.

Once on the sidewalk, she strode at a quick yet disciplined pace so as not to attract undue attention. She stopped and gaped at what had been her friend's house, now consumed in a cloud of dust and rubble still settling from the second explosion. All the while, the wail of sirens of emergency vehicles became louder as they converged on the scenes of utter mayhem and destruction.

"What happened?" Alicia shouted at a man crouched behind a tree sheltering his whimpering dog.

"A gas explosion I suspect," he yelled back.

It can't be, she reflected in an ever-heightening state of vigilance. *There was no gas hooked up to her friend's house. Not only that but the main gas line ran parallel to the sidewalk on the opposite side of the street.*

Alicia retraced her steps to the garden shed in her back yard. A second group of emergency vehicles could be heard approaching as flames mixed with acrid black smoke from her burning SUV shot above the roofline of what had been the kitchen in her house but was now just a structure in shambles. She retrieved a metal box hidden behind a false wall in the shed. She emptied the contents into a satchel with methodical haste: credit cards, Canadian, American and European Union currency, a Canadian and European Union passport, the latter with French diplomatic designation, other essential identification papers, and a cellphone with a European Union SIM card and continental charging cable. All were linked to that life she had temporarily left behind barely two years earlier. As the emergency vehicles arrived, she stealthily departed as she had entered through the back door of the garden shed, then fled into the shadow of the dishevelled hedgerow in the direction of a safehouse.

So much can be suppressed in the silence of a safehouse, a sanctuary, an echo of peace and quiet, camouflaged in the anonymity of suburbia. It had become a footnote to her previous life, forever linked by the vow of silence taken among colleagues.

She sat quietly for a moment staring out of the window at a solitary autumn leaf as it surrendered its grasp on a barren branch and drifted silently to the ground to join others blanketing the lawn. *Was my life becoming a recollection of forgotten photographs from seasons past like those black and white pictures my mother had tucked away in old shoe boxes carefully packed in the storage bins of memorabilia in her now abandoned basement?* she wondered. A scar of doubt lingered but her momentary reminiscence vanished in the stark reality of the current circumstances in which she found herself.

From the secure wired phone in the safehouse that could not be electronically traced to her, she called her travel agent. Together they reserved a flight from Victoria to Vancouver to depart in less than four hours. That would barely give her enough time to minimally recharge the cellphone with the European Union SIM card that she had hurriedly stashed in her satchel. She reassessed her strategy. She adjusted her makeup to better reflect the photo on her Canadian passport. Using her Canadian cellphone, she attempted to text and email her husband and the children, but the network was not responding. She called her service provider from the secure wired phone.

"Neither my email nor text messaging seem to be working on my cellphone," she explained.

"What is your account number?"

"I'm not sure. I'm mobile at the moment using another phone. Can I just give you my name and cell number?"

Alicia provided the additional security information requested.

"You are on a family plan that was cancelled effective midnight yesterday."

"Cancelled? By whom?" she retorted, astonished by the promptness of the exacting reply of the service provider.

"Marc Bolibar. He is the other name on the account."

"Can you reactivate just my cellphone?"

"Yes. It will take a while. If you have backed up your data to the Cloud, you will be able to download it but that will take longer."

Using the same wired phone, she then tried to call the friend whose house had been damaged by the second explosion. It rang but there was no answer.

CHAPTER 2

Her brief connecting flight from Victoria to Vancouver was uneventful, not that she expected otherwise. But she had also not expected a blast that destroyed her SUV to demolish her kitchen. Her cellphone boogied across the side table in the Air Canada Maple Leaf Lounge at the Vancouver International Airport from the vibration of an incoming email. The data download from the Cloud had completed. Her domestic cellphone was once again operational. She did not recognize the email address but she did recognize the subject line text which read 2CV. Her heart jumped. Her chest tightened. Her breathing quickened. The only person to use 2CV was Sophia, her youngest stepdaughter with whom she had bonded more closely than her older sister. It was their innocuous secret code solely for use in times of imminent threat.

"Do I know you?" Alicia replied to the email.

"No. But you may know a young girl who asked to use my cell to send a brief email to her mother from the Vancouver International Airport. Are you her mother?"

"Yes, I am her mother. When was this?" Alicia asked, relieved by the contact but increasingly worried by the brevity of the e-communication. The girls would not have the wherewithal to travel alone. Someone would be with them, more than likely their biological father, her husband, Marc Bolibar.

"About four hours ago. She followed me into the ladies' washroom. She explained that her cellphone had crashed. She seemed anxious but I figured that was normal with young girls when they became inexplicably separated from their social networks. She said she was with her older sister. It didn't seem too strange so I lent her mine. She calmed down a bit after that."

"Thank you for being so kind," Alicia replied. She ended the email and again tried to call the friend whose house had also been blown up. As before, there was no answer. Not knowing was worrying. There could only be two good reasons for being incommunicado. First, she was dead. Second, she was alive but unable to communicate because she was disabled as a result of injury. Or perhaps a third explanation. She had been taken hostage. In order of probability, first, she was dead; second, disabled; third, held against her will. Given her status as a retired MI6 employee, like Alicia's father and herself, the latter was a distinct possibility – remote but feasible.

Alicia reflected on her own circumstances. Why had she been a target for assassination? Where was Marc? He wasn't in the house. There was a strong probability his status would mirror the girls'. It just didn't add up. She didn't want to consider the alternative, that Marc was solely responsible for the attempt on her life. Could he have been a co-conspirator?

Even after a long career with MI6, her father had not been able to fully retire and walk away from the long-reaching tentacles of the arcane world. She was her father's daughter with far less time in the shadow of the trenches. She wasn't naïve. She knew she could not fully retire either. John Le Carré's fictional character, George Smiley, had been threatened with the loss of pension and benefits if he did not testify about errant details of a prior incident in which he had been involved. These circumstances seemed different, though. She was not being asked to account for dangling details associated with a previous case. Yet, she was once again in the crosshairs. Someone wanted her dead for whatever reason she did not know or for another contrived reason also unknown to her at this time.

Her mind drifted back to the image of her SUV exploding and her instantaneous reaction. Nowhere in her response was calling

9-1-1 an option. She had more confidence in the Keystone Cops than in the local constabulary. Spending time providing a statement and attempting to explain why she had become a target for assassination was not a survival technique. Ironically, her comfort zone was back in the fray among experienced colleagues. There she would be provided with the tools of the tradecraft to help level the playing field.

Out of habit, Alicia found herself assessing the haunted looks of others in the departure lounge lost in their own worlds, giving nothing away. Some were hiding behind newspapers and raised laptop monitors, their heads popping up, eyes calculating, then clandestinely emerging in possible parallel surveillance as either friend or foe. Still other expressions were like empty fireplaces yawning and veiling the thoughts they wished to keep hidden.

A man in his forties, yet seemingly much older because he had no one to impress, stared at other women but not at his wife who sat passively opposite him. A female in her mid-twenties had spent considerable time in front of her mirror applying mascara and foundation to complement her self-administered hair colour in a futile effort to look natural. This female appeared like an orphan. A younger girl sat beside her, head down, timidly attempting to cover up self-administered faint parallel lines on her teenage wrists. Bruising on her upper arms cried out for protection from those who did not see or did not wish to look. Both females were masking defiance and the scars of too many failed relationships. Were others experiencing a similar sense of hollowness that allowed them to cast doubt, at this moment?

The business class pre-boarding announcement diverted her attention. As she rose to proceed to the check-in counter, she glanced back at the teenager who failed to return her gaze. She too needed tutored confidence and access to tools in order to help level her own playing field. At another time and place, Alicia would have reached out and wrapped her in a protective cloak, defended her until such time as she could stand in confidence against all that had brought her to the perilous precipice of sharp-edged instruments. There, the young girl could look down at her scars of despair with endurance and determination, never to return. Instead, she would be a beacon of hope to others who had experienced the unrelenting onslaught of demeaning abuse as had some of Alicia's childhood friends. *I can't save them all,* she ruminated regrettably.

The short stroll along the boarding walkway from the check-in counter to the front door of the aircraft allowed her the brief yet sufficient time to transition back to the reality of her uncertain circumstances. She showed the flight attendant her e-ticket on her cellphone whereupon she was directed to the private business section, first on her left. Although there was ample space in the large overhead storage bin for her satchel, for security purposes, she chose to keep it close at hand in the cavern of the extended foot rest of her private singular sleeper pod. There, it would be virtually impossible for anyone to stealthily access it should she extend the bed to join Wynken, Blynken and Nod sailing on a river of crystal light in search of much anticipated sleep.

CHAPTER 3

As the aircraft gained altitude enroute to Toronto with a connecting flight to her final destination – Paris Charles de Gaulle International Airport, Alicia found herself reflecting on her vows of silence which were in conflict with her wedding vows. She was aware but did not want to admit that when you decide on a lover to share your bed, you accept anecdotes presented with candour, merged with fabrication. The demarcation is rarely obvious. Often the naïve partner will be recruited for a role in a play for which they had not knowingly auditioned. More problematic, if the deceitful partner tweaks the script after the curtain rises in order to sway the storyline in their favour, the narrative doesn't flow as smoothly as the initial playwrights had intended. Not yet aware the script had been clandestinely modified, the second partner is foiled by the improvised lines and unrehearsed scenes. After too many deviations from the intended script, the duped partner simply becomes accustomed to the folly, or leaves the stage altogether. If they are still interested in the theatre as a life-time pursuit, as opposed to the façade of the theatrics, separation and divorce becomes the inevitable solution.

In retrospect, Alicia had not been wholly honest with Marc before or after their marriage. She was good at keeping secrets about secrets. It was in her espionage DNA, fine-tuned by her tutored upbringing.

She was the only child of a well-established British family and had spent her formative years in Weymouth on the south coast of England. Her father had worked for British Secret Intelligence Service's foreign intelligence agency, MI6. The family had moved to Canada upon his retirement, a transition which left Alicia filled

9

with guarded anticipation, and pessimistic optimism, like an initial offer of full-time employment. She had returned to England to complete her graduate degree in mathematics and computer science at Oxford University before briefly following in her father's footsteps. She spoke neither about this initial foray into the enigmatic world of espionage and intelligence nor the esoteric vocation which she had subsequently pursued on the continent.

Marc, on the other hand, had been more elusive about his family roots near Donostia-San Sebastián in northern Spain on the Bay of Biscay – Basque Country, only alluding to faint assertions of Spanish sovereignty. His parents had separated. Although he maintained a distant relationship with both, he spoke little about his childhood. He had two daughters from a previous relationship, Sophia now aged 13 and Camilla 15. He explained that his wife had been killed in a boating accident on the Spanish Riviera. Sometime later, he departed with his daughters to begin a new life half a world away on the Pacific West Coast of Canada.

Both Alicia and Marc were in their early- to mid-thirties when they met and exchanged wedding vows in a civil ceremony in Victoria. She was happy to adopt what would appear to be a maturing family without the anguish of morning sickness and stretch marks. It was not so much a marriage of convenience as a fitting façade within an established suburban setting.

Recently, however, Marc had become withdrawn. He had begun to turn away from her more often in bed as if a veil had been progressively woven, preventing her touch. Of greater concern, he had become increasingly aggressive toward her and the girls. Alicia could not pinpoint the source of the stress. Their relationship had deteriorated rapidly in the past several weeks. Today, it could best be described as turbulent. They had talked about the possibility of a trial separation at a date yet to be determined. With their disappearance, she presumed, rightly or wrongly, he had arbitrarily made this decision to depart with the girls without forewarning.

Like the vacant business class seats, her life felt eerily empty, one previously scripted by others. She had inherited the house from her father and legally adopted Camilla and Sophia. Now, the house was in shambles and both Marc and the girls were gone. Reestablishing contact with them would be her second priority at this juncture. The first would be identifying and neutralizing the threat to herself which she surmised was linked to her former arcane exploits beyond the hedgerows of her secluded Victorian Pemberton Estate home.

The intricacies of returning to the intelligence fold after a hiatus, however brief, were never taught as part of tradecraft curricula. Both parties assumed the employment would be full-term or until death do one of them part, invariably the employee. An attempted assassination negated these unwritten rules of engagement. The terms of the initial contract would be renegotiated. If linked to a previous case file, discussions would be premised on mutual benefits. Alicia would first need to establish that link. Second, she would need to demonstrate that the threat to herself was not just a risk to the employer, but that the employer was in imminent peril. Third, eliminating one threat would ideally eradicate the threat to both for the foreseeable future. If not exactly happily ever after, life would at least be less precarious and stressful.

For now, the flight from Toronto to Paris would provide her with the uninterrupted luxury of listening to a medley of her favourite Joan Baez folk tunes composed at the time of the American involvement in the Vietnam War and the subsequent peace protests. Alicia's current circumstances seemed to pale in comparison with the perceived threat to global peace of the sixties and early seventies. It had been fabricated by politicians and generals who put their careers ahead of the lives of thousands of soldiers and civilians, and countless others maimed physically, mentally and emotionally. It echoed the brutality and carnage orchestrated for the entertainment of plebeians and patricians in the Roman Colosseum. The lyrics and the unmistakable voice of Joan Baez, the iconic folk singer made her reflect – *We both know what memories can bring; they bring diamonds and rust.*

Like a couple of light years ago, Alicia recalled lessons her father had taught her. There was more truth in stories than detail in facts he had reminded her repeatedly as if once was not enough. Stories had to be interpreted, facts just had to be memorized for the simplicity of what they were. She was very good at remembering, gifted as had been her mother. Stories interpreted, in contrast, were a matter of deduction, having first considered all the facts. But drawing inference from what? She did not have all the facts, instead just suppositions.

Had she been away from the fray too long, her ability to think critically lessened, eroded unlike diamonds which do not rust? She had escaped the explosion more by providence than skill. The consequences of challenging premonition devoid of critical analysis could be deadly, not only for herself but for others in her sphere. She needed answers. Why had she become a target for assassination again?

CHAPTER 4

"Ladies and gentlemen, we will be landing shortly at Paris Charles de Gaulle International Airport. In preparation for landing, please ensure your luggage is securely stowed, your table trays and your seat backs are in the upright position and seatbelts are securely fastened. The local time in Paris is 9:55 a.m."

"Welcome back to Paris, Madame." The security officer stationed in the priority booth spoke with a brusque nod having reviewed Alicia's French diplomatic passport with a cursory glance.

"Thank you," Alicia replied, her voice an unassuming whisper. Her accent was cultured and continental, acquired after academic terms as an exchange student at the University of Paris, Sorbonne. She had spent hours immersed in the ambience of the cafés, fashions and gastronomy in the City of Lights, and summers vacationing in Monaco, Cannes and Marseilles on the French Riviera.

She had returned to France several times since moving to Victoria, describing the trips to Marc and the girls as business related to her father's estate and his previous home in Weymouth on the south coast of England. Some flights were direct from Toronto Pearson International Airport to Paris Charles de Gaulle Airport. Others were through London Heathrow Airport with a Eurostar connection from London St. Pancras Station to Paris Gare du Nord. Varying her itinerary provided additional secretive facets to her business consulting cover story. The trips had been financed through her private Banque Nationale de Paris debit account to keep Marc from finding out, another deception in their marital relationship.

She hailed a taxi to drive her directly from Paris Charles de Gaulle Airport to the Gare du Nord rather than taking the Metro because it avoided prying eyes scrutinizing passengers arriving on international flights. She boarded the TGV high speed train from the Gare du Nord to Gare de Metz-Ville in the province of Alsace-Lorraine, while starlings and sparrows pecked at crumbs left around the bench-style seats abandoned by the parade of passengers who had joined the scrimmage for regular seats on the train. Alicia, in contrast, boarded the first-class car and settled into her reserved, more spacious seat on the upper deck. This vantage point allowed her to look above the berms at the passing countryside. Initially, she had considered purchasing a small farm like some she saw but came to the realization that any location in France was too close to her haunting past. When the earthen sound barriers obscured the view, she withdrew into pensive interludes marked by less tangible thoughts.

Once at the Gare de Metz-Ville, Alicia took a taxi to an out-of-the-way refuge, another safe house in Place Saint Louis. Through lead-lined stained-glass windows and Alsatian lace curtains in the turreted garret suite, she had 270-degree unrestricted surveillance of the comings and goings in the square. Those who frequented the plaza in the cool of the summer evenings to sip Perrier or Pinot Noir were thankful the pigeons and doves no longer followed the flight path of their winged ancestors to the pigeonnier that adorned the turret under the shale roof tiles.

One of her favourite brasseries serving the best boeuf bourguignon and an exquisite selection of Côtes du Rhône wines was located directly across the square. She had spent many hours sipping cappuccinos while reading novels by Jean-Paul Sartre, Virginia Woolf, Albert Camus and Simone de Beauvoir. Conveniently, this exquisite brasserie had an equally unfettered view of the square. Of operational importance, it provided direct getaway access, as needed, to a delivery lane via a back door, more frequently used by harried employees capturing a quick nicotine fix or enjoying a fleeting amorous rendezvous.

She adjusted her appearance once again to match the regular French passport which she exchanged for her French diplomatic documents.

⚔ ⚔

ALICIA STROLLED ACROSS PLACE SAINT-JACQUES IN THE old district of Metz, stopping briefly in front of an antique shop as if window shopping. She smiled, her scrutiny surveillance alert. The backgammon board had been turned, indicating he had arrived. She entered the adjacent shopping arcade from the Hôtel des Fleurs entrance and descended the escalator. Out of habit, she tapped in the code and pressed her thumb on the recessed reader. It seemed as if no time had passed since she had spent hours here analyzing intelligence data for patterns and anomalies, in addition to patterns of anomalies.

"Good morning, Daan," Alicia said as she extended her hand to Daan Segers, the director of the European Union Intelligence Unit. He exuded cultivated elegance. As always, his dress and deportment were flawless, complementing his athletic physique. His azure blue eyes were as magnetic as they were disarming. She noted the hair on his temples had adopted half a dozen shades of grey since they had last talked face-to-face. Recalling the French fashion designer, Coco Chanel whose mantra was 'dress chubbily, they remember the dress; dress exquisitely, they remember the woman.' Accordingly, she dressed to be remembered.

"Well, you are a pleasant sight for weary eyes." Daan rose from his ornate boulle mahogany desk with a welcoming smile followed by a gentle hug and a kiss on both of her cheeks. The advantage of sharing space with an antique boutique was first choice of items dropped off as consignment for sale. "What brings you back to my doorstep? Do you want your old job back?"

"Be careful what you ask for because you just might get it," Alicia replied, trying to maintain a light disposition.

"What can I do for you?" Daan enquired.

Alicia showed him a photo on her cellphone.

Daan squinted through wary eyes. "There's an ugly ghost from Christmas Past. Where did you get it?"

"You recognize him?" Alicia answered with a faint edge to her voice and a falling tone.

"His name is Marc Bolibar, also known as Santiago López. Since you took your leave of absence, we learned he was and may still be an active Basque separatist." Daan paused, letting the revelation hang before filling in the final agonizing details.

"We have also learned that he murdered your former fiancé, Jacques Bernard, three years ago. He disappeared sometime afterward and his trail went cold."

Alicia screamed silently. She stood frozen in stunned shock at the realization that Jacques' assassin had shared her bed for the better part of the last two years. The glaring mental imagery was horrifying.

Her soul had died the same day as Jacques. Although he was dead, her memory of him was not. At this moment, distant recollections of joy shared with Jacques collided with overwhelming feelings of vengeance that consumed her every fiber. She had reflected on the events leading up to his murder more often than she cared to remember. Despite her gift of clear analysis, she could not identify who had pulled the trigger or why Jacques had been targeted. She repeatedly reviewed all combinations and permeations of the facts known at that time. Nothing seemed to make sense.

"I can confirm that he is married and has two children," Daan continued. "His estranged wife, Elana, is also a member of the

Basque separatist movement. More revealing and assuredly more problematic, she was a Russian informant. She subsequently joined the FSB as an agent whereupon she was sent by Moscow back to Basque Country in northern Spain to stir up discontent. Elana is still active, recruiting internationally for the Basque cause, although we do not know her exact whereabouts. We surmised that Marc, Elana and the girls had disappeared with the aid of Moscow perhaps to lay low as a sleeper cell. Subsequent intelligence suggested otherwise. They had gone their separate ways. With no trace of the girls, we believed Elana had taken them to Moscow where they would not be recognized. Perhaps Marc had become a freelancer off the grid somewhere."

I'm married to the murderer of my fiancé and a bigamist. Alicia shuddered in disgust at the reality of that revelation. She felt numb, suspended in time by the realism thrust upon her. That thought was so repulsive it had never entered her mind, let alone been considered as a contributing factor in the recent dissolution of their marriage. She struggled to catch her breath.

Marc had been a maestro of deception and seduction. But did he know about my background? Could I have been that naïve? Does love make us that blind? Her mind buzzed at such dizzying speed she could not perform calculations in elementary school maths let alone forensic calculus.

Her reaction did not escape Daan's scrutiny. He had often observed her withdraw when conducting analyses of case file data and then rejoin the discussion with solutions in rank order of probability. She was elsewhere at this moment, in another space he did not recognize.

Alicia broke the protracted silence. "I may take you up on your invitation to end my leave of absence and actively rejoin the European Union Intelligence Unit. But you may decline my overture and for very good reason."

Daan held her gaze without speaking. He had been tutored in the richness of patience. His open smile morphed into a non-judgemental expression of collegial encouragement and support.

"Talk to me," he quietly invited, his voice as appealing as it was disarming.

Shrouded in a shadowed world within worlds like Matryoshka Russian dolls encased in successive replicas that conjured unspoken truths and emotions, she replied in a faltering voice, "It's complicated."

She had reluctantly taken a temporary leave of absence to deal with her personal affairs, the circumstances of which had been impairing her ability to make rational decisions. After Jacques' death, she had become a liability to herself and her colleagues. Daan had agreed and granted her request for a temporary leave of absence. Although no time had been set when she would have to either return to the fray or resign, it was agreed that she would keep in contact. Hence, she had developed the cover story for the business trips from the sanctuary of her Pemberton Estate in Victoria to Daan's den above the Metz antique shop. The trips also allowed her to update her French diplomatic and regular passports, European Union SIM card and other documents.

CHAPTER 5

"Complicated may be an understatement," Daan commented after listening to Alicia's account of her life since taking an extended leave of absence from the European Union Intelligence Unit after Jacques' murder. "Grief can be messy." He allowed a moment of silence to linger in respect. "I now have a better understanding of your response and desire to re-join our merry band of brothers and sisters. I need to clarify one point. What is your primary motivation?"

"Why am I a target of assassination after all this time?" Alicia replied without hesitation. "What has happened that the fight has been brought to my front door, literally? Once that unknown has been unveiled, I am confident other truths will be revealed."

"Understandably, I sense a whiff of vendetta. The *raison d'être* of the EUI Unit is to protect the European Union from internal and external threats, not to provide carte blanche for personal revenge. My final question is simple. Can you control your urge for reprisal should you confront Marc?"

"I can't cover up my primal instincts to shoot that son of a bitch in retribution for Jacques' murder. But that wouldn't shed light on the answer to my primary question – why have I become a target for assassination after all this time."

Again, Daan allowed her a moment to consider the magnitude and consequences of the information he had provided, in addition to her motivation to re-engage.

"In response to your question, yes I am confident I can control my primal urge to retaliate." Like the Siamese cat she had once had as a child which could maintain a trance-like state with its blue eyes wide open, Alicia reflected with an equally impenetrable

19

gaze. She reflected. *Had I been too much my father's daughter and not enough of my own self? How many times had I felt eclipsed standing in the enigmatic shadow of his espionage silhouette? I had been good at mirroring successful mannerisms. My parent's marriage had been successful, at least to all outward appearances. The British family had perfected that façade of maintaining appearances, the stiff upper lip with a typical English sense of propriety and a generational code of silence when it came to details of family secrets.*

She had mimicked those performances, the husband, the two children, the house in upper-class suburbia despite the fact the marriage had been a private civil process, the children adopted not truly hers, and the house, although lawfully hers, never really a true home. Genuineness had been absent in her marriage.

As a gifted child, more her mother's daughter than her father's in this regard, she found contentment in the solitude of her mind. She never saw herself as a dutiful devoted spinster. After her mother's death from cancer, she and her father merely shared the accommodation, each in their own mental space most of the time. Yet, after his death, Alicia realized she was truly alone for the first time. Escaping into the solitude of her mind was no longer sufficient. She didn't need a soulmate, whatever that was. She didn't need a father either – perhaps just a partner, someone with whom she could engage in conversations that mattered yet unrelated to her chosen vocations and inherited background.

She furrowed her brow. She tightened her lips, admitting for the first time that genuineness had been absent. She paused, abandoning any pretence. Internal change needed a catalyst. Daan's revelation about her husband's true identity, Marc's deceit, his dishonesty was now that catalyst. Now, her own admission, her anger, her horror, her sorrow, her railing against betrayal, was her motivation. It opened the gateway for her to allow the possibility of change and to relinquish her grasp of the haunted memories – the lyrics of Joan Baez, the diamonds and rust.

"Not sure if you have had a chance to catch up on international news?" Daan's prompt caused her to refocus.

She leaned forward slightly, looking inquisitive. The initial detail had left her in deficit mode, her confidence faltering but not defeated. How much more shocking could it be?

"Enlighten me," she replied, her response less a question than a statement.

"Quiet, staid Victoria is now on the front page of the international news. An Islamic State of Iraq and Syria – ISIS – cell has supposedly taken responsibility for the bombing of two houses. You are reported to have been killed along with an unidentified occupant of the second house. Marc/Santiago has been identified as the suspected bomber because of his supposed Middle East sympathies. His arrest is the number one priority for Interpol. He is also on the Europol radar."

She took a deep breath before responding. "He may be tangentially involved somehow. I just don't know. But he wouldn't carry out the bombing of his own house. And his mysterious disappearance without notice is completely out of character. Yet, it is connected somehow and is one of those unknowns. He loves his daughters and would go out of his way to protect them physically, mentally and emotionally, not place them in harm's way, although he has a strange way of showing his affection on occasion."

"How certain are you?"

"I'm still a good judge of character, less so of male amorous intentions apparently. After two years of living with him, I can state emphatically that he would not affiliate with ISIS. Basque and Islamic philosophies are at opposite ends of both the religious and secular spectrums. Those hard-held Iberian hatreds are innately grounded in Spanish history. No more so than in Basque resentments that date back to when the Moors invaded Spain in 711 A.D., bringing with them their Islamic religion, caliphate and culture. Marc would become enraged anytime he heard news items about ISIS or Islam in general."

It was Daan's turn to reflect. "Yes, the EU Council in Brussels also has its doubts about any ISIS connection. It's too convenient. Whoever is spreading this rumour has ulterior motives. I'm convinced it is connected to the recent simmering dissidence, still unidentified, which has an inherent anti-EU undercurrent."

Daan went quiet as he contemplated the options to counter this latest threat to the European Union. Alicia knew enough not to interrupt him. She remembered the many times he would stare upward focusing on nothing in particular while the embryo of an idea was born.

"You bring to the table first-hand knowledge of Marc's personality and, more importantly, of his Basque penchant for planning, better than any confidential informant or espionage source could. That is invaluable and may tip the scales in our favour to neutralize this threat. Other sources suggest that it is international in scope so we have not yet envisioned the true magnitude of its devastating potential, like a viral pandemic in its infancy."

"How can I help?" Alicia offered, her question posed in earnest.

"How would you like your old job back? It may be to our and your advantage to be reported as one of the two cadavers recovered from the bombed houses in Victoria, at least for now."

"Happy to accept your invitation. When do I start?"

Daan handed her a hotel business card embossed with a reservation number. "Please proceed to this hotel in Vaduz, Liechtenstein as soon as possible. There you will meet up with your new partner who will introduce himself as 'the professor'. I will join the two of you once I have finalized some details and received formal authority with budget approval from Brussels. I will bring your identification documents and toys of the profession."

"I would like to make one stop here in Metz before I leave."

"Fort de Queuleu?"

Alicia stood quietly, acknowledging her superior's recollection of history and her family connection.

Daan nodded solemnly. "Depart as soon as possible." His direction was forthright yet compassionate. He was acutely aware of her motivation for a brief detour.

Before being made aware of her family's heritage, her life had been simple, surrounded by teddy bears and dolls, and friends who shared common British values and some secrets in her diary. After learning about family secrets, she was more careful about what she shared, what she wrote. She thought long and hard before she spoke. She had fewer friends as a result, because she was seen as being introverted like a librarian, not eager to take on a commanding leadership role in the classroom or on the sports field, or support others with great enthusiasm.

Inwardly, she had not changed. She was still Alicia, the inquisitive highly-intelligent girl who believed in equality, fairness for all and environmental causes. Eventually, she shunned others in response to their rejection of her and what she believed in. It wasn't right but it just happened naturally. She found solace in individual achievement. As a gifted child, she excelled particularly in maths and sciences. A myriad of trophies and awards adorned her shelves and walls, bolstering her ego and confidence. The secrets were still there, though, and she was very good at keeping secrets about secrets.

She gained solace from the fact that she knew things that others did not, details that she had learned on her own. It was not a matter of arrogance felt from lording knowledge over the heads of others. Instead, it was satisfaction experienced from solving the crossword puzzles with uncanny speed and accuracy, and the subsequent confidence that she felt. She didn't need constant praise, so to speak. Often, she found such accolades to be demeaning.

But why had she recently become a target of assassination after all this time? Not knowing all the facts was frustrating. She found herself unable to logically deduce the answer, like not being able to decipher the calligraphy of the legend which she had meticulously scripted. Worse, she didn't know the reason for the impasse. Celtic culture taught that our ego was the dragon holding us back. She needed to slay the dragon. There were advantages of being a Star Wars lone Jedi. Now was not one of them. Luke Skywalker had Yoda. Perhaps her new partner, the professor, would fill the role of an Obi-wan.

CHAPTER 6

Alicia presented Daan's business card to the receptionist at the hotel in Vaduz who immediately summoned a gentleman from the hotel manager's office. He was dressed as one would expect of a distinguished representative of a five-star European hotel spa. There was no mistaking his professional bearing, which was that of a seasoned warrior, approachable but unforgiving if crossed.

"I am Alicia Dupuis. You must be Professor Lucas Peeters. I understand we will be working together on a research project."

He extended his hand, his grip confident but not overpowering. "Apparently so," he replied, with a restrained yet relaxed tone. Intuitive students attuned to disciplined processes of communication could learn more from his demeanour and how he spoke framed in the milieu of the knowledge he passed along within the context of formal lectures but more importantly the informal gestures. Marshall McLuhan was correct. The medium is the message. Professor Lucas Peeters was such a medium.

"We will have your luggage taken to your room," the concierge politely whispered.

"The journey from Metz to Vaduz can be a bit circuitous, especially as Vaduz is the only European capital without an airport or railway station. For our purposes, it is advantageous when keeping track of who comes and goes from this fairy-tale principality. A little light refreshment?" he invited.

Alicia followed him into the lounge while scanning the décor that added to the venue of excellence and ambience of intelligence. The message was subtle but self-evident.

"Come into my office," he gestured as they approached a discrete alcove with two high-backed plush leather chairs positioned away from potential prying eyes and attuned eavesdropping ears. An expansive Victorian bay window framed against a rich mahogany-panelled wall provided a breath-taking view of the snow-capped Swiss Alps.

Alicia chuckled to herself at his choice of words, "Come into my office." She was reminded of the opening line of Mary Howett's 1829 poem, *The Spider and the Fly*: "Will you walk into my parlour said the spider to the fly…" Lewis Carroll later parodied the expression in The Mock Turtle's Story in *Alice's Adventures in Wonderland*. Was Lucas a spider? Did she need to be careful of his intentions, his invitations, his inducements?

Lucas noticed Alicia's careful surveillance of a waiter who had shadowed them at a discrete distance.

"Although Liechtenstein was a neutral country during the Second World War, Nazis would spend time in this hotel enjoying a little rest and relaxation," he explained. "It was said that the waiters would be paid three times. Once by the hotel in meagre wages, once by patrons in generous gratuities, and multiple times greater by all those keen to know what other guests had quietly discussed. Compensation for the latter often exceeded the combined former a hundred-fold. Today, the waiters are scrupulously vetted by the management for their integrity and discretion, and only compensated by the hotel and tipped by the appreciative patrons. I'll elaborate a little later."

Alicia acknowledged his explanation with a discrete bow. "I like your taste in furnishings," she added warmly.

"What is the pleasure of your palate?" Lucas enquired.

Was this the spider curious as to the habits of the fly? she pondered. Lewis Carroll had coined the statement, "curiouser and curiouser" for Alice to cry out. Alicia would merely muse instead.

"Côtes du Rhône?" Alicia, not Alice, respectfully replied with a cautious yet curious smile.

"Ah, a lady with a refined taste for the virtues of the exquisite fruit of the vine. We have something else in common besides research into Basque culture."

"A professor of which discipline?" Alicia enquired.

"Middle East and North African culture. At least that is what I lecture on at the University of Leuven."

"Leuven, if I'm not mistaken, is where Daan retired to after a distinguished career in military intelligence."

"You are correct. He lectured for a short time as an associate faculty member at the University of Leuven. That was where we first crossed paths. Shortly afterward, he answered the bugle call from Brussels to head the European Union Intelligence Unit and be their Europol representative."

"And your association?" Alicia inquired. "I sense you have more than an academic affiliation in common?"

"Correct again. Initially, I was an academic advisor to the EUI Unit. At Daan's behest, I followed him into the fray as an agent but kept my professorial appointment with the university as a cover. I'm still on the register as a faculty member but officially listed as being on sabbatical. As Daan explained, the EUI Unit employs agents. Those bent on destroying the European Union dispatch spies. The difference is subtle but very important."

"One last inquiry if I may?"

"Certainly," Lucas replied with an encouraging response.

"The receptionist summoned you from what appeared to be the hotel manager's office." Alicia raised her eyebrows. *How many hats was he wearing?* She pondered. *His talents seemed multi-faceted, like Daan and others she had worked with prior to taking her leave of absence. It was a prerequisite for success in the arcane tradecraft.*

"Two of Daan's colleagues, our colleagues in the EUI Unit, own this rather elegant hotel spa, hence, the preferred status. Any time you need to establish a low profile or engage in a little rest and relaxation from the stress of the profession, you merely have to quote the reservation number listed on the business card. There are a few secure suites permanently set aside. It's a perk of being one of the comrades in arms."

Alicia scanned the lounge, then rested her gaze on her new partner. Both spoke of integrity. When she had first been introduced to her previous partner, Jacques, she had a similar awareness of his professionalism. From that initial introduction, she surmised that Jacques would cover her back if push came to shove. In contrast, she had never really felt that level of support and assurance with her colleagues in MI6. They seemed more interested in climbing the corporate espionage and intelligence ladder at the expense of their peers. One fewer colleague translated into one less rung to compete for.

Her father had forewarned her and, in retrospect, the incessant backstabbing while feigning friendship was her primary motive for transferring allegiance from Her Majesty's Secret Intelligence Service to the European Union Intelligence Unit. She and Jacques had created a professional ambiance when first introduced, which unperceptively evolved beyond collegial to intimate. Her assessment of Professor Lucas Peeters at this first meeting was also professional. She would keep it that way. She sensed he would cover her back if push came to shove. Time would tell though.

"Daan briefed me on your background with just basic facts regarding your colleague's murder. I understand that it was related to the Basque file which brings us together."

Alicia held his probing gaze over the rim of her wine glass but did not add further details. Her mind was elsewhere. She was adept at keeping secrets.

After an awkward interlude, Lucas picked up the conversation with a friendly yet measured exactitude in his manner. "I appreciate the sensitivity of the circumstances surrounding Jacques' death. You know more than I the hazards associated with this line of work. In addition, you bring a wealth of first-hand experience and knowledge to this case. If we are to work together successfully, we will need to establish protocols for dealing with the elephant in the room."

Alicia held his stare as if in suspended animation. Memories overshadowed their conversation. She sighed at the reality of being in combat with herself, once again. The dichotomy inherent in such recollections had plagued her on nights too numerous to count with cryptic images portrayed in technicolour on the giant flat screen monitor of her mind.

"Daan's latest text indicated he will be arriving by helicopter tomorrow morning to brief us on the file with suggestions as to where we might begin. May I propose that you join me for dinner this evening? I'll make reservations for seven. I would like to confirm with Daan that we have the trappings of a collegial working relationship in place by the time we order crème brûlée, cappuccino and cognac."

Alicia nodded without hesitation. With renewed engagement she confirmed, "Sorry about that pause, partner. Yes, it is still a sensitive issue. Yes, I will join you for dinner. Yes, we will establish that protocol. Further, you have my permission to whack me on the back of the head if you get an inkling of hesitancy from me. Seven it is. *Jusque là* – until then."

As they left the lounge, Alicia was drawn to the familiar rattle of the dice. Six and a five, the lovers leap, she mused as she looked down at two elderly guests playing backgammon while sipping cognac from Swarovski crystal snifters.

Noticing her attention drawn to the board, Lucas murmured with an inviting smile, "You play?" The sole purpose of his enquiry was to get to know his new partner better. If that led to a friendly match also over cognac or other libations, so be it.

"I've been known to play a friendly game or two, in addition to a few tournaments. I sense you have also known the enjoyment of throwing the ivories in a relaxing environment." She spoke more in the tone of a challenge not to be ignored, than a bland response to a close-ended question. "And you?"

"Some have described me as being an avid backgammoner," Lucas answered.

"Avid. I like an avid challenge. Perhaps we can play a game or three or more."

"That sounds as though you have dropped the gauntlet," he replied, smiling in anticipation of a joust.

"Jusque là," she responded with a welcoming smile, countering the challenge from the high ground she knew she held. Her genial response trailed off as a tactic to a tournament that might never have an ending, best of five, seven, nine, ninety-nine. She sensed from their initial meeting that Lucas would not, could not back down. He had gallantly yet perhaps naïvely picked up the gauntlet she had demurely dropped. She had learned more about him in this exchange than the spider had deduced about the fly.

"Please excuse me. I have some business to conclude." Lucas returned to the manager's office.

Alicia acknowledged his departure with a courteous bow. From the lobby, she sauntered into the library where she was welcomed by the sound of crackling logs burning in a huge fireplace the likes of which she had not experienced since accompanying her father to old English country estates owned by colleagues from the British aristocracy, some of whom had close affiliations with Her Majesty's Secret Service. While their host and her father adjourned to private conversations behind closed doors, she had scanned the titles of ancient books, some rare, a few priceless, amassed on equally impressive aged oak library shelves. She had judiciously accessed a select number whose spines did not appear to have ever been broken, an indication of their contents. On careful examination, there were single folded sheets of less contemporary tissue paper concealed, some inscribed with sequences of numbers or references to verses of poetry penned by English poets in earlier centuries. Her father had been accurate if not always straight forward in his furtive directives to her.

She had made a mental note of the numeric sequences by two-dimensional column and row as much an exercise in memorization as mental gymnastics to be applied when thinking in the multi-dimensional abstract and asking probing questions. She could always remember numbers and codes, a talent she had been born with. She had mastered the art and science of cryptoanalysis from hours of intense concentration as an adolescent when shunned by her school chums for being different. In every adversity, there were the seeds of its opposite. She just needed quiet time alone in her own mind to accommodate her curiosity about solving problems by rearranging complex mathematical sequences and theories or creating innovative formulae. She was her father's daughter after all.

Unlike her father, Alicia was less adept at recognizing and intuitively employing appropriate social skills. Her long blonde hair, tall sleek physique and keen wit ensured her dance card was always full, signed by eminently eligible suitors. Unfortunately, many became easily intimidated by her superior intellectual prowess and cerebral episodes when she would withdraw to ponder like Pooh Bear over a pot of honey.

Lucas seemed different, certainly not intimidated by her portfolio but impressed by the myriad talents and credentials she brought to the table. When she disengaged at their first meeting, he brought her back not with an ultimatum but a challenge. If she wanted to find out why she had become an assassin's target, she would need to work with him, alongside him. As an equal partner, she had invited him to whack her on the back of the head if he sensed she was withdrawing. He had accepted that challenge and her invitation to play a few friendly games of backgammon. She found that approach appealing, reassuring, comforting, refreshing.

CHAPTER 7

"Good morning," said Daan, handing Alicia a secure tote bag. "Here are your updated documents and tools of the tradecraft."

Alicia scanned the identification papers and confirmed the safety status of the Glock 9 mm model 19 pistol while Daan and Lucas exchanged confirmatory looks. Her hand on the pistol grip seemed as warming as her inward smile. It felt good to be back in the fold, perhaps ironically more secure, more protected from the assassin's focus. Images of the destructive impact of the exploding SUV in her driveway in addition to her kitchen in shambles seemed more distant yet were only days old.

"We have the makings of a new crime-fighting diamond duo?" Daan suggested.

Alicia and Lucas looked at each other and then at Daan. They nodded in unison like disciplined synchronized swimmers completing the opening movement as a segue to their performance.

"Excellent. As this will be your first file working together, allow me to set the stage and bring you up to date on the rules of engagement. Then we can discuss the file and finally consider some options for a preliminary operational plan. Questions before we begin?"

"We're good to go," they replied in unison.

"We can deal with a cancerous threat in one of two ways or both simultaneously. We can infiltrate the malignancy and kill it from within, or surround it and, in doing so, starve it of all life-sustaining nutrients. Basque Country is ill-defined and has no formally mapped borders so it would be exceedingly difficult to surround, like a nebulous fog bank advancing and retreating with the forces of nature. A focused approach might be more useful. But that means navigating the uncharted labyrinth of clandestine relations reaching back into Celtic and Druid folklore like the *Quer*, a secret society."

"We face an added challenge if the cancer has metastasized because we will need to repeat the process for all configurations of mutating cells," Lucas commented. "From a more pragmatic perspective, we need to find an agent and follow that person to the center of the cell in order to eradicate it."

"Marc Bolibar, a.k.a. Santiago López," Alicia suggested in a matter-of-fact voice. "If he has been detached too long, I am confident he will lead us to someone more current."

"I agree." Daan raised his eyebrows. "That brings me to my first point. The raison d'être of the EUI Unit is to counter all threats to the European Union from within, acknowledging that the source of these threats may not be solely internal to the European Union. In the brief period since you left, Alicia, externally sourced threats have increased exponentially. Their modus operandi has been to agitate potential provocateurs as their proxy agents of unrest. The EUI Unit formally takes over, once inside the borders of the European Union. It is the responsibility of other enforcement organizations to extinguish the external threats within their respective jurisdictions. Today, Europol acts as the coordinating body for policing within the European Union and the liaison for external police forces including but certainly not limited to Interpol."

"The waters have already been muddied with known players both internal and external," Alicia conceded. "No change in context, just content."

"Agreed," Daan acknowledged. "We suspect that Elana, Marc's estranged partner and mother of the two girls, attempted to kill you in Victoria. But why?" Daan queried, looking at both Alicia and Lucas for input. "What would be worth killing and dying for, connected to Alicia, to make her such a high priority target of assassination?"

Lucas reflected. "Because Alicia was instrumental in the capture of another Russian agent masquerading as Basque and a close colleague of Elana's? Is that worth killing and dying for though, making Alicia a target for assassination halfway around the world? How would Elena have known where Alicia lived? The connection has to have been Marc Bolibar, a.k.a. Santiago López."

"Another motive could be maternal," Alicia proposed. "Elana may want the girls so badly that she will go to great lengths to eliminate all competition or obstacles. I don't believe she knows I have formally adopted the girls, which would give me some legal recourse, although international family law has been reluctant to back up such claims across some borders. Like your suggestion, Lucas, how would Elana have known where I lived? That link can only be Marc."

"Would she go so far as to murder you, her perceived surrogate maternal competition?" Lucas followed up. "That seems extreme."

"Maternal instincts run deeper than any other. In nature, mothers sacrifice themselves for their young more than their mates do," Alicia proposed.

Daan added, "I'm waiting to hear back from a source who has strong connections to Moscow, both the old KGB and its successor, the FSB. I have asked her for a personality profile of Elana and, specifically, to comment on how far she would go."

Lucas glanced over at his new partner who was maintaining a pensive, resolute expression as if the existing threat to herself was a matter of routine and not overly worrying, let alone reason to shy away. He was gaining confidence in Alicia's ability to remain objective in the face of peril. He responded to her brief gaze with a terse nod.

Daan continued, "The media has reported Alicia as one of two victims in the Victoria bombings. Once it becomes known she is alive and back on the EUI Unit payroll, Elana may redouble her efforts to hunt her down and kill her. Such a subsequent foray would be made easier with Alicia here in Europe instead of half a world away."

"With that probable scenario, Alicia will become the bait," Lucas concluded. "I don't like the sound of that prospect."

"It is an inevitable outcome of the reality that Alicia is now on Elana's trail," Daan pointed out.

"Once the predator, Elana will have to acknowledge the tables have been turned. She has become the prey. With that realization, she could become more cautious, more circumspect, more than likely to second-guess her own choices," Alicia proposed. "We use that to our advantage. Follow Elana and she will probably lead us to Marc who, in turn, will lead us to the nucleus of the Basque separatist movement."

Don't allow fear to become your limitation, her father's words echoed. *Face the fear, become focused on your plan of action because that action will dispel the fear.* That had always been her resolve, not to cocoon herself in a shroud of trepidation but reconfigure her determination. *De l'audace, encore de l'audace, et toujours de l'audace* – audacity, more audacity, and always audacity. She had learned well from her tutor the discipline of keeping her heartbeat in cadence with each systematic step forward. It was essential to maintain great respect for the lethal potential some opposing forces could unleash.

"Another factor," Daan advised, "Marc and the girls entered the EU thirty-six hours ago via Paris Charles de Gaulle International Airport. CCTV shows them at the Gare de L'Est thereafter. We could not determine their whereabouts after that sighting."

"Marc occasionally spoke fondly of the old districts in Strasbourg, specifically the district around the Cathedral on the

Grande Île, so I suggest we start there," Alicia offered. "To our advantage, the girls will slow him down and make him easier to identify and track."

"I have contacted another informant who has direct links to the Middle East and North Africa to sniff around. Once we hear back, I'll let you know," Daan added. "That may be a starting point for Lucas to renew acquaintances with some of his academic research colleagues."

"I've already started to cast my net," Lucas confirmed. "The Mediterranean Basin has historically been a cauldron into which all cultures have poured ingredients. One merely needs a seasoned palate and an ability to differentiate subtle flavours. It becomes slightly more challenging when regional herbs and spices have been mortared into a paste. That's when we employ individuals nurtured and schooled in each culture to interpret the nuanced details such as language dialects."

"The last point," Daan announced, "we know Beijing has been financing some ISIS activities. We also have strong suspicions that Beijing may be funding more recent agent provocateurs either directly or through ISIS financiers. The link may be Elana or one of her close associates."

"That's worrying," Lucas muttered.

Daan nodded. "This file is multifaceted. So, we need to be open to any and all possibilities. We cannot assume that our previous suppositions and strategies will apply today. As always, let's be safe."

Alexandra Belliveau approached with her hand out. "Daan, I sincerely hope that your guest is enjoying our accommodation."

Daan rose from his chair. "I am pleased that you could drop by."

Alicia followed his lead.

"Please, don't stand," Alexandra requested as a gentleman sauntered in alongside her.

"Alicia, may I introduce you to Doctors Alexandra Belliveau and Paul Bernard. They are the proprietors of this jewel in the crown of the Principality of Liechtenstein. They are also our colleagues in the European Union Intelligence Unit."

"Daan is correct about our affiliation with the EUI Unit," Paul confirmed. "But for now, we are on a sabbatical, so to speak, something like Lucas's more recent affiliation with the University of Leuven. If we can make your stay with us more comfortable, please do not hesitate to ask."

"Thank you," Alicia smiled, gauging their relationship with Daan and Lucas. She sensed she *was* welcomed, albeit a novice addition to the seasoned team that had earned their credentials under fire. It would be incumbent on her to earn her spurs amongst her present company. Although it had only been a brief two years since Alicia had served with the EUI Unit, the dynamics of the organization and the dimensions of the threats to the European Union had grown exponentially like mutations of a virus in ways that had not been imagined as possible when she had temporarily started her leave of absence after Jacques' death. Much of the unprecedented change was technology-related. Two-dimensional battlefields were now multi-dimensional battle spaces. Wars could be won or lost without a single bullet being fired. Explosives with the potential for mass destruction with loss of life and limb remained as effective in psychological warfare as the cyber threats to infrastructure such as electrical power grids, and financial institutions. The common denominator was the fear generated by the perceived yet unseen threat. Fear was the unknown. Action dispelled fear.

"Alexandra and Paul bring special talents to the table. Although on a temporary leave of absence, I have asked them to be available," Daan confirmed.

Daan's pragmatic request was for Alexandra and Paul to be available to assist. Their equally swift response was affirmed.

Daan's request to Alicia was clear: *Why did she want to re-join the European Union Intelligence Unit?* Her response was equally straight forward: *To find out why she had become a target of assassination after all this time.* She was good at making pragmatic decisions based on fact, unencumbered by the quagmire of emotion.

Her second priority was to find Camilla and Sophia. This posed a moral dilemma, putting the response to her personal objective above and beyond the health and safety of Camilla and Sophia. Was the choice an either/or decision? Either one was first, or the other was. Alternatively, should it be a both/and decision – identifying why she had become an assassin's target and ensuring the girls were safe. She was not as good at making choices involving sentiment. She returned to her decision-making model. If she was dead, she could not provide a safety net for the girls. The priority of choices was obvious. Finding out why she had become a target of assassination would remain her top priority. There could only be one first choice. She felt a tinge of remorse.

CHAPTER 8

Alicia gazed out of the turreted window of her hotel room in the old district of Strasbourg – la Grande Île – and lamented as she watched young mothers pushing prams. Although her two stepdaughters were a temporary family, she felt a maternal affection for them, especially the younger, Sophia, with whom she had developed a closer relationship. *Were they safe?* Neither had accessed their social media accounts since the day Marc had taken them away. This was completely out of character for Camilla, who, although two years older than Sophia, was emotionally far less mature and had become chronically dependent on Twitter and Facebook. Without her medication to deal with her panic attacks, she would be unable to concentrate for more than several seconds, a minute at most. Finding the girls and establishing a safety net for them remained a secondary but still pressing priority.

"You seem a bit distracted," Lucas commented. "Need a whack on the back of the head?"

Alicia chuckled. "There are too many loose ends in this case, which are worrying. I'm not a control freak, but I am bothered by some inconsistencies and their potentially lethal consequences. On the edge are the menacing unknown unknowns. The laws of quantum mechanics, especially entanglement theory, suggest everything is connected to everything, somehow. I'd be more comfortable if we could establish a risk-management strategy for each of the variables." She knew she had a habit of mulling over intervening variables, occasionally over-thinking scenarios, but it tended to pay dividends.

"Talk to me," Lucas said. "What concerns you the most?"

"I referred to the other person whose house was blown up

in Victoria as my colleague. In fact, she was one of my father's protégés from his MI6 days. I am unaware of her nom de guerre. I knew her only as Jane, as in plain Jane. But she was far from simple. Although not my formal trainer, Jane took me under her wing as a favour to my father for all the time he had spent guiding her. She retired from Her Majesty's Secret Intelligence Service just as I was becoming involved with the Basque file."

"Why do you believe Jane was a target of assassination like yourself?" Lucas probed. "What's the connection, if there is one? Was the bombing of her house merely coincidental, unrelated? We don't have all the facts yet. So, what is your intuition telling you?"

Alicia gazed down at the floor while taking a deep breath. She had realized as an adolescent that intuition is never wrong. It is only the misinterpretation of intuition that sends us down the wrong path. She looked up briefly before responding. "Was it directed at me? If so, then I could surmise that whoever blew up my SUV and subsequently the back of my house might have known of our relationship, friendship." She paused momentarily. "But then again, perhaps not."

"Fair assessment," Lucas confirmed. He wasn't necessarily agreeing with her, only validating her proposition. In doing so, he was encouraging her to explore other avenues of explanation.

She shrugged her shoulders and turned both hands upward. "Perhaps most worryingly, did they also know about our MI6 connection and Jane's relationship with my father? This is all too convenient to be coincidental, like blaming ISIS and connecting Marc to the Middle East. There is an ulterior motive."

"When the two of you chatted, did Jane allude to anything related to MI6 that caught your attention?" Lucas probed.

"Yes and no. I always had the impression she and my father were involved in a case of dire significance. But neither spoke to me about it. It was this complete absence of information that piqued my concern. As you are aware, under the *Official Secrets Act*, we were sworn not to discuss any files, not even among colleagues still serving or retired. Accordingly, we didn't talk in detail. Jane and my father did chat in general though, about other less important cases. Before my father died, he told me about a file which could still come back to haunt me. But again, he did not divulge any specific details. It was as if he was apologizing to me in advance. But neither of them talked about that one file which caused such foreboding."

Alicia lingered with a vacant stare searching her memories for yet unidentified clues that might suggest a connection, a segue to events past and present. She drew a blank. She had learned that the absence of the evidence did not mean that there wasn't anything to find. Instead, it indicated that she merely had not been examining the known facts in a way that could shed light on unknowns still stealthy lurking in the recesses of her memory banks.

"You are correct. In the clandestine world of duplicitous intelligence, nothing exists in the absence of context. The same applies in academic research," Lucas admitted, endorsing her uneasiness.

"What was and perhaps still is the context of their most secret MI6 file and our Basque case?" Alicia pondered aloud. "I'm convinced there is a link to Jane and to the Basque unrest either directly or indirectly. I can feel it in my bones. I think I need to get back to what remains of my house in Victoria, which I inherited from my father. Perhaps not just the building and the land but his MI6 legacy. In this context, I inherited all that embodied him and his secretive life."

Her slight hesitancy shed flickers of peripheral light on her deduction like sparks of distant fireflies dancing in the midnight blackness itself devoid of context or patterns – there, somewhere, consistently inconsistent. "My father was too meticulous not to have left some clues for me to find." She dwelled on her query again. Her perception was more focused, sharper, warier. "On several occasions, he would quietly refer to needs for a rainy day. He repeated these words on his death bed as an invitation with a caveat. I concluded I had no option but to follow Lewis Carroll's White Rabbit down the tunnel to accept the quest and solve the riddle."

Lucas maintained eye contact in an effort to assess the nuances in her tone and decipher innuendos in her mannerisms. He had perfected this skill after spending countless hours coaching doctoral students as they sought the elusive dissertation topic that would consume their lives until they had successfully defended their thesis, and many moments thereafter. "What else is troubling you?"

"My father had worked out of the U.K. embassy in Rabat, but spent most of his time in Casablanca, the economic and business center of Morocco. Whether by reputation or happenstance, more foreign agents seemed to prefer to conduct business in Casablanca most likely because it was the chief port on the north Atlantic coast which made it easily accessible by sea. In addition, it is one of the largest financial centers on the African continent. With a population of approximately three million, it was easy to get lost and remain anonymous. While there, he had developed a relationship with a young Moroccan who eventually became one of his most productive assets. I got the sense this person was also connected to the ultra-secret file my father and Jane had worked on."

"What about Marc? Do you believe he is somehow connected?" Lucas probed, trying to identify additional missing pieces of the mysterious puzzle.

"The unannounced disappearance of Marc is a problem but Marc was a troubled soul as I found out later. There was a dark side to him I discovered after we were married. But more problematic is the abrupt disappearance of the girls. Their social media accounts are completely dead. I had established a secret code with the younger daughter, Sophia, to use in the event of an emergency, an immediate threat. She borrowed a stranger's cellphone at the Vancouver International airport and sent the clandestine code, 2CV, to me. No further details and nothing since."

Lucas sat quietly mulling over his partner's growing concerns and conundrums. There was something unsettling about her father's file, but Lucas was more perplexed about what Alicia referred to as the abrupt disappearance of the girls rather than Marc, who had a dark history punctuated with outright lies. That misleading behaviour could be explained, given his life and their respective worlds of intelligence and espionage. However, the unexplained disappearance of the girls seemed to insinuate a more menacing intimation of a foreboding complexity.

Lucas observed her closely, seeking clues that might lead to answers unrevealed and questions unasked, and what she referred to as unknown unknowns. He did not want to seem forceful so he explored tangential issues. "What else is on your mind?"

"Marc was deceitful about his background but he could not completely hide his emotions, although I must admit I didn't always notice them immediately. From our conversations about his family, I am convinced the Basques are not a major threat to the European Union. They just want their claims to Basque Country recognized. Yet some are raising havoc. I'm convinced these supposed terrorists are being provoked by a third unknown party, like Churchill's SOE, his Special Operations Executive, created to sabotage, subvert, and stir up anarchy in Nazi-held territory. I'm convinced the recent Basque separatist motivation is deeper than just heritage land issues. The apparent agitation may even be a red herring."

"And apart from all this, Mrs. Lincoln, how was your evening at the opera?" Lucas laughed.

Alicia returned his smile. She felt the strain in her neck subside ever so slightly. "I like the humour. On a positive note, we can eliminate John Wilkes Booth as a suspect in our file."

"And which people of interest can we really exclude?" Lucas asked, hoping her analytical process that had brought them to this point could be tapped into for one more nagging factor.

"Interesting question. Perhaps too early to say at this juncture but let's keep analyzing."

Their cellphones buzzed simultaneously with a text from Daan: "Heard back from my source who advised connection is not Moscow-directed but instead Moscow-related. Nothing is beyond birthmother's capacity, including eliminating surrogate parent. My source will delve further; will get recent photograph of Elana. Be careful. Play safe in the sandbox."

"If Marc and the girls are in Strasbourg, where might they be?" Lucas asked. "We need a starting point. From there we can expand our search in a patterned grid, starting in the old city center."

"Marc is an ancient history buff so we start from the Place Gutenberg just around the corner from our hotel. Sophia also loves Old World Europe so she would have an influence on him. If Camilla isn't glued to her cellphone, which appears to be the case, she will follow her sister's suggestions, because Sophia has a calming influence on her when her anxiety disorder goes ballistic. That is why I chose this hotel as our base of operations."

"What about Elana?" Lucas asked. "How will she react when she realizes the hunter has become the hunted – that you are alive and on her trail? What will she do when she has lost the element of surprise, the wary warrior edge in this lethal game of cat and mouse?"

"I'm not sure. It's doubtful she will raise her hands and simply surrender. If she has never been in the crosshairs before, I suspect she will reconsider, perhaps withdraw briefly, in order to re-evaluate her strategy. The more familiar strengths of friendly forces will prevail over the weakness of unfamiliar resources and tactics of enemy forces."

"You have changed your identity. So, I think Elana wouldn't immediately recognize you. It would not be unreasonable for her to have asked Marc for a photo of you. Thus, she might look twice if she saw you, scanning her mental Rolodex file in the hope of putting a name to a face. That would be a routine procedure of her FSB training. She doesn't know you. On the downside, you don't know her."

"Good point. If she believes the media report that I was killed in the explosion, she may not be looking and second-guessing. As we do not know what she looks like either, we can only scan for a lone female appearing both cautious and curious."

"True," Lucas affirmed, "but if she is the source of the false media release?"

Alicia interjected, cutting him off. She needed hard facts to analyze. "Another unknown," she muttered, wrinkling her nose. "Let's start from the knowns or at least the strongest probabilities."

Lucas proposed an option. "First, the girls are with Marc and probably here in Strasbourg as you suggest. Second, the girls will be agitated because they have been cut off from their Twitter and Facebook accounts. So, Marc will do his best to keep them entertained sightseeing in the old part of the city. I agree with your deduction. That is where we start."

Alicia nodded. "Elana may not have contacted Marc, which means we keep a lookout for a lone female scanning every face. I can recognize the girls, but they might not immediately recognize me with my different hair colour and style. Marc might not recognize me at first glance either."

"Let us press on to Place Gutenberg. Excuse the play on words," he chuckled. "An added advantage to us," Lucas said, "is that neither Marc nor Elana would expect you to be with a male partner.

So, I suggest we present ourselves as a couple. Are you comfortable with that proposal?"

"Not a problem," Alicia replied without hesitation, her words deliberate and unhurried. "Thanks for confirming. I appreciate your sensitivity."

A thin half smile accompanied his tic of a nod, an expression of discretion. *One less elephant in the room to contend with,* he mused. *But one less variable with potential intimations albeit veiled at this time. Best not to eliminate completely.*

The EUI Unit Delta teams had confirmed their strategy to provide cover while Alicia and Lucas conducted a grid search of the old city of Strasbourg. Mobile units were strategically positioned along the route which they had logged. Likewise, surveillance teams of two would mingle amongst the tourists and leapfrog between hotels. At least one in each team would carry a cup of a beverage which would provide a cover for their thumb microphones raised to their mouth. The other would carry a cellphone camera which would allow them to raise their hand to their face when they spoke. Coffee cups or other beverage containers had always been a diversionary tool of the tradecraft. Advances in technology had made it easier to use mobile phones and cameras to conceal intentions, the latter making it simpler to record and simultaneously share images in real time. It was a fashion statement to wear brand-name ear plugs.

These contemporary aids to surveillance had their limitations. Immediately, they could not identify and ultimately neutralize the unknown and known threats, Elana and her nefarious intention to assassinate her target, her nemesis. Only Alicia could confirm the ID and only if she could create a link to Elana via the girls or Marc. A near *Catch-22*.

CHAPTER 9

I am confident that Marc will pose an immediate threat to Alicia directly or indirectly, Lucas ruminated. *He may appear to be conciliatory on the surface. But by virtue of the fact that he left Victoria with the girls under a shroud of secrecy strongly suggests that he has some unresolved issues. According to Alicia, he has already demonstrated traits of an abusive personality. Accordingly, I surmise that he could become violent. Alicia's reaction to Marc when they meet, however, will be an untested unknown. If that scenario unfolds, should I move closer to Alicia in support and, in doing so, be better positioned in the event the encounter goes sideways? Marc might perceive me as a challenger if in close proximity. I am confident that Alicia will de-escalate any public display of conflict, particularly if the girls are present. Or should I keep a discrete distance when Alicia confronts Marc, and play the role of an inquisitive independent bystander? And then there is the known threat, Elana. If she recognizes Alicia, I would have to intervene to prevent another attack with an increased probability of direct and fatal collateral consequences. There are too many unknowns, vagaries, and relentless duplicities in this ruse de guerre.*

Lovers transition, mutate, and accommodate over time, Alicia mused like a Shakespearian philosopher. *Regardless of the intensity of a relationship, it will inevitably wane if the partners have not grown together. Marc has changed and so have I. Confronting Marc is a given, be it today or another occasion. Who would he be and what role would he play? In my renewed function as an agent of the European Union Intelligence Unit and with my new objective partner, my reaction will be different if I were to act in my previous role of quasi-domestic spouse. That scenario is no more and never will be again. Had the Pemberton Estate home in Victoria been my real life or was my real life that of an intelligence gatherer and espionage agent, now in the early stages of renewal? Confronting the unknown known, Marc will be easier to read than engaging with the unknown Elana threat. If confronted together, would Marc back his first partner and birthmother of his children or his second partner and current wife and adoptive mother? Here as well, there are too many unknowns, vagaries, and relentless duplicities in this ruse de guerre.*

"I have a map pulled up on my cellphone listing all the hotels on la Grande Île in the old city," Alicia advised. "There appears to be just over a dozen. As we wend our way through the serpentine cobblestone streets, we can ask at the reception desk of each hotel if they recognize the photo of Marc and the girls which I have as a screen saver. We should probably have started with our hotel but we can do it last."

"Sounds like a plan. We should be done by lunchtime," Lucas speculated. "We just need to advise our protection detail so they can provide surveillance and security."

Alicia added, "Marc has a sweet tooth so we can also show the photo to clerks at the various chocolatiers."

"He can't be all that bad if he holds the cocoa bean in such high esteem," Lucas quipped.

Alicia gave him a sarcastic look. "I suppose I could blame his deceit on his veneration for and worship of the chocolate gods."

※ ※

"It's interesting, perhaps puzzling," Lucas observed, "that no hotel clerks in the old city recognized the photo, yet one of the chocolatier clerks definitely identified him. Hotels outside the old city are too numerous to check at this juncture". He was seeking options with his voiced summary of their search.

"You live two years with someone and can only recall their addictions and shortcomings half the time," Alicia responded. "What does that say about our ability to predict behaviour of those closest to us? Perhaps familiarity can become more of a hindrance. We don't see the trees for the forest."

"Fifty percent is good. I wasn't even that accurate. If I had been better, perchance I would still be married," Lucas conceded. "Our separation came before I formally joined the ranks of the EUI Unit with Daan. So, I can't attribute the breakup of the marriage to this arcane vocation that keeps me on the road," he murmured regretfully.

Alicia was a bit taken aback by his candid disclosure of personal circumstances. Her description of Marc was pragmatic, meant to contribute additional detail to the psychological profile they were building on their primary target. Lucas's brief admission was purely personal.

"Cappuccino and an opportunity to rest our weary feet?" Lucas asked as they re-entered the Gutenberg Square where they had started their enquiries. Foreign tourists who had been transported by the busload on a systematic schedule were hurriedly taking e-pics of the statue of Johannes Gutenberg, inventor of the moveable-type printing press, and the Notre Dame Cathedral of Strasbourg from every angle in the belief they could capture and preserve the ambience that, in reality, could only be absorbed tacitly and first-hand.

Alicia and Lucas rested in their own space seated in the patio of the restaurant Aux Arms de Strasbourg overlooking the Place Gutenberg, reflecting more on their own mission rather than the reality swirling around them. Alicia maintained her gaze and supportive smile, not wanting to probe for further personal details when prudence was appropriate. Should he wish to invite her into his private life, it would be of his own accord; if not now, perhaps in the fullness of time. Their working relationship was not wholly dependent upon knowing every detail of the previous worlds they had frequented. She certainly had more ghosts than a bedroom walk-in double closet could hold. Such spirits never die or completely go out of fashion.

A moment passed. And then another as he composed the Coles Notes version of his two lives: his home that, like Alicia's, didn't exist beyond the façade of his house, and his profession, his vocation, his fluid career with as many disguises as were warranted.

He transferred his gaze back to her. "My parents were farmers just south of Leuven which is where I grew up, a sedentary lifestyle," he said proudly. "Our life was not what you would describe as affluent but the farm brought in enough to pay for my education. One town, one school, one lifestyle. In contrast, my ex-wife was the daughter of German diplomats. She had lived in many places, attended many schools and lived a nomadic life, as she described it with mixed emotions. We met at the University of Leuven and married a month after graduation."

Alicia quietly maintained her neutral expression, supporting his decision to elaborate on his formative years and marital circumstances. All the while, she silently suggested further disclosure wasn't necessary.

Lucas continued, "I wanted to travel the world. She wanted to stay at home in our cottage. At first, she came with me when I started to attend international conferences but it wasn't long before I was making reservations for one. I was an extravert and, in my element, presenting academic papers. She was an introvert, happiest puttering in her garden. In the end, I concluded I was married without a wife. She concluded she was married without a husband. In retrospect, there was room for reconciliation but neither of us chose that path. The divorce decree was without complications. She kept the cottage. I kept the family farm. I moved on and became an agent for the EUI Unit. She retained her position as a librarian at the university." Alicia sensed there were other explicit details he did not and would not divulge.

Alicia intervened in his self-conscious hiatus. "Let's take an early lunch. But first I'd like to go up to my room to refresh."

"I'll do the same. Knock on my door when you're ready."

CHAPTER 10

As Alicia was about to enter her room, a piercing voice echoed up the winding staircase leading to the top gabled floor of their newly renovated heritage hotel.

"You can't escape. There is nowhere to go. You might as well come back right now."

Alicia and Lucas turned in the direction of the sound of running footsteps as they crossed onto the final upper-level landing where they stood. Alicia stared at Sophia's frantic face and quizzical expression. Initially, the girl didn't recognize Alicia, who whispered her name as she pointed to the fire escape sign on the wall above a hatch on the hallway floor. It read *manche d'évacuation* – evacuation sleeve – with instructions to an escape route to the fourth floor below. Lucas quickly opened the hatch on the floor and gestured to Sophia to descend. As he closed the hatch, a spindly woman with hollow cheeks framed by thinning dishevelled hair stormed onto the landing from the staircase.

"Where's the girl?" the woman demanded sharply.

"What girl?" Alicia replied calmly. She scanned the narrow hallway as if surprised by the question.

"Excuse me," Lucas addressed the woman as he attempted to negotiate the tight space around her.

"Get out of my way," the woman demanded as she attempted to push by, her scowl defiant. She glared with ferret eyes at the four closed doors of the recently revamped attic, and at Alicia and Lucas who were the only other people on the landing.

"I followed the girl up here. You have hidden her," she blurted out abruptly.

"There is no girl up here. See for yourself," Alicia replied gesturing at the limited hallway space. "Now, you need to calm down and leave or I will call hotel security."

"The elevator is over here." Lucas pointed immediately on the heels of Alicia's calm yet precise explanation. "I'm heading down to reception. Let me help you." The woman transferred her attention to Lucas.

Once the sliding door closed and the elevator started to descend, Alicia scampered down the winding staircase to the fourth floor where she located the exit doors labelled *manche d'évacuation*. She softly tapped on the doors and quietly called, "2CV, you can come out now. It's safe."

Sophia gingerly pushed the door open and stared awestruck. "MUM!" she gasped in a faltering whisper. "Where did you come from? How did you get here? Boy, am I happy to see you! What did you do to your hair?"

Alicia held her index finger to her lips and motioned Sophia to follow. They dashed up to the fifth floor and entered Alicia's room. Alicia quickly texted Lucas, "We are in my room." She then hugged Sophia and fondly stroked her hair until she heard Lucas's soft knock.

"Lucas, this is Sophia. Sophia, this is my good friend, Lucas. You can trust him completely."

"How was the ride in the evacuation sleeve, Sophia?" Lucas asked with a supportive smile.

"Very cool," she replied, still whispering. "But!"

"But we are here and together, and you are safe," Alicia assured her calmly, still stroking her hair. "Tell me what happened from the time your father announced that you were all leaving our home in Victoria."

Lucas stood sentinel by the door where he could hear any voices or footsteps approaching in the short hallway. He looked from

Alicia to Sophia and back again with a composed uplifting expression. Sophia needed answers.

Sophia was happy but confused, unsure but secure, calm in Alicia's protective embrace but still apprehensive about the stranger. She closed her eyes and gathered her thoughts. She was thirteen going on thirty when it came to accepting responsibility.

Alicia continued to hold her closely in her arms as much a reassurance for Sophia that she was safe as for herself that there was one less unknown to complicate her muddled mind. Sophia could provide some answers. But where was Camilla? Alicia couldn't leave without her. Her priority had been to first find out why she had become an assassin's target, then find the girls. With Sophia secure although their circumstances perhaps less so, it was no longer a matter of either/or but now both/and, both find out why she had become a target and transport the girls to a secure location. Camilla couldn't be far.

Alicia looked at Lucas who provided a guarded pose, perhaps not Horatio at the gate so to speak but at least at the door. His command presence filled the frame. It was comforting to have a partner who she could depend on and look to for viable options. She chuckled to herself. Marc had never been there for her under far less precarious situations in the two years they had lived together as husband and wife. Being responsible for virtually all domestic decisions, kept her current and strategic in situational and risk analysis. It was second nature, in her DNA.

Sophia took a deep breath. "It's been a crazy time, Mum. Did you get my emergency message? My cell wasn't working so I borrowed a lady's phone who was in the washroom at the Vancouver International Airport. I did what you instructed me to do. I put 2CV in the subject line. I didn't leave a detailed message because I knew the lady would be able to read what I wrote and I wasn't sure if it was safe. I knew you would be worried but it was all I could think of."

Alicia gave her a comforting hug. "Yes, I got it, dear. You did exactly as we planned. Well done."

"It was crazy weird, Mum. On Friday, Dad said we were going on a short trip. He had our bags packed. We flew from Victoria to Vancouver where we stayed in a really nice hotel at the airport. I tried to text you but my phone still wasn't working. Camilla's phone wasn't working either. Dad explained the network was down. He also said we couldn't use the phone on the table in the room because it wasn't paid for with the hotel reservation. The next morning, we got on an early flight to Toronto where we boarded another flight to Paris. Then, we took a really fast train here to Strasbourg. I mean really fast, over three hundred kilometres per hour. We moved into this hotel. Our rooms are on the third floor, 303 and 305. Camilla and I share one room, 303. Dad has the next room. I heard him talking with someone in his room, the woman who chased me. They were talking in loud voices. She threatened to take us away. Camilla got scared and ran out. Her anxiety is really bad, Mum, 'cause Dad didn't pack her meds. Dad is acting really weird. He's not himself. He's really stressed. He still yells at us but not as bad. Can you help us, Mum?"

Alicia maintained her gaze with an encouraging expression. "Yes, dear. Lucas and I can help. That's why we came." She glanced toward Lucas who returned her smile all the while listening for footsteps or voices in the narrow hallway. Lucas smiled at her.

"I'm so happy you're here, Mum. I was so worried. How did you find us? I don't think Dad told you."

Alicia looked at Lucas as she continued to embrace Sophia. "Don't worry about that now, sweetie. Lucas and I will get you and Camilla out of here to a safe place, away from the woman who chased you."

"I've texted Daan," Lucas murmured. "The cavalry is on the way. ETA five minutes with transport and reinforcements."

"Have you had anything to eat?"

"Not since breakfast, Mum."

Alicia ruffled through her satchel. "Here is one of my gluten-free bars. There is some cold water in the fridge."

"Thanks. I figured you'd have one. You always do. Do you eat gluten-free bars, Lucas?" Sophia asked.

"Not yet, but I may try one on your recommendation, Sophia."

"Can I borrow your cellphone, Mum? I'd like to post my friends on Facebook to let them know where I am and that I'm OK."

"Best not right now, dear, until we can get you and Camilla to a safe place. We don't want that woman to know where you are."

"Right, Mum. 2CV."

"Exactly, dear. 2CV."

"And Dad?"

"I'll contact your father once you are safe."

"Thanks, Mum. You're the greatest. I knew you'd save us. Just like Superwoman."

"What name did your father call the lady who chased you?" Lucas asked.

"Elana. I don't know what her last name is though."

"That's OK, Sophia. Thank you. You are very brave and very smart."

"Mum taught me," she replied as she looked up in admiration at Alicia. "She's the greatest."

"She sure is," Lucas confirmed as he glanced at his partner. "The greatest." He reflected back on his initial assessment of Alicia. He now had no qualms about her potential. Once the girls were safe, he would confirm with Daan that he and Alicia were a diamond duo ready to take on all challenges.

Lucas's cellphone buzzed with an incoming text message: "Delta 1 in the lobby, at service entrance and on sidewalk outside front entrance, Delta 2 at north side by service entrance. Dark blue SUV there." He caught Alicia's attention with a terse nod.

"Time to go and find Camilla, Sophia," Alicia announced.

They walked down the staircase with Lucas in the lead, quickening their pace past the third floor. At the main floor, he surveyed the hall and dining room from a window in the door, which he held ajar. He signalled all was clear. Alicia and Sophia followed close by. He then checked the alley. The driver of the SUV gave the all-clear.

Lucas signalled back to Alicia and Sophia who promptly hopped into the vehicle. The driver cautiously pulled ahead to allow a view of the main entrance to the hotel from the street. Delta 1 confirmed their status.

"There's Camilla," Sophia said excitedly.

"Call to her to jump in, Sophia," Alicia instructed as she quickly slid the side door of the SUV open.

"Camilla, over here. Get in, quick," Sophia yelled.

Looking confused, Camilla paused and then ran toward Sophia in the SUV.

Elana saw them and yelled with venom in her voice, "You get back here, now."

Camilla flashed a stare at Elana then Sophia and jumped in beside her sister. Continuing to appear puzzled, she exclaimed, "Who are these people, Sophia?"

"It's Mum and her friend, Lucas. You can trust him."

Camilla stared in disbelief at Alicia. "Mum?" she blurted out as the SUV sped away from the hotel.

Elana drew a pistol and shot at their SUV, striking the back window. "Get after them," she yelled at the driver of a black Mercedes

A Class which had pulled up alongside her. Elana jumped in. It immediately sped after the SUV.

At the first intersection, a second SUV pulled into traffic between the two accelerating vehicles and abruptly stopped, preventing the Mercedes from continuing the chase.

"Ah, cool, Mum," Sophia laughed.

Still confused, Camilla asked her sister, "What's going on, Sophia?" She then burst into tears. "What's going on, Sophia?" she repeated in a broken voice. Tears flowed down her cheeks. Her hands began to tremble.

"It's OK, Camilla. Mum has saved us. Mum is really Superwoman."

Alicia placed her arms around both the girls and held them close.

Lucas glanced in the side-view mirror and whispered, "We've lost them. We're in the clear."

"We'll be at the safe house shortly," the driver announced.

Daan read the new text message: "We have two girls, identified whereabouts of Marc. ID'd Elana, who did not recognize Alicia. Need to move out of hotel rooms now. No doubt Elana knows we engineered escape. Suggest air evac for girls and us to Vaduz. Can you arrange for proprietors to meet and attend to girls? Need to get Camilla's prescription for anxiety refilled soonest."

Daan replied: "Well done to you and Delta team. Agree with your move. Will arrange for Delta 1 to recover your luggage. Helicopter will transport you to Vaduz. Prescription will be filled."

"We will be taking a jet helicopter to a really cool hotel that has a really nice swimming pool," Alicia explained. "There we will introduce you to two more of my friends, Alexandra and Paul. They will take care of you and make sure Elana doesn't find you. You will stay with them for a few days because Lucas and I will be away. You need to take care of each other and do what Alexandra and Paul ask you to do."

"Aw cool, Mum," Sophia exclaimed again. "Can we get new cellphones?"

"Not until Elana is no longer chasing after you. I can't say when but it shouldn't be too much longer. But Alexandra and Paul will take you shopping for new clothes or whatever else you want."

Alicia kept eye contact with both until they agreed. Sophia's nod was more confident, Camilla's tentative but still confused. The prospect of shopping brought smiles to both youthful faces.

At the safehouse, Alicia whispered to Sophia, "Can you talk to Camilla and explain it is *very* important not to use Facebook or Twitter or any other social network like Instagram? It is still too dangerous right now. 2CV."

"OK, Mum, 2CV. Superwoman can't be everywhere. I'll talk to her," Sophia reassured her.

⁃ ⁃

"WHERE ARE THE GIRLS? THEY'RE NOT IN their room," Marc confronted Elana.

"They got away, ran away."

"What do you mean they ran away?"

"The older one ran out of their room. The other one ran upstairs and disappeared. I lost her somehow. They won't do that again once I get them back to Moscow."

Marc glared at her. There had been no mention of Moscow only Basque Country in her threatening communiqué.

"I went down to the hotel lobby and then onto the street to watch the entrance. The younger one was in a SUV and yelled at her sister to get in as soon as she saw her walking toward the hotel. The older one jumped into the SUV, which took off. I fired at it and then gave chase, but we got cut off in traffic and lost them. They had help. A man and a woman."

"What!" Marc yelled. "You put their lives in danger by shooting at them? By the way, their names are Camilla and Sophia. You fool! You idiot!" He glared at her with rage. She knew that expression and the consequences.

My God, Moscow, he reflected in horror. *What have I done? How could I have been that foolish? Where is Camilla? Sophia?* His heart descended to depths he had never experienced before. *Déjà vu.* A flood of terrifying images darted before his eyes, seemingly unrelated yet all connected. *That is why I killed Jacques. Elana told me he was a Moscow double agent gone rogue. But was he? That is why I disappeared to Victoria with the girls, to protect them from all this mayhem. But to safeguard them from whom? Too many unanswered questions. Could it be? But she is dead. Killed in the house explosion. The media reported it. There were fatalities, two women. False news, again? The first casualty of war is the truth.*

Elana stepped forward and embraced Marc with an affectionate hug in an attempt to calm him down. She transformed her demeanour from argumentative and confrontational to subservient and conciliatory, then intimate. Her effort was futile. He pulled back. She approached again. Again, he rebuffed her advances. He seemed out of control, beyond her influence. She became acutely aware of the consequences. The FSB psychologist had warned her. She needed to disengage for her own safety before he took his anger out of her. She had witnessed the consequences with others. He needed space. She would grant him his request, but from a distance, close enough to supervise yet not so close he would become increasingly violent. It had been a little over two years. She could only hope the control tactics that the Russian psychologist had implanted while he was under hypnosis would still be effective without the intimacy which he had just rebuffed. In the past, conciliation alone had never been wholly successful.

CHAPTER 11

"Are you OK?" the subject line read on Alicia's cell. It was signed, Jane.

"I'm OK. Thought you were dead, blown up. The media reported two deaths," Alicia texted back.

"A neighbour was killed in the explosion but I'm OK, only dazed from the concussion. Just released from hospital. Someone is feeding false information to the media."

"Can you call the accountant and arrange for Pemberton Property Management to board up my house and secure with regular patrols?" Alicia requested.

"Yes. Where are you?"

"With my previous employer."

"Your previous or our previous?"

"My previous."

"We need to meet soonest regarding the file your father and I worked on. Are you closer to Metz, Geneva, Graz or Colmar?"

"Colmar."

"On my way. I'll text when I arrive."

"I'll provide detailed instruction regarding rendezvous location when you text next. In the interim, activate tracking device."

※ ※

"Looks like a dilapidated rabbit warren," Lucas said as he stared through the gates at the Colmar property wedged in a corner of the cloistered courtyard, which vied for space with adjoining structures. There was nothing pretentious about its functional façade. Access at its entrance was limited to two adjoining narrow cobblestoned one-way lanes defined by medieval stone archways and stuccoed walls, topped with serrated shale. These structures impaired easy access and line of sight into neighbouring houses except through wrought iron gates constructed at the corners of the courtyard to accommodate the tapered horse-drawn carriages of yesteryear and today's modern compact vehicles. A stone path worn down in the center from centuries of trampling feet hugged the perimeter.

"It's not what it seems. It's actually well maintained in an unkempt condition deliberately," Alicia explained. "The courtyard provides natural security. The caretaker lives across the square in what is the refurbished carriage house. Thus, no neighbours complain or question what goes on. The adjacent house, just outside the courtyard, is part of the complex and also well maintained. The Delta teams can set up surveillance there in the carriage house and updated barn."

"Convenient neighbourhood," Lucas commended as they entered the courtyard and circled to the left behind what appeared to be the derelict structure to the reinforced backdoor.

Alicia monitored an incoming text and replied with directions. "Jane has just arrived at the Gare de Colmar," Alicia confirmed. "Her taxi should be here in fifteen minutes."

"Radio check," Delta Leader announced.

"Delta 1 confirmed. All feet posing as tourists."

"Delta 2 confirmed. Vehicles at both entrances."

"Delta 5 confirmed. All visual and audio surveillance working."

"Subject has entered the lane," Delta 2 advised.

"Entering the courtyard," Delta 1 confirmed. "The taxi is departing. She is pausing in the portico surveying the courtyard, now entering the house."

Jane scanned the eclectic interior decor which resembled used furnishings one might find in a bric-a-brac in the 3rd Arrondissement Marais district of Paris. "It's good to see you alive and well," Jane hugged Alicia. "Who is your friend?" she asked, looking cautiously at Lucas while exhibiting open distrust. He reciprocated with equal edginess, a behaviour consistent with the tradecraft.

"Likewise," Alicia replied. "Lucas is my new partner. Uneventful trip?"

"I'd like to say yes but have the feeling I'm being watched. Nothing positive. Just a sensation. They are professional whoever they are. So, we need to talk quickly." Her eyes nervously darted between Alicia and Lucas and back to Alicia who attempted to calm her concerns with a reassuring nod.

"Heard that," Delta 5 confirmed. "Deltas 1 and 2 keep your eyes peeled."

"Did your father talk to you about a source he had, the Moroccan from Casablanca?" Jane asked guardedly. "He was known as Aziz or just the Moroccan. At least that was one of the names he used."

"Yes, vaguely."

"We need to find the Moroccan and fast," Jane insisted. Her anxiety revealed the need for urgency and wariness. Her posture emphasized priority be dedicated to tapping into that source while remaining vigilant.

Alicia held her stare, her breathing slow but deliberate. She and Jane had engaged in many conversations that mattered over the years. She remembered none with such gravity as the one they were having now. "I'm sensing somehow there is a connection between the explosive destruction of our homes in Victoria, the unrest among select Basque factions, and my father's elusive communiqués which mentioned a mysterious file," Alicia proposed. "Why was your house blown up?"

"I don't know," Jane replied in a neutral matter-of-fact voice. Her detached almost impartial expression gave no outward indication to the contrary. Yet Alicia sensed otherwise.

"There has to be a connection between both attacks literally within minutes of each other," Alicia insisted. "If not mere coincidence, the common denominator has to be MI6 where we both served albeit never worked together on any file. Else, coincidence is too remote. I continue to refrain from using superlatives like always and never."

Jane shrugged her shoulders, knowing the question from Alicia would be forthcoming. "I have drawn a blank with my link analysis. I'm at a loss. With your brilliant mathematical mind, I was hoping you would have an inkling of a probable explanation."

"The only other link common to both of us is my father. You served with him. I lived with him." Alicia maintained her gaze, mirroring Jane's blank response. She sensed Jane was attempting to divert the conversation back to the Moroccan who was a tangible lead unlike speculation about the two explosions. Alicia quickly exchanged glances with Lucas, seeking confirmation of his intuitive response thus far to Jane's presence. He blinked once confirming her request, his stare seemed impartial yet cautious.

"I am learning more about the Basque file but I know virtually nothing about my father's cases or how he might have been involved, if at all. You need to fill me in," Alicia said in the form of a directive more so than an open-ended request or an introduction to a relaxed convivial chit-chat.

"There is a document in an envelope hidden in the tunnel between your house and the garden shed," Jane revealed. "But I don't know the exact location or the contents. Your father referred to a tunnel in one of our conversations when his health was failing. The Moroccan is the link somehow," Jane confirmed. Her reference to the Moroccan seemed less informative than deliberate, as if Alicia would provide more detail than she would share.

"How?" Alicia retorted. She wanted to press for an immediate response before Jane could manipulate facts, if that was her intention. Alicia was probing for feelings because emotions lead to truth exposed in tone and texture which are more difficult to hide. She was looking for a structural weakness, a chink in Jane's façade which would expose her ulterior motivation. In Jane's steady gaze, she sensed a veiled forewarning.

Lucas watched his partner as she and Jane jousted as if in a medieval tournament. Jane seemed to be seeking more information than she was prepared to surrender. Alicia held the higher ground, analyzing every word, every innuendo while probing for additional data to enhance her analysis. He read her mind as one might do after drinking from the Fountain of Delphi. What was the prophecy of the Oracle?

"It goes further, relating to your father's work. It involves Middle East militancy, Beijing and your ex-fiancé, Jacques," Jane added.

"Jacques?" Alicia interjected impatiently. *Was there more to Jacques than Daan had revealed? Was there more I hadn't known, that he hadn't shared with me, even during those intimate moments and quiet dialogues of a future life together?* Or was Jane throwing out bait that she knew would cause Alicia to respond emotionally more than objectively. The former certainly had been activated. Alicia remained as neutral as possible.

Jane elaborated. "Moscow money is being funnelled to ISIS. I am convinced it is Beijing capital being supplied, and through ISIS, to a small band of agitators deceptively presenting themselves as supposed disgruntled Basque separatists. The courier to the Basque might have been a disgruntled former Russian KGB agent who set up his own intelligence consultation consortium somewhere on the Spanish Riviera after he wasn't asked to transfer to the new FSB. The Moroccan will elaborate. He is the only one who can fill in the blanks. That is why we must find him soonest."

"I recently learned that Marc had assassinated Jacques," Alicia declared. Admitting personal fault lines had never been one of her strengths. Through reflection, she had become conscious that the more she resisted her feelings, the longer she would remain blocked.

Jane raised her eyebrows and took a deep breath. "I'm not surprised to hear that. There are too many conglomerates and lone wolves with conflicting loyalties and agendas associated with this case. It goes with the turf. The greater the importance, the greater the secrecy and the greater the number of individuals actively seeking anything to do with the file. Here I refer to all agents from all organizations in addition to freelancers who market in intelligence like the ex-KGB agent living on the Spanish Riviera. The colosseum can get crowded quickly with gladiators, some disguised as wild beasts. The proverbial question is: Who are the good guys and who are the bad guys? Better still, which ones are masquerading in the clothes of their nemeses assuming there are more than one? Who is the errant defector?"

"How do we contact this Moroccan?" Alicia asked.

Jane handed Alicia an envelope. "This is the last known information I have about him. Introduce yourself as a colleague of Friar Tuck. Your father used this cover name, amongst others. If the Moroccan is prepared to meet, he will reply: 'Little John looks forward to sharing bread.'"

"There is what appears to be an Asian tourist mingling around the entrance to the courtyard," Delta 5 announced. "He is reaching into his oversized backpack." Delta 5 shouted a warning. "Alicia and Lucas vacate immediately! MOVE NOW! MOVE NOW! MOVE NOW!" he yelled in rapid succession like a machine gun spitting out hollow-point bullets.

"We need to get out of here fast. Follow me," Alicia barked.

As they rose, the Asian tourist pulled out a hand-held mini rocket launcher and fired into the safehouse. The projectile struck Jane as Alicia and Lucas fled behind a reinforced barricade and into the adjacent house. Delta 1 converged on the assailant while Delta 2 pulled their vehicles into the lane blocking the two entrances. The real tourists ran for cover.

Delta 5's frantic voice cracked the airwaves: "Everyone down. He is wearing an explosive pack."

Within minutes, Colmar police had cordoned off the courtyard. The fire brigade was standing by to wash down the walls of buildings and the cobblestone lane pitted by the shrapnel that decades earlier had escaped similar damage during the latter months of the Second World War only now to incur vestiges of the ferocity of the Cold War. The only forensic evidence was blood splatters on the walls mixed with fragments of bone. Delta 1 had swiftly commandeered what remained of the backpack and mini rocket launcher bearing embossed Russian identification markings.

Alicia and Lucas left through the front door of the adjacent house which was outside the police tape. Tinnitus screamed in their ears. Disconnected thoughts swirled in their muddled minds from the contained concussion of the explosion in the safe house. Headaches and blurred vision lingered with both. Every step they took tripped successive somatic detonations along a myriad of hyper-active brain cells and neural pathways, reminding them of their mortality.

"Debrief," Daan's text read.

Alicia and Lucas both knew they would need to rest before they could gather their thoughts in any semblance of order. For now, they would return to their hotel where they would tend to their thundering headaches, screaming tinnitus and blurred vision. Images of her exploding SUV in her driveway flashed on the flat screen monitor of Alicia's mind. Lucas would immediately text Daan their status and location. Delta teams would provide perimeter security for them. Other team members would provide security to the courtyard which contained a sundry of debris from the explosions.

Life before returning to the EUI Unit and becoming a partner with Lucas had been relatively peaceful for Alicia. The hiatus was a period of reflection. In retrospect, though, Alicia missed the challenges inherent in the arcane discipline. Her motivation to re-engage was the mental stimulation, part of which was engaging with colleagues in conversations that mattered. She would not be content being a soccer mom. That was now readily apparent.

Alicia had never been in the line of fire with either MI6 or her initial stint with the EUI Unit. Such experiences demanded mental acuity different from data analysis. She had excelled in the world of academia. She had shied away from the colosseum where she could not always excel as a lone gladiator. Survival in this arena depended upon her being accountable to others of equal and greater competencies in their own right.

Jane had been a friend. Lucas was a partner. Alicia had used those terms in a cognitive context. Jane was now dead. Lucas had barely escaped the scythe of the grim reaper, as had she. There was nothing intellectual about this scenario. She had crossed the Rubicon and immediately engaged the reinforced enemy positions on the opposite bank.

CHAPTER 12

"How are you, Alicia?" Alexandra asked with a sympathetic greeting. "You have survived two explosions in as many weeks. Your friend, Jane, wasn't so lucky the second time. I am so sorry for the loss."

"Thanks for asking. I'm still processing the events and nursing a wicked headache, as is Lucas. The reinforced wall absorbed the shrapnel and deflected most of the blast into the ceiling baffles. But I have concluded I'm not twenty-one anymore. The bounce-back spring still bounces back but not with as much oomph as it once did. Put another way, I've got a feeling that we're not in Neverland anymore," Alicia jested in a resigned tone.

"An accurate analogy." Alexandra assured her. "Good that you have retained your sense of humour. Reservations at our R&R resort spa are confirmed for as long as you need."

"It would be glib to say it comes with the turf, but it does come with the turf," Alicia admitted. "And I'd be dishonest if I said that I didn't miss staid Victoria and the serene backyard of what was once my secluded Pemberton Estate. That is a past life now, not to be replicated, at least not in the sanctuary of the Pacific Coast. For now, I will follow the doctor's instructions and take a little more down time in my new favourite five-star accommodation in Liechtenstein."

Alexandra said nothing. Her support was evident. In her former profession as a forensic psychologist, she had learned the attuned art of silence and patience as a preferred means of therapy.

Images of the SUV exploding in her driveway and the subsequent shattering of the façade of her house were lodged firmly in her mind like the penetrating shards of glass and splinters of wooden window frames that had destroyed the kitchen. The structure could be repaired. Her relationship with Marc was irreparable. She accepted the fact her past blurred the present and distorted the prism of the future. Fear, like grief, can transform your DNA and that of your offspring. It was part of her culture, how she perceived others, who she was, her father's daughter. Making peace with the ghosts of the past and establishing a sense of clarity for the future would be a work in progress.

"My major concern is for the girls and their safety. How are they?"

"Doing well. Loving the swimming pool and modelling all their new clothes to the staff at the hotel. Sophia is a jewel, supporting Camilla whose anxiety seems to be abating now that she has her medication. She is getting through the worst phases of the abrupt withdrawal from being a young teenager without a cellphone and the overwhelming blitz of mindless social media. One of our older staff members has become their governess, watching over them like a protective hen. She is teaching them about the history of Liechtenstein and how to speak German."

"I cannot thank you enough," Alicia replied with genuine gratitude in her tone.

"I have recently become a new grandmother to a delightful granddaughter in Paris, so I'm quite enjoying being around young girls. Speaking of mother hens, Daan is herding the gaggle. We can talk more, later."

※ ※

"THANK YOU FOR ATTENDING AT SUCH SHORT notice," Daan welcomed them. "I would like to re-introduce Yolina Lambert, our lead at the European Union Commission in Brussels, and Commandant Benoit Parent from Police Nationale Counterterrorism and Terrorism Cyber Units. I also welcome our EUI Unit colleagues, Doctors

Alexandra Belliveau and Paul Bernard who have cut their sabbatical short in order to assist. And thank you, Commandant Parent, for hosting this meeting. Yolina, the floor is yours."

"Our file on recent Basque agitation has expanded beyond the EU. The European Council has expressed deep concern over recent events. Security remains the top priority. We are all gathered here because of the attack in Colmar which has demonstrated an exponentially increased threat from entities beyond the borders of the European Union. We have seen this before but recently the threat has become multidimensional with grave geo-political overtones. You have all read the Colmar briefing notes. We need to establish a coordinated stratagem by the time we adjourn."

Daan continued the discussion. "Benoit, top priority is an IT strategy to tap into, monitor and, as necessary, disrupt the cyber-crime communications without leaving any telltale traces. From an operational perspective, it is imperative that we understand what they are thinking and what their next moves will be."

"I've already established a network of electronic eavesdropping akin to what folks in our HUMINT – human intelligence and watcher service – do. You won't be surprised to hear there has been a flurry of cyber traffic in the past forty-eight hours. In contrast, you may be surprised to learn the greatest increase has been between two independent hackers with known Beijing and Tehran affiliations. Yet they are neither Chinese nor Persian; instead, new kids on the block with fast fingers for hire in the criminal cyber zone. We suspect they are currently working out of Islamabad but are mobile. Their chatter confirms they are active with ISIS cells in the EU, most recently in the Marseilles region of the French Riviera. We have distributed digital photographs."

"Do we need to put them under full-time physical surveillance?" Daan asked, concerned about the increased demand on resources already over-stretched. If needed, it was opportune that Yolina was present to authorize immediately the expenditures.

"I recommend not at this juncture. We know they are new to the hacker game because they have virtually no keyboard discipline. Nor have they been well tutored in the art of codes and encryptions. As a result, their e-signatures are very easy to identify and trace. We don't want to spook them into modifying their identities or MOs."

By noon, Daan had co-ordinated Europol assets. The priority of strategies had been forged and the European Council had committed to the requisite funding. Alicia and Lucas had been authorized to cross the EU border into North Africa, specifically Morocco, after an all-too-brief respite in Liechtenstein and visit with the girls. Travel to other locations around the Mediterranean had received tentative approval subject to prior notification.

As the meeting adjourned with a successful strategy in hand, Yolina approached Alicia with a warm smile. "I am pleased to hear you have returned to the fold. When Daan asked for funding, I immediately approved his request. I've been acquainted with Dr. Lucas Peeters for a few years and am confident the two of you will make a formidable team. It goes without saying I am bothered by the circumstances that have brought you back to the EUI Unit, particularly the two recent attempts on your life."

"Thank you," Alicia replied. "It is good to be back among colleagues." The tone of her response was overshadowed with conflict. She had been relatively content half a world away on the Pacific Coast of Canada despite the motivation for her temporary leave of absence. Her return was welcomed by both Yolina and Daan, and herself, although it brought back unresolved memories of Jacques' murder. She was determined to find out why she had become a target for assassination. Yet that opened a Pandora's box now filled with emotion of Marc's marital betrayal. The elephant in the room would be the ultimate confrontation with him to face their differences and to deal with the final blow to their relationship. She knew how she *should* react but did not know how she *would* react. Not being in the know had always been her nemesis. The scales were not tilted in her favour. She reached for her pistol. Her grip tightened.

"Have you taken the time to visit Fort de Queuleu?" Yolina enquired softly. Her manner was calm although cloaked in a never-ending desire to resolve past injustices.

"I have. And you?"

"As time permits, I pay my respects. I'm humbled by the recent commitment of the French government to preserve the ramparts and the structure in the name of the Vichy betrayals amongst others, despite the efforts of some to desecrate them. Rest assured, the European Union Parliament will do whatever is necessary to keep alive the memories of those whose fate were forever sealed by betrayal and forced one-way passage through the gates. We can talk more, later." Yolina encircled her with an affectionate hug of a mother for a favourite daughter about to leave the security of the hearth for perilous forays. "Listen to your intuition," Yolina whispered. Her eyes reinforced her abiding affection and guarded apprehension.

Alicia recalled the many quiet conversations she had had with her father and the tone of cautiousness that shrouded those solemn occasions. It wasn't so much the words he had spoken to her as the connotation of innuendos he had imparted as if a bequest. Although he had crossed the English Channel to France on several occasions, he had never travelled to Fort de Queuleu or to the family home south of Metz since the end of the War. The pilgrimage would have been too raw. The memories alone bore a burden too heavy for him to continually carry. That was a part of her inherited DNA. Her own journey had been shorter in time but no less onerous than Yolina's, just different by tainted circumstances.

CHAPTER 13

The café in Casablanca where they had arranged to meet her father's informant, the Moroccan, was crowded with too many searching eyes and attuned ears like finely adjusted radar to foreign nuances in gestures and expressions. Alicia was reminded of Lucas's explanation of the roles the waiters in their Vaduz hotel had played during the Second World War when Nazis frequented that facility for periods of supposed rest and relaxation. Covert liaisons appeared to be the motivation for some individuals of differing political persuasions in this wary Moroccan ambience. On many occasions, she had watched the 1942 black and white Hollywood film, *Casablanca*, starring Humphrey Bogart and Ingrid Bergman. A rerun could have been filmed here today with no additional props needed, not even a classic piano brought to life by those all too familiar with the fifty-two ivory and thirty-six ebony keys.

"I am a friend of Friar Tuck," Alicia said quietly. She wasn't confident about how her introduction would be received so did not identify herself initially as her father's daughter.

"Little John looks forward to sharing bread." The Moroccan's discreet reply was masked by the muffled din of the conversations of patrons and the high shrill bartering of the street merchants. Regardless, Alicia sensed that the intent of their visit was known in advance as if the agenda for their communication had a wide distribution list with no regard for security clearance. Where was the perceived leak, if there was one? And only one?

"Who is your colleague?" the Moroccan followed up as he led his guests into a back room behind the bar. The same eyes followed them as they had done when they first entered the café. Although their discussion would be beyond the range of eavesdroppers at the tables, the secluded room would be within range of any microphones planted to troll for intelligence and sold thereafter at a negotiable profit.

"My colleague is an academic associate. We are conducting research into Basque history," Alicia explained simply. Her reply was purposefully simplistic and devoid of specifics. She was a novice in this North African primarily Islamic culture, and at assessing its ambiance and the potential response of their Moroccan host. Jane had assured her the Moroccan was a trusted friend and colleague of her father. But could she trust Jane? She hadn't in the past, at least not completely.

"And what brings you here to my doorstep?" the Moroccan asked in a gentle, disarming manner, almost too benign to garner immediate confidence. She wondered whether her father had that confidence. If so, to what extent. She was not aware if Jane had actually accompanied him on any of his liaisons to Morocco and meetings with Little John. She doubted it for two reasons. First, her father only spoke to her of solo missions. Second, a generation ago, women rarely if ever negotiated with men in this North African culture, especially Muslim men. Islamic tradition had not changed since her father crossed the curtained entrance of this café and perhaps this meeting room. Today, she was the only female in this male-dominated establishment. By being here, she had violated a sacred tenant by her mere presence. Had she not been with Lucas, her safe access and egress would have been tenuous at best. This was not an occasion to appear either timid or bold.

"Before my father passed away, he suggested if I ever needed help, I should contact Little John. One of my father's associates, Jane, also spoke highly of you."

"Ahhhhh," the Moroccan sighed. "He had spoken of you with great fondness. You have your father's eyes and honesty. Welcome."

Alicia met his gaze with a discerning smile. Her initial concern was mitigated by his cordial reference to her father. The Moroccan was correct. She did have her father's eyes. Others who knew her father from his MI6 service had made similar observations, some as compliments, others with wariness. Secret Intelligence Service ghosts conjured suspicion amongst its ranks. Trust had been irrevocably violated by Kim Philby and other associates of the Cambridge Five. Those who were former Special Operations Executive only trusted each other at the best of times. Now rarely, if ever, with complete trust.

"How can I help the daughter of Friar Tuck?" His willingness to assist showed in his quiet, relaxed bearing. A double handshake confirmed his sincerity and finesse in disarming her lingering unease. "Let me assure you this is a safe place to talk. Please sit." Alicia and Lucas followed his invitation while he poured them tea.

His handshake seemed sincere as did the glint in his eyes and tenor in his voice. But such explicit expressions could be learned through training and disciplined practice, each a two-way venue – what was felt physically in concert with expressed facial features and audible tones. When in doubt, intuition would be the deciding vote. Alicia's initial assessment was to remain neutral, until proven otherwise. She needed to work more with Lucas in order to tap into his implicit yet pragmatic evaluation. For now, she would simply garner layers and layered effects of facts for subsequent analysis.

Under ideal conditions, there would have been briefings based on the most current intelligence acquired from HUMINT – human intelligence, in addition to electronic monitoring before an asset entered an area of operations. Alicia had the benefit of none as she entered this café, with the exception of Jane's verbal recollection of events, which had not been vetted for accuracy and trustworthiness from Alicia's perspective within the North African regional context. In the final analysis, it was all about money and profit in the marketing and subsequent sale of resources in demand, intelligence being just one of many commodities.

Alicia opened the conversation. "I need to know everything about the case the two of you had worked on. Jane passed along some details but said you would know more. Unfortunately, she was killed recently in an explosion. I have also become the target of an assassin's bomb after a few years. Yet, I do not know why. I suspect it may be linked to my father's service with MI6 or related to my own files."

The Moroccan nodded, suggesting he had become aware of the increase in what were reported as focused terrorist attacks. "I gave your father some photos of a Beijing agent, and maybe a Basque contact lurking on the periphery. I no longer have copies of them. More photos were sent to me after your father's time." He reached into a satchel and retrieved an envelope. "Here are copies. I apologize for the poor quality. They have not been stored in the best of conditions. In addition, the copier was also of poor quality."

Alicia hastily scanned the black and white photos before passing them to Lucas. One of the images caught her attention. She lingered almost imperceptibly, faintly touching the tip of Lucas's index finger. That tentative pause of recognition did not go unnoticed by Lucas who carefully scrutinized the details, all the while maintaining his attention on the Moroccan. He was practiced at assessing individual intentions but the Moroccan's were proving to be increasingly challenging.

"This man in the background with the fedora pulled low over his forehead as if wanting to hide from public view," Lucas pointed to one of the photographs. "Is he one of those you refer to as lurking on the periphery?"

His enquiry was received favourably despite the fact the Moroccan had focused his attention mostly on Alicia. The Moroccan studied the mysterious figure whose expression was as enigmatic as his own. "Not sure. I don't think he was ever introduced to me. It was safer not to ask. He was with a Basque person. Maybe he was the kingpin but wanted to mask that role. I surmised he was just someone you did not want to cross. I think he was not true Basque because he did not display Basque features of broad shoulders and powerful legs from climbing goat trails in the Pyrénées. In addition, he did not have the chiselled face of a Roman or Greek god common among men of that culture."

Lucas transferred his gaze to Alicia, seeking a possible endorsement of his line of enquiry like a sorcerer's apprentice, a protégé pursuing validation from his mentor. She certainly had more intimate and practical experience with the Basque although she seemed reluctant to share it at the moment. Perhaps she was seeking clearer recollection of events woven into the fabric of old memories, the veiled pattern that had not yet been fully revealed. Or perhaps the distant recollection haunted her like the howl of Arctic wolves which could be locked up but never silenced like secrets of secrets.

"We first met in Beirut," the Moroccan continued after a period of silence. "A few weeks later, we met again in Valencia on the Spanish Riviera in the company of a retired KGB agent. Curious man. He sat on the beach drawing caricatures with charcoal – cartoonish faces of tourists – while talking to them. Maybe that was what he wanted to do. Drawing was an excuse, a cover for his real reason for being there, to listen to stories, to gather intelligence. There is always more truth in stories than detail in facts. Or he might have been there as an intermediary. Sorry, I have no photo of him," he concluded as he shrugged ever so slightly and raised his eyebrows in an inquisitive manner.

There is more truth in stories than detail in facts, she mused. Her strength was in analyzing facts gleaned from a myriad of sources. She tended not to trust the synthesis of stories conducted by others. Instead, she preferred to listen to the stories first hand, to hear the spoken words, to observe the lips of the raconteur, to see the eyes, to judge the tone, and to sense the mood. Within lay the truth.

"What was discussed at these meetings?" Alicia asked, curious to gain a better insight into the motivation of all the players. The details might also shed light on why she had recently become an assassin's target. She wished to remain humble in the company of the proud Moroccan man who seemed to fluctuate between an enigmatic sage and an unpretentious merchant of knowledge, both fishing for and providing wisdom regarding the most opportune repository of advice where specifics were scarce. Intelligence provided without wariness had its own landmines, even for those experienced in the tradecraft. The daughter of Friar Tuck was not Friar Tuck.

The Moroccan studied the context of her request. "Some conversations I did not hear. What I heard was talk of armaments, Soviet surface-to-air missiles. Today, the Chinese are more involved and want to sell weapons to Middle East and Basque contacts. Their plans were part of long-term, geo-political strategies, not just one-off deals. I was surprised to hear the Basque wanted to buy weapons. I had never before heard about aggression from any Basque people. It did not make sense. The Basque, for the most part, are relatively docile except when agitated by outside interests, provocateurs, regarding land claims. Unlike Chinese dynasties or the millennial vision of the Nazi Third and Fourth Reich, the Basque never had global ambitions with visions of vast resources. They tended to focus on their Druid and Celtic roots, not on future global empires acquired at great expense and loss and suffering."

"Who are the other people in this photo?" Lucas again asked, pointing to one of the more recent photos. Again, his enquiry was received in the same tone as Alicia's, perhaps because she was present. The Moroccan appeared to be a trove of intelligence when searching the distant recesses of his mind for scarce inventories as opposed to exact facts. What wasn't initially disclosed appeared to be richer in clues. Any hesitancy on his part was as a result of trust more so than a dearth of detail.

"The Basque woman seemed to be a go-between," he elaborated. "Her Russian name was Nadia. She went by another name – a Basque name, Elana. I say supposedly because she didn't strike me as being solely loyal to the Basque cause. She had a different agenda, perhaps partially scripted by another party. I deduced a mixture of personal and professional, the latter being contractual."

Alicia and Lucas exchanged glances. This gesture did not go unnoticed by their host who took the opportunity to top up their tea before continuing with his identification of others in the recently acquired photographs, while casting his own net for validation.

"The Chinese man was referred to as Liu. He was quieter. I needed to be careful. He appeared to be more distant, harder to read. He needed to be treated with more cautiousness, respect if for no other reason than he seemed unpredictable. I didn't know what he might do. He seemed to be unstable. Perhaps it was his culture. The Mediterranean-looking man was referred to simply as Mohammad. I never asked about his family of origin although I believed he was Egyptian. I am sure that you can appreciate it was best not to enquire. I was known to them only as the Moroccan. It was safest that way. Again, I apologize for the dubious details. The photographer was an amateur. His camera was old."

"And the Russian who sketched tourists?" Lucas followed up. "Was he ever there, at these meetings with Elana and the man in the fedora?"

"Dmitri was the name he sometimes used. But you need to know that, like me, these people used false or code names more often than not and sometimes more than one code name."

"Understood," Lucas acknowledged with an appreciative nod. The absence of verifiable accuracy was sketching an ambience of intrigue that by itself reflected a dearth of individual detail. But combined, it was rich in potential background knowledge and motives.

"What was my father's primary interest?" Alicia pressed.

The Moroccan held her gaze although his attention seemed elsewhere. "Difficult question. Maybe three interests. One, who were the players? Two, what were the connections. Put another way, who were the associates? Identifying their motivation and intelligence is revealing in itself. Three, what were they doing with armaments, some surplus Second World War, some more modern. Money was a big motivator. But there was more than profit or commerce. Ask yourself why there was a need for so many brokers? I mention motivation. It was certainly a consideration in long-term strategy. It was regional for some and global for others. Your father was interested in global geo-political ramification. The Cold War was about to boil over back then, and now too. Your father talked about World War III and Armageddon. He was very worried, that the eleventh hour fifty-ninth minute was approaching too quickly. It was as if he could see the future but was powerless to intervene, like the Cassandra effect in Greek mythology."

"And the Russian? If he wasn't present at all these meetings, what was his interest? What role was he playing? Was he brokering any deals?"

"This Russian who did the caricatures described himself as a free agent, an intelligence entrepreneur who played the field working for both Moscow and Beijing, and anyone else who could pay his consulting fees. He was also connected to other Far East Asian players somehow, a few of whom had reputations for being exceedingly nasty. At least two were on his payroll as snipers." The worrisome frown on the Moroccan's face was in complete contrast to his initial welcoming demeanour.

"Is he still in Valencia?" Lucas enquired with equal curiosity and caution, taking the Moroccan's forewarning to heart.

"No. I heard he had been murdered by one of his Beijing associates who subsequently tried unsuccessfully to blame the hit on Moscow. A hazard of the tradecraft when you play one vindictive vengeful client against the other," the Moroccan concluded. "In all of this, there is a constant that is often overlooked – the financial. Players make more money creating confrontation, because it is and always has been an influential industry. There is virtually no profit in peace. Even in supposed peacekeeping missions devoid of declared war. Military commanders like to prolong missions because it allows them to get their tickets punched, an operational prerequisite for promotion."

"What is your sense of the players today? Traditional and newcomers?" Lucas followed up respectfully.

The Moroccan contemplated the question. He poured more tea as he considered his reply. "The Russians were once considered to be the best along with the British and Americans, all of whom relentlessly jousted for top billing. The Russians are still very good but now there are other more venomous vipers hiding amongst the bulrushes in the swamp. One was an agent with olden Druid and Celtic roots who had infiltrated French Counter-Intelligence. He disappeared mysteriously around the same time the ex-KGB entrepreneur, Dmitri from Valencia, was killed. The Chinese are good but do not fully understand the culture. That is a major short-coming for them. As a result, they are defining the global arena within the context of Mandarin philosophy. There are some other minor players. Time will tell what they will do. Regardless, the most prominent variable today is not so much cultural or regional but technological. That is the game changer. Even the Dark Web and big data have their limitations. I have been around a long time and witnessed constant transition. I can assure you the eyes of the drone in the cyber world bring a new dimension to the battlespace, but they will not replace traditional eyes of HUMINT, the one-on-one human intelligence gatherers. Technology may detect more readily but conversations confirm more accurately."

CHAPTER 14

Alicia mused, "The West has been fighting with and, more recently, against the Russians much longer than the Chinese so we know them better, but still not completely. Ask again in the next millennium and we will know the Chinese better if we haven't destroyed ourselves by then."

The Moroccan held her gaze. What he did not say was more telling. What followed revealed the richness of their discussion. In it could be found the essence of his wisdom. "I miss playing backgammon with Friar Tuck. I trust he taught you the intricacies of the game." The Moroccan's transition held the seeds of implicit knowledge that Alicia needed to attend to. It also signalled the end of their meeting.

"That he did," she replied. The Moroccan's question caught her curiosity. She sensed her father's presence. She could only imagine how discussions between Friar Tuck and Little John would have transpired as the two played multiple games of backgammon. Their respective strategies would have transformed the direction and format of their communiqués, each an enigma without a codebook yet every move an individual encryption of a code. The translation was in the game, best of three, five, seven, never pre-set, just known.

The mention of backgammon tweaked Lucas's attention. The game originated in the Middle East, Persia, what is now Iran. If the Moroccan played with her father, both would have been world-class experts. Had Alicia learned from her father, an expert in the actual strategies of the game and interwoven innuendoes? They would need to talk at length.

As they bid the Moroccan adieu and left the café again under the scrutinizing eyes of its male patrons, Lucas commented, "You seemed to recognize someone in the newer group of photos."

"Or something," Alicia muttered with a tinge of irritation. "Memories can be fleeting just when you need them to be detailed and accurate. They require a fertile context to rebloom."

It wasn't a time for a whack on the back of the head. Yet, Alicia seemed to withdraw ever so slightly – a trigger point. "In the photo, to the right of the person wearing the fedora, the distant figure appears to be the Great Sphinx of Giza, the oldest known sculpture in Egypt, directly facing west to east into the rising sun," Lucas offered.

"That's what is confusing me. The man in the fedora could be Jacques, my ex-fiancé. But he was never in Egypt to my knowledge, so I doubt it's him."

"How do you know he was never in Egypt?"

"He would have told me. A visit to Giza and the pyramids is not an everyday event in one's otherwise mundane life." She stopped short of a conclusion. "Unless it might have been a frequent occurrence." She lingered a moment. *But how could that be? I knew Jacques, or I thought I did.*

"Let me play the devil's advocate," Lucas proposed. "Perhaps he withheld it for reasons you never knew or he did not want you to know."

"That proposition is preposterous," Alicia snapped back in disbelief. "What are you suggesting? That I didn't know my fiancé?"

Lucas continued in a calm, measured tone. "Did you know everything there was to know about Marc after two years of matrimony? How long had you known Jacques? Months?"

Alicia's glare needed no further clarification. "Leave it alone," she snapped.

Lucas let it simmer but did not abandon it altogether.

"Why would he be there?" she questioned after an awkward

silence. "Another unknown." She didn't need more perplexing questions to gnaw away at her already waning self-confidence. She was seldom self-conscious. After a moment of reflection, she shook her head.

Lucas's probing stare mirrored her mounting annoyance, a manifestation of the tradecraft when analysis does not suggest a viable solution or reveal at least potential scenarios.

"If it is Jacques under the fedora, the operative question is why. Why was he there?" she reiterated in a more collegial tone.

"Perhaps he had a suspect under surveillance," Lucas proposed. "Or it wasn't a one-off tourist event but something more underhand that, if it was publicly known, would have had ill-omened, perhaps lethal consequences for him, for you, for others. Was he protecting you? Potentially more problematic, we do not know when the photo was taken, before or after the two of you met. Each scenario would have a different consequence. Without that data, we are hard-pressed to create an accurate context. Without the context of the timeframe, we are left with speculation less any credibility."

She countered, "Another unknown being heaped on the growing haystack? Another distraction?"

"Is the elephant still in the room?" Lucas asked. She seemed to have drifted into another realm, propelled by recollections, triggered by the possibility that the man wearing the fedora was Jacques.

Alicia sighed in frustration. *To be loved, needed, desired. That was all I sought in a relationship, not deceit, dishonesty, betrayal. Were my intimate relations with Jacques and Marc nothing more than a convenient affiliation for them, tactics with ulterior outcomes? Tools of the covert tradecraft? Merely individual fiefdoms where my emotions had been held in fief, in fee, for sale each with their own price determined by the feudal lords of the manor?* Her lips trembled in disillusionment at the thought. She grimaced in repulsion as she glared at the myriad of images projected onto the flat screen monitor of her mind. Her contemplative reflection cut through the distant clamour that had been holding her hostage.

Lucas maintained his quiet supportive stare. His intent was not to distract her, not to increase her frustration to the point when she exploded. Instead, he wanted her to concentrate on the growing evidence, some complementary, some contradictory, none simplistic and complete.

"The elephant is no longer in the room although its smell lingers," Alicia declared in resignation. "Thanks for the whack on the back of the head. Sorry for the bark. Let's get back to the basics of this case."

"Is there just one case?" Lucas proposed, unsure himself of the precision of the truth. "Or are we dealing with more than one, each overlapping the others and layering the complexity? The destruction of your house in Victoria may be a common denominator, or your father and his MI6 service. Is the common denominator a geo-political factor?"

"Any or all three could be possibilities. It is safe to say Marc was involved directly or indirectly in the destruction of my house," Alicia replied confidently. The explosion of her SUV in the driveway seemed a lifetime away yet barely a fortnight had passed since her kitchen had been reduced to shards of rubble and she had scrambled down the stairs and into the tunnel. She emerged into her previous life. Lucas was correct. Somewhere amidst the debris was the common denominator. What had the Moroccan said, what small inference had he knowingly or unknowingly alluded to that could shed light on the next tunnel to explore? He had answered their questions in a manner that seemed to be forthright and pragmatic. A common denominator

– he had played backgammon with her father during which time they had engaged in many conversations that mattered. She had done the same when she rattled the dice with her father. And then there was Jane. She had also played many games with her father. What had her father confessed to all of them yet separately? *So, was my father the common denominator or at least the nexus, the hub from which all spokes radiated outward to the rim that connected all surfaces together?* She pondered.

"What about the ghost of Jacques? Jane? Your father?" Lucas questioned. "Their deceased status is common amongst them. Enough to qualify as a common denominator? On the flip side, you are a common link to all three."

Was Lucas suggesting a correlation or a causation? If he was, he needed to keep his distance. But that was too late. I don't like the sound of either, she mused. "Once we identify the link, I'm certain these variables will be connected. Right now, they are just merging fog banks, not even quasi-distinguishable fuzzy dots."

"Let's start from what verifiable facts we know and work out from there. Then, we can focus on what you refer to as the fuzzy dots. Within those parameters, we can look at timelines – which events have to precede others. The Basque file should be easier to investigate in some respects because it's active. In addition, many of those involved are alive."

Alicia caught herself in a moment of silence. The photo of Jacques wearing a fedora and standing by the Sphinx in Giza caused her to reconsider her criteria. "Let me qualify that last statement. *Some, perhaps most* of those, are alive. My father's MI6 file is older and we know less. Two people involved, my father and Jane, are dead. As our link analysis regarding the Basque file progresses, we connect the two. As far as we can confirm at this juncture, the Moroccan is the only live link."

Lucas nodded in agreement with her logic. "The Moroccan

discussed players from the Middle East and North Africa. I will follow up with one of my colleagues from Cairo University. Together, we had researched and presented a paper on traditional North African trade routes. Our other known living breathing links are Marc and Elana."

CHAPTER 15

"Speaking of Marc," Alicia acknowledged, "One of us needs to contact him if for no other reason than to let him know that the girls are safe. I owe him that much."

"Let's think that through," Lucas cautioned. "We don't know what his relationship is with Elana. We do know that Elana did not recognize you in the hotel when we rescued Sophia and Camilla. We need to conclude that by now she has associated us with the disappearance of the girls. We can also conclude that she and Marc have discussed that encounter. You know Marc. How would he have reacted?"

"He loves his girls. He would have been furious with Elana for allowing them to leave the hotel on their own into a community and a language they did not know. He would be speechless with rage if she told him she had shot at our vehicle as we took off from the hotel."

"OK, an unknown. What overwhelming influence would Elana have over Marc to get him to bring the girls to Strasbourg? Enough influence to get him to leave the safety and tranquillity of your Pemberton Estate house in order to blow up the only stable family environment the girls have ever known, and to kill you, the only real mother they have ever known? Was Marc a co-conspirator? You have mentioned a few times that he loves the girls more than anything. Where do his loyalties lie?"

Alicia searched for answers, clues, any quantifiable data to analyze. "Having made too many errors in judgement regarding my relationship with Marc, I conclude that I'm too close. I need to defer to you."

"I understand and that is why we are a team. If I were Marc, I sense the one unrelenting factor to get me to travel here would be an imminent threat to the girls, communicated by Elana. Correct?"

"Correct."

"The girls are safe in Vaduz. The probability of him knowing that right now is infinitely small. If we were to communicate to him the fact that they are safe, then Elana's hold on him would be reduced, possibly eliminated. Correct?"

"Correct."

"The thought you may be alive must have crossed his mind by now. Who else would know the girls are here? Who else would go to the ends of the earth to rescue the girls? Just you. Correct?"

"Correct."

"If he had a choice to side with the woman who is the greatest threat to the girls or side with the woman who, like him, would do everything possible to keep them out of harm's way, who would he partner with?"

Alicia responded with a slow, deliberate nod. "I follow your logic."

"An unknown for both Marc and Elana is your confirmed status. You must be either dead or alive. Unlike Schrödinger's cat, you can't be both at the same time. That is why it is referred to as a paradox of logic. The related interpretation of quantum mechanics has its limits. You are either deceased and in a morgue in Victoria or very much alive with me walking the streets of Strasbourg. I can assure you, you are very much alive and present with me. Correct?"

"Correct."

"OK," Lucas concluded, "I suggest I contact Marc and let him know the girls are safe. They have not been kidnapped and there is no ransom demand. I say nothing about you. If he asks, which I suspect he will, I'll sidestep the answer. To validate my information and calm his concerns, I'll tell him something only he and you would know. What would that be?"

"He forgot Camilla's prescription medications to control her anxiety. It was on the dresser in her bedroom. The prescription has been renewed and she is coping much better. Sophia continues to be a positive influence and is helping Camilla through her most anxious moments."

"OK. I will make contact and request a meeting with him. What response can I expect from him?" Lucas followed up.

"He will agree to meet and ask to see the girls. You will tell him you will not expose the girls to further danger so will not have them with you. To confirm they are safe, you show Marc an e-pic of the girls. We can ask Alexandra to take a photo with a nondescript background and forward it."

"I'll set up the meeting," Lucas confirmed. "We will have Delta 1 provide security. You can stay in the surveillance van with Delta 5. I'll be wired so you can monitor the conversation and provide me with any prompts. Ultimately, we want to know if he will work with us. I'm the front person on this one and you have my back. Agreed?"

"Agreed."

Lucas leaned forward and looked directly at her. "I have full confidence in you, Alicia, don't ever forget that. Your intimate knowledge of this case relating to Jacques and Marc is invaluable. I can only imagine the emotional turmoil you are going through."

Alicia smiled briefly. "Thanks. I can assure you the elephant is no longer in the room, just the foul smell." Her thin smile expanded to her eyes for the first time since they met in the hotel lobby in Vaduz. Her breathing became more relaxed as did her general demeanour. Thinking back, she could not recall an occasion when Marc had ever supported her emotionally. She asked herself: *What had I seen in him? Why had I ever married him? Really dumb decision on my part.*

Until recently, Alicia hadn't been aware of the burden she had been carrying all her life. Relationships had been a never-ending challenge. Those she wanted but never had, and those she'd had but should never have entered into. Like the fable of the frog in boiling water, she had been blind to the gradual escalation of danger until it was too late to jump out. Thus, she played with relationships on the periphery. Even then, the weight of the steady change tilted the scales out of alignment, to her disadvantage. Perhaps now she could attain a more balanced perspective, one day at a time. In the interim, she would be content to defer such interpersonal interpretations to Lucas.

Her IQ had been assessed several times in her school years. The results were consistently in the 150s, highly gifted range. Highlights in other various aptitude testing were her proficiency in all the maths – trigonometry, algebra, geometry, calculus – in addition to the hard sciences of physics, chemistry and biology. She had also excelled in languages, mastering French and Spanish on her own, in addition to Russian and German in class. Emotional intelligence was another matter altogether. She had consistently struggled with team sports and in-class group assignments. She could now add marital relationships to that list. But without them, what would fill the space? There was genuine emotional exchange between her parents. With an audible sigh, she caught herself again. She had always referred to them with the distanced collective noun, parents, never as father and mother. Never had she called them dad or mom. That closeness seemed not to exist. When introduced, they had always said, "this is my daughter." Rarely had they used her name, Alicia, when addressing her directly.

She recalled her father holding her mother's hand and shedding sorrowful tears as she relinquished her final breath to the ravages of lung cancer. He refused to leave her side in those final hours when it became apparent the Grim Reaper was knocking at the door. In contrast, Alicia merely stood behind her father, not wanting to impose, not knowing how to respond emotionally. She had never cried, not even at the graveside. She had been bothered not so much by her mother's death but by her own reserved reaction, not cold, not indifferent, just unsure, unaware of what emotion would be appropriate. When her father had died, she never shed a tear, either. Instead, she felt a profound loss for a friend, a colleague, a close associate, her sage. She had lost her Yoda, the legendary Jedi Master from *Star Wars*, not Darth Vader the father figure who wielded evilness.

To this day, she was bothered more by the presence of his absence – the reminder on a daily basis he was dead, than by the absence of his presence – every so often recalling what he had done, what they had done together. The parade of elephants had traipsed through the cavern unabated. She needed not only to banish the elephants but replace them, her father's ever presence, with appropriate emotion in order to move on. Lucas's gentle probing was the right reminder at the opportune time. Increasingly, she was experiencing greater contentment, greater relaxation, more frequently.

CHAPTER 16

"Daan, do you have a moment?" Lucas asked.
"Always. What's up?"
"You knew Jacques Bernard, Alicia's fiancé, as well as anyone. Did you ever authorize him to travel to Egypt, specifically Giza?"
"Our mandate is the European Union. We have no authority beyond our borders. Brussels would not have authorized the travel except under extraordinary circumstances, which I would have had to recommend. I never did. Why do you ask?"

Lucas showed Daan the photos from the Moroccan. "The man wearing the fedora. Do you recognize him?"

"Curious, if it is who I think it may be." Daan turned the photo over in search of a date or inscription which might shed light on the images and context. There was nothing, not even a faded date of the developing process. This was a rather poor copy of the original print. "Perhaps as a tourist but if he was on vacation, there was no notation of it in his security clearance file. I can't recall, though. Where did you get it?"

"From the Moroccan. It was one of several photos but one which immediately caught Alicia's eye. If it is Jacques, Alicia cannot recall him mentioning anything about a trip to Giza on business or for pleasure."

"How did she react when she saw the photo?"

"As I would have expected. She was defensive at first but then questioned her self-confidence. She thought she knew all there was to know about Jacques. In retrospect, she thought she knew all there was to know about Marc too. She has now concluded otherwise."

"I will review Jacques' file and get back to you. Like all our agents, an in-depth security clearance had been conducted on

Jacques. It wouldn't be the first time we missed something. Perhaps with the passage of time, an unknown unknown will become known." Daan could not readily recall Jacques identifying any physical possessions of particular value relating to Giza. Objects are connections to culture. In retrospect, Jacques had none. He was a lone wolf. *How had I missed that,* he critiqued himself? "We never did determine why Marc assassinated Jacques. It could very well be connected. If so, it's perhaps one more enlightening piece of the Basque puzzle."

Lucas raised his eyebrows and slowly nodded his head in endorsement of Daan's preliminary assessment.

"Talk to me, my friend. What is your pragmatic academic mind telling you?" Daan probed. From the first time they had worked together as colleagues at the Katholieke Universiteit Leuven, he had been impressed by Lucas's analytical skills. He missed the times when they had engaged in profound conversations over snifters of cognac in the faculty lounge, or better, in their favourite café facing the Grote market square, the 15th century gothic edifice of Saint Peter's Church and the majestic Leuven town hall.

"As you mentioned in your initial briefing to us in Vaduz, we need to approach this file with fresh eyes, and analyze every detail again. I have complete confidence in Alicia to do so. I sense she is challenging and reassessing all the facts as she perceived them to be three years ago. But she is also questioning her ability to make accurate decisions when her emotions are involved. She now defers to me on such occasions and that is good. I would do the same if I were in her shoes."

"And what is your intuition suggesting?"

Lucas reconsidered the factors. "There are too many high-stakes players involved, including the Russians, Chinese and ISIS, and a handful of other lesser players for it to be simply a few disgruntled Basque provocateurs grumbling about ancient land claims."

"And the MI6 implications recorded in some notes supposedly squirrelled away by her father in a tunnel in Alicia's backyard?" Daan speculated.

"Both she and Jane mentioned them so I think there is some truth in the story potentially with dire geo-political implications," Lucas conjectured. "In the brief time we met with Jane, I surmised she was genuine with what she communicated with us, perhaps for different reasons. Jane appeared to be a bit unsettled with me in the room. That could have been a factor. She was reluctant to divulge everything she knew but her concern for Alicia seemed sincere and her father's missing file considerably more so. However, like most who play in this field, there was something mysterious about her. It was a game and she wanted to know more than she was prepared to reveal. Had she lived, I am confident she would have debriefed Alicia at length after our interview with the Moroccan, pressing for answers to questions she hadn't asked us in Colmar. I'm not sure how much she knew about this case Alicia's father had worked on. I'm less sure about her motivation to find out. In retrospect, I am convinced Jane wanted Alicia to interview the Moroccan alone certainly without her being present."

"Having a secreted cache in an elusive tunnel would be highly irregular, if it existed," Daan speculated. "But nothing surprises me anymore. If Alicia's father was suspicious of a legacy associated with the Cambridge Five or other disloyal MI6 colleagues, he might have felt it safer to retain some semblance of intelligence off-site, if not conclusive evidence of foreign spies among MI6 spies. The significance of the implications must have been astronomical for such extraordinary measures. That in itself is sufficient for me to give credence to the probability of its existence. What about the Moroccan?"

"He was candid in all his responses to our questions, mostly because he immediately connected with Alicia as the daughter of his old comrade, codename Friar Tuck. He shed light on some issues but identified additional unknowns like Jacques' presence in Giza. It's not like today when anyone can doctor an e-photograph to place images of people in places they never were. You and Alicia have confirmed that Jacques is the man in the fedora standing near the Sphinx. The Moroccan wasn't sure if the photo had been taken before or during Jacques' tenure with the EUI Unit. The latter would be more worrying for us."

There was no hesitation in Daan's response. "Marc needs to be interrogated while he is emotionally upset because of his girls being threatened by Elana and now captured from under his nose. Details relating to Jacques' death are crucial to our investigation because they relate to the importation of armaments and the players involved. What motivated Marc to assassinate Jacques? Was he working alone or was he under orders from someone else to pull the trigger? I will have our resident forensic psychologist, Alexandra Belliveau, undertake that interview, if you don't mind. No doubt she will want to speak with Alicia first to get a sounding on Marc's personality. Both of you can monitor the interrogation."

"May I suggest we dispatch a team to Victoria to search the tunnel that connects Alicia's house to the garden shed in the back yard for the notes Alicia's father allegedly hid?" Lucas offered. "As each fact comes to light, it becomes increasingly evident that this MI6 file and our Basque case may be connected either directly or indirectly."

"I have two colleagues in mind who can attend to that. One has a KGB/FSB affiliation, but recently came in from the cold. It is from this source we learned a connection to our case is not Moscow-directed but there is a Moscow-related relationship. The other contact is from the Middle East and has a background in Turkish Military Intelligence. Both worked with us on a previous case and, although not completely candid all the time, they provided invaluable services and intelligence when needed. We have them on a retainer fee for intelligence gathering. Alicia may have crossed paths with them in Victoria and not realized it."

"The ex-military intelligence colleague from Turkey – is he referred to as the Knight-errant with roots to the Knights of Malta?

"One and the same," Daan acknowledged.

"Small world," Lucas added. "The Moroccan mentioned an ex-KGB agent in Valencia who was affiliated with some interesting people doing interesting things in interesting places. I got a sense this Knight-errant maneuvered on the periphery of the agent's world. The Russian was allegedly killed by one of his supposed Beijing snipers. I say 'allegedly' because the Moroccan was vague about the accuracy of these details."

Daan's subtle smile confirmed Lucas's projection. Providing invaluable services and intelligence, although not always candid about the details? There is more truth in stories than detail in facts. Where fiction has to make sense, facts just need to be confirmed through logical link analysis.

"Would this Turkish ex-military intelligence colleague have known about the Moroccan? Jacques? Marc? Elana?" Lucas asked.

"We think alike, my friend," Daan chuckled. "I will send him copies of these black and white photos the Moroccan provided and ask if he can identify any of the players and contribute further background information."

"And Alicia? Lucas queried. "What if these enquiries reveal Jacques was not what he appeared to be? In a worst-case scenario, a mole with differing ideological and political stripes? Clearly, he was deceptive in his security declaration regarding his background activities. Such a fabrication suggests there were potentially other incidents where he was deceitful. I can conclude that everything about him is suspect and, as a result, it would be naïve to suggest his enigmatic profile was a viable explanation for this short-coming. This begs the question: what were the common interests among Jacques and his allies – the supposed Basque separatists, the Russians, and/or Chinese, and/or Middle Eastern, and/or North African contacts? To his disadvantage, he may have had one too many nefarious associates which left him with one foot on someone else's flypaper. Sloppy tradecraft," Lucas shrugged his shoulders. "Just my interpretation."

"We need to ensure Alicia remains focused, so I will keep her here to assist Alexandra with the interrogation of Marc. Having her return to Victoria right now would muddy the waters. But at some point, she will have to come to terms with that reality if the evidence confirms beyond any reasonable doubt that our suspicions are accurate. We'll cross that bridge when we come to it."

Lucas agreed with Daan's summary. That psychological bridge for Alicia might not be far over the horizon. He would prepare her, as best he could, for that eventuality.

"Let me add that you are doing an excellent job as her partner. But given the emotional implications associated with Jacques and Marc, in addition to the two assassination attempts on her life, I'd like to increase her face time with Alexandra who can provide appropriate psychological support," Daan proposed.

"Wise investment," Lucas agreed. "I get the impression Alicia would like to remain with the EUI Unit after this case has been concluded. But she has to deal with the conflict between reality and loyalty to the girls. The likelihood of her reuniting with Marc at this time is so infinitely small it would be safe to say never. Yet, where Marc goes, the girls will more than likely follow. After we interrogate him, we will have a better understanding of his plans. Regardless, Elana remains the wild card."

Daan stared at Lucas with seasoned eyes. He had gained great respect for his ability to balance his pragmatic academic discipline with his implicit intuition and emotion. How Lucas deduced the facts was a combination of applied logic derived from careful analysis and intuitive sensations of the mind. The latter was wisdom older than consciousness itself. On one occasion when they were engrossed in conversations eased by Rémy Martin, Lucas had described the aptitude he had inherited from his mother. Only he and his father knew she was of Romanian ethnicity with roots reaching back to the 16th century kingdom of Transylvania with Romani people also known as Roma. Daan had observed Lucas on several occasions reading tea leaves and Tarot cards with uncanny accuracy. It sent a shiver down his spine just thinking about it. This was one of those times. Their mutual gaze was sufficient.

"The living skeleton riding a white horse and carrying a black flag embossed with a white pattern, the Tarot card of death," Lucas whispered. "Not Alicia," he reassured Daan, who sighed with relief. "But death will soon ride like the Four Horsemen of the Apocalypse with all manner of cadavers in their wake, some deserving while others not. Advance knowledge cannot alter fate, the inevitable. It can only beckon those who listen with intuition to pay homage to voices older than time itself."

Daan lifted his head, searching like radar into the multi-dimensional distance beyond, attuned to what the silence was saying. Launching missions was his least favourite and most difficult undertaking, especially when tentacles reached beyond the borders of the EU and into the murky espionage cesspools populated by all manner of treacherous traitors. What had he forgotten, omitted in his strategic analysis and subsequently in his briefing? He was all too familiar with the reputation of Hydra, the multi-headed serpent of Greek mythology that resided in the depths of Lake Lerna, guarding the entrance to the underworld. Decapitating all the mythical heads of Hydra had been a penance of Hercules, now Daan's own atonement, his cross to bear.

Threats to the European Union had migrated from individual

lone wolves with personal grievances to terrorists with political agendas. Both were homegrown for the most part. Both had morphed into threats against the EU facilitated by third parties with their respective global geo-political motivations. Mission success, like the battle space, was multi-dimensional. Gathering intelligence was essential. Assessing the source, critical. Verifying the reliability, integral. Overlooking critical caveats, potentially lethal.

Truant weapons of war were being amassed on European soil, with more en route. Daan had been forced to set aside the adage of Emperor Augustus – *festina lente* – hasten slowly. He was being pressured by Brussels to hasten as the primary tactic without rashness except as an ultimate priority in order to avoid costly casualties on a much larger scale. That would mean modifying tried and true strategies and tactics. Shortcuts in some circumstances would have to be taken, which he could not formally approve but must tacitly sanction. It was not his preferred modus operandi. Regardless of his own misgivings, he had complete confidence in his people, as individuals and as a team.

CHAPTER 17

"Marc has been picked up by the Delta team for questioning. I need you to brief me on what I might expect from him," Alexandra asked Alicia.

Alicia gathered her thoughts. "In brief, he is a pro in the art and science of deception. His Achilles heel is the girls. He loves them and will do whatever is necessary to protect them. He is more than likely anxious over his decision to take them away from their secure home in Victoria. At least there, he was able to provide an anonymous sanctuary until the secrecy was breached. Here in Strasbourg, he could not assure even a modicum of security for them. We need to remember he has killed and is capable of killing again. He can be terribly charming. But if pushed too far, you will see a cold calculated persona emerge, first in his eyes which will deepen like an abandoned subterranean passageway devoid of a destination. He may then become depressed and disassociate from others."

"Multiple personality or bipolar disorder," Alexandra speculated.

"That's possible. Perhaps just a conscious decision to disengage. But I'll defer to the psychologist for a professional diagnosis," Alicia responded.

"I think I should open the interrogation by assuring him that the girls are safe. Thoughts?"

"Yes. I suspect he will reply by asking, or rather demanding, to know where they are. In the same breath he will probably ask if they are with me. He should become a bit more relaxed and cooperative if you verify that fact. You will notice him interlocking his fingers when he is tense. He rests his chin on steepled fingers when more tranquil and pensive."

"Consider another scenario," Alexandra posed. "How would he react if he is a co-conspirator in the bombing of your house and perhaps Jane's?"

Alicia pulled gently at her hair, forming ringlets around her index finger as she considered that possibility. She focused on Alexandra. "He could be one big lie. If that is the case, then his entire façade and everything he says will be a falsehood, a fabrication in an effort to deceive you. He will blame, project, deny, and fail to take responsibility. He will appear cooperative in his manipulating manner. However, he does not lie when he talks about his love of Camilla and Sophia. He truly loves them in his own weird way. That will be your benchmark for truthfulness."

"Thank you for being candid. I know from personal experience with betrayal in a marital relationship that accepting reality is a very rough journey. On a positive note, you will be able to watch and hear the conversation. I'll be wired so you can suggest to me what I might want to ask or watch out for."

※ ※

"Marc, thank you for agreeing to speak with me," Alexandra welcomed him in a professional yet cordial manner.

He frowned sarcastically at Alexandra. "I wasn't aware I had a choice."

"Before we start, I can assure you that Camilla and Sophia are safe. Camilla has her anxiety meds you forgot to pack in your rush to leave Victoria."

His cynical tone changed to concern at the mention of their names. He sat up straight and leaned toward his interrogator. "Where are they? Who has them? You cannot keep them from me. I want to see them. Now."

Alexandra cut off his questions in an effort to maintain dominance of the discussion. "They are safe. That is all you need to know for now."

"Who are they with?"

Alexandra reacted with a reassuring smile but did not respond. Knowing the answer but not divulging it assured her of continued control. She could negotiate or demonstrate good faith by replying, but only on her terms. She experienced a tinge of remorse as she reflected on her own childhood. French counterintelligence had kept her mother from her on all those camouflaged business trips that separated them. Her aunt and uncle had been her surrogate parents. Too many times, she longed for her mother's touch. Perhaps Marc was experiencing similar empty feelings.

"Are they with their mother? They are not safe with her. You need to get them back before she takes them away to Moscow," Marc pleaded. His breathing kept pace with the increase in his heart rate.

"Yes, with their mother, Alicia, who loves them. You will probably find that difficult to acknowledge after you attempted to kill her by blowing up your home in Victoria, the only real home Camilla and Sophia have ever had. That is one of the things we will talk about, why you attempted to murder her, the mother of Camilla and Sophia. You say you love your daughters yet you try to murder their mother and expose them to danger."

"Alicia!" he exclaimed sharply. He leaned further toward Alexandra. "Is she OK? You need to believe me when I say I didn't know they were going to do that, to attempt to kill her. Where is she now? I need to talk to her, to explain what happened. How I was threatened, coerced into bringing my girls to Strasbourg."

"We will get to that. But for now, let's start by telling me everything you know, including why the house was blown up. You probably know that INTERPOL is looking for you because Canada has issued a warrant for your arrest on murder and terrorism-related charges. If that warrant is executed, you may never see your daughters again."

He bowed his head and momentarily broke eye contact with Alexandra. His face darkened. His eyes darted around the room. The surveillance cameras recorded his clasped hands under the table with fingers tightly interlocked. Alicia was correct.

"I swear that I didn't know their plans were to kill Alicia. I would not have gone along with it had I known. She threatened to kidnap the girls and, as I just recently learned, take them to Moscow. I was told to bring them to Strasbourg."

"Who are *they*? Who is *she*?" Alexandra pressed before Marc had a chance to take a breath and unleash another salvo of questions.

"They are provocateurs who are instigating armed retaliation against the Spanish government through some supposedly disgruntled Basque. But they are not Basque. She is Elana, the girls' birthmother."

"They? Specify?" Alexandra interrupted again, keeping him from gaining control of the interrogation with another burst of questions.

"It gets complicated. Let me go back twenty years. Elana and I were from the same town, Donostia-San Sebastián on the coast of the Bay of Biscay. We became involved in the furor of the Basque independence movement against the Spanish government. It was all about our land, Basque Country. And then non-Basques took over and promoted violent revolution as a means of achieving our goals against Spain and the European Union. If Madrid wouldn't negotiate, they would make Brussels come to the table. I was against violence but Elana embraced it wholeheartedly. It was around that time she became pregnant with Camilla and then Sophia. But we were never married. Elana seemed to be the link to money and weapons. The thought of guns and explosives frightened me."

"So, why did you return to Strasbourg?"

"Elana threatened to harm the girls, kidnap them. I initially thought she wanted them back. I agreed to bring them to Strasbourg so they could meet her in the guise of a holiday. She then blew up our home and spread the word I did it. That way, I could never return. Unknown to me, she planned to kill Alicia. That would have been my last link to Victoria. I would have no connections to that life I had made with Alicia and the girls. I just wanted a peaceful life-style for Camilla and Sophia."

"What about the explosion of the second house in Victoria?"

"I don't know. There is something else going on I am unaware of. I only know what I read in the newspaper and saw on the television news. Someone is blaming me, trying to connect me with ISIS. I swear I know nothing about it."

Alexandra showed Marc a photograph on her cellphone.

"That's Elana," he replied. "She blew up our house, not me. I swear. You have to believe me," he protested in earnest.

"Help me on this, Marc," Alexandra pleaded. "You said the girls' birthmother, Elana, contacted you in Victoria and threatened to kidnap Camilla and Sophia if you didn't cooperate and do as she directed you to do."

"Yes, that's correct."

"Cooperate with what? I appreciate a threat to the girls caused you some anxiety. But what did Elana want you to do? She could have just as easily arranged to see the girls in Victoria if she wanted to reconnect with them as their birthmother. There had to be another reason to get you to come to Strasbourg. Look at it from my perspective. There has to have been more." She shrugged her shoulders, puzzled.

"I don't know," Marc stressed. He stalwartly held her stare. His eyes transformed into an aggressive glare. His jaw tightened. His breathing slowed. He leaned back. His persona became aloof, cold and detached.

"Are you still a member of the Basque revolutionary cause?" Alexandra asked in an effort to change tactics to keep him off-balance.

"If you are asking me if I still believe in an acknowledged Basque Country, the answer is yes," he barked back, raising his chin in an arrogant Benito Mussolini pose. *Who does she think she is, trying to manipulate me?* he reflected. *I have been trained by the best in counter-interrogation by foreign agents. She doesn't realize it but I am in control.*

"How far are you prepared to go for Basque independence after all these years?" Alexandra insisted.

Marc squinted more intensely but said nothing, maintaining his aloof stare.

"Are you prepared to kill again? Be a co-conspirator in the planning and execution of Alicia's murder? Is that what Elana has over you – to reveal to the police all the details of this homicidal plot? Is that why the Canadians have a warrant out for your arrest on terrorism charges? You have to agree that an international arrest warrant would not be issued on the basis of speculation alone or hearsay evidence."

"I don't know," he replied, increasingly callous and detached.

"His hands are clenched under the table with fingers intertwined," Alicia advised Alexandra through the earpiece. "The son of a bitch is lying. He has that cold distant look in his eyes. Be very careful. He is wound up like the mainspring on a grandfather clock. He could physically strike out against you. Delta members have positioned themselves outside the door if he moves against you."

Alexandra nodded slightly indicating she had heard Alicia's point. "No doubt you are aware France has also issued a warrant for your arrest. You have been charged with the murder of Jacques Bernard."

"Where are you dredging up all this false information? France has no jurisdiction in Basque Country. Nor does Spain," he smirked as he arrogantly leaned back in the chair and crossed his arms over his expanding chest.

Alexandra felt slightly safer from an imminent physical attack with the distance he had established with his hubris pose. She had experienced other attacks in her years as a forensic psychologist while interviewing sociopathic suspects. She dug in her heals and grasped hold of the table from the hidden frame in preparation for a potential frontal assault. She would lift the table at him in response, which would give her support team ample time to rush into the interview room and intervene.

"You admit to killing Jacques but in Spain."

"Wrong again. I shot him in Basque Country where only the Basques have jurisdiction, not the Spanish or the French. They commended me for defending Basque Country from a cowardly traitor. I am a Basque patriot," he proudly proclaimed.

Alexandra showed him the black and white photo of the man wearing a fedora in Giza standing beside the Sphinx.

Marc laughed. "Jacques was screwing Elana. And worse, he screwed the deal. What you don't see in this picture is Elana. She is off to the side somewhere making a deal with her Russian friends."

"What deal?" Alexandra countered before he had an opportunity to take another breath. She knew that he wanted to, needed to seize and maintain control of the interrogation, the conversation. He could only accomplish this by talking. In addition, he needed to explain his perceived version on what had taken place in Giza. The sphynx would bear witness to his version of the truth.

"To get resources that would allow us to fight for independence, to define our Basque borders once and for all."

"Why didn't you shoot Elana if she was a willing partner in the sexual betrayal of your relationship with her, in addition to the Basque?"

"That's pretty obvious." A spiteful hiss emanated from his throat. "She is the mother of Camilla and Sophia. How could I deny the girls their true mother?" He glowered with an arrogance that left no doubt about his attitude which changed as quickly as his darkening complexion.

"But you were prepared to kill Alicia, the only real mother Camilla and Sophia had ever known," Alexandra rebutted. She glared at him with greater intensity. "Was the deal about getting guns and other armaments from Moscow?"

A numbed silence filled the room. He had backed himself into a corner with his emotional responses. He acknowledged his female interrogator had won this round in the oratory exchange. He needed to seize the upper hand to not only grasp the initiative but not allow her to succeed again in the subsequent dual of words. He just had one more demand to make before ending the interrogation, turning the table in his favour. Round two, the final engagement in the ring, would be his.

CHAPTER 18

"I want to see Camilla and Sophia," Marc demanded. A second personality emerged in his appearance and demeanour. A distinctive change in the tone of his voice morphed simultaneously.

"When we have finished talking," Alexandra responded. "Let me ask again, who is Elana?"

Marc did not respond. Instead, he sat erect, cold-faced.

"Who is Santiago López?" Alexandra added.

"We are finished now," he snarled as he glared and leaned across the table at his interrogator. He then sat back defiantly with crossed arms while tightening his clenched fists. "I'm not answering any more questions until I see my girls," he uttered with malevolence in his tone, indicating the end of his part in the discussion. Mutual mistrust filled the space between them. Both were aware of what their respective next moves would be. Neither were wholly aware of how the other would respond.

"Why don't you just sit here and think about my questions and your options? Consider the fact Elana knows you are here telling us everything because we have Camilla and Sophia and you will say anything to see them, to get them back. She might conclude that you orchestrated the escape of the girls from the hotel from under her nose. How do you think she will react? Think about it, Marc."

Alexandra left Marc to ponder on this as she joined Daan and Alicia who had been observing and listening to the interview.

As she rose from the table, he blurted, "*Euskal Autonomia Erkidegoa* – autonomous community of the Basque Country." With a deep baritone voice, he then broke into the anthem of the Basque Country as if in a different place and time.

"Thoughts?" Alexandra asked Alicia.

"You handled him superbly. I thought for a moment he was going to explode over the table at you. I knew Marc had a dark side but I never saw such evilness in him before. He only saw Elana as their rightful mother, not me. What else have I misjudged about him?"

"Some personalities remain well-hidden even from parents, partners, best of friends, and psychologists. What you just witnessed you had already suspected. You noticed the signs and symptoms and were astute enough to give him space. So, don't beat yourself up. Switching between expressing love for his daughters and a remorseless craving to kill, all in the same moment, are typical psychopathic behaviours."

"Daan, your thoughts?"

"He provided answers to some of our questions. He admitted to killing Jacques supposedly motivated by infidelity in addition to Jacques botching a deal to import guns into Basque Country from Russia. An important question remains. What were the details of the deal? Just smuggling arms into the Basque Country? I think there has to be more."

"He consistently denied culpability in any violence. Instead, he projected it all on Elana and her colleagues," Alexandra added.

Daan concluded, "I have a strategy. Let's just hold him for now. I want to send an e-copy of the interview to Commandant Benoit Parent, the head of France's Counterterrorism Unit and the French police representative to Europol because of the terrorist implications."

Alicia looked at Alexandra with tired eyes. She then reached up and momentarily covered her face with both hands before slowly drawing her fingers down. Her disbelief and repulsion at his coldness were palpable.

"I need a cappuccino. Interviews can drain me sometimes. This is one of them. Care to join me?" Alexandra invited Alicia with a warm smile.

"Can our pasts blind us that much? Who we are? Who we will become?" Alicia asked. She followed up after a pensive troubled reflection, "Am I condemned to the DNA of my ancestors, not just my father but his heritage?"

Alexandra qualified her response. "There is more truth in stories than detail in facts. Those truths are what we perceived them to be when they were formed, influenced by all that we were, all that made up our lives at that moment, from conception to birth and beyond. Each time we recall them, they pass through our present-day filters. That is when we have the opportunity to see the truth and mould our future. In response to your question, are we condemned by our DNA? Not necessarily."

"How could I have been so wrong about Marc and Jacques yet be such an excellent investigator?"

"Trained analysts make pragmatic decisions devoid of emotions for the most part. Our relationships with people are about emotions. The emotional part of the brain which determines our ability to make decisions is formed during adolescence. It becomes our default mode, so to speak. That's the good news. Once we realize that, we can choose not to follow the default but instead make different decisions. Once I realized my first marriage was the worst decision I had ever made because it was purely emotional, I changed the way I made decisions and never looked back. Paul would say the same thing about his first marriage."

Alicia sat back as she sipped her cappuccino. Her shoulders relaxed more. Her face returned to its natural composure. Her gaze calmed. Her breath mirrored the relaxing cadence of her heartbeat. Yet her ghosts of an Ebenezer Scrooge's Christmas past continued to remind her of her heritage, just less hauntingly so.

ALEXANDRA RETURNED TO THE INTERROGATION ROOM WHERE Marc sat. He did not acknowledge her presence.

"Alicia has no desire to see you," Alexandra bluntly advised Marc.

He squinted at her but said nothing.

"Can you blame her, given the fact you were involved in the conspiracy to kill her? Camilla and Sophia will remain with Alicia, their legally adoptive mother. Their location will remain a secret. Their safety is of the utmost importance to Alicia, and clearly not yours."

He broke his self-imposed silence. "You can't keep me away from my girls," he shouted. The octave of his voice had deepened such that Alexandra did not recognize it initially.

Alexandra sat back with her arms crossed across her chest, mimicking his pose. "I doubt any court would give a self-confessed murderer and sociopathic separatist custody of the girls. We could give them to Elana to take to Moscow or leave them with Alicia," Alexandra suggested nonchalantly in a counter offer.

Marc sat staring at the floor, seething at the only possible option. He didn't like it but the alternative was worse – Elana taking Camilla and Sophia to Moscow. He would take the time to plan his escape from his temporary confinement. He hadn't noticed any bars on the windows or heard any locks on any of the three doors closing behind him as he was ushered into the interview room. The only obstacles were those who had detained him and escorted him into this room. He hadn't noticed them carrying any guns. He had escaped from more restricting spaces before and would do so again.

He would show Alexandra who was superior, who was in charge. She thought he was inferior, one to be manipulated. Elana had treated him with the same disrespect, believing she could control him by being submissive when she wanted him to follow her suggestions. In reality, he could manipulate her also, get her to do as he wished merely by being charming. He did the same to Alicia. When she was being difficult, he would become aggressive. She would then back off and give him space, which was what he wanted. Camilla and Sophia were quick to learn. They sensed when he was about to bark at them with the aggression of an agitated Doberman Pinscher. At that juncture, they escaped to Alicia's apron strings. He wouldn't have to eliminate them.

Basque Country exists on no maps except those which are known only to Basque people. Yet people have died defending it. Likewise, their pantheon is as indefinable as nature's spirit. The Basque underground network had been an integral part of its intangible culture. With the aid of his Basque contacts, he would travel the underground highway to his home in Donostia-San Sabastián. There he would re-arm himself and engage the enemy of Basque Country once again. He would home-school Camilla and Sophia on the history of the Basque and their obligation to follow in his footsteps.

CHAPTER 19

"Daan, Benoit Parent. I viewed the interview with Marc Bolibar alias Santiago López. My compliments to Alexandra. We can proceed with a murder investigation with this confession. I sense you want to leverage Marc's admission to the broader arena."

"Correct," Daan confirmed. "There are larger implications relating to criminal conspiracy and international importation of armaments. I'm not talking about a few handguns. I have reason to believe we are dealing with surface-to-surface and surface-to-air missiles, and rocket launchers in addition to large quantities of high explosives."

"What are you thinking?" Benoit asked for more detail, sensing the resources being considered would be beyond French borders.

"I'd like to release Marc and then keep him under electronic and physical surveillance. I am convinced he will head directly to Basque Country. Elana will follow him because she will rightly assume he traded information regarding Basque separatists in exchange for access to his daughters. How much, she won't know but will want to find out. If you agree with my strategy, we will need to work closely together to establish and coordinate a joint task force including a multi-jurisdictional surveillance team. We also need to have your Counterterrorism Cyber Unit alerted to increased e-traffic in the region. In brief, we need Europol to activate an Integrated Command Center."

"This is timely because we have noted recently a significant increase in e-traffic," Benoit acknowledged. "Several of our intelligence sources are reporting an upsurge in activity with connections to Beijing and the Middle East. As a side, have any of your people been snooping around the Mediterranean region, especially North Africa, Morocco?"

"News travels fast," Daan confirmed. "A source alluded to a potential confederate in the European Union intelligence network. I'm following up as we speak."

"I support your initiative," Benoit said. "As you are aware, we will need approval from the top floor because of the international implications and budget. I'll call you back soonest."

⋈

THE INTEGRATED COMMAND CENTRE WAS OPERATIONAL WITHIN the hour. Benoit's team would provide surveillance in France, with the EUI Unit shadowing. The Spanish would take on the primary role if Marc crossed into Spain and Basque Country. Benoit would liaise with his Spanish counterpart. The Counterterrorism Cyber Unit would monitor all multi-jurisdictional e-traffic.

As Daan suspected, Marc travelled directly south over the Pyrénées and through Andorra upon being released. His first Spanish stop was at Casa de las Hermanas Sagradas in Pamplona. No one responded to his repeated pulling of the bell cord. He left a note on the door, "Sorry to have missed you, Mom, S." He then headed north to Donostia-San Sebastián on the Bay of Biscay where he entered his father's house.

Elana was stalking his every move. An inactive Russian sleeper cell and a less well-known Asian couple posing as tourists, seemingly aware of Elana yet unaware of each other, followed as if in line astern.

"Dad," he called out.

"Get out. I no longer have a son," his father bellowed with a belligerent snarl. He turned his back on him, gesturing with a dismissive wave of his arm.

"Don't be like that, Dad."

"Don't tell me how to be. You are a traitor. You abandoned our Basque Country years ago. Now leave before I throw you out."

"You want to talk about abandonment," Marc erupted like molten magma from Mount Vesuvius, yelling at the top of his voice and shaking his fists in threatening gestures. "You abandoned my mother after you beat her to the point when she had to be hospitalized," he roared with rage. "She almost died."

With that challenge, his father lunged forward in a drunken challenge for dominance, forcing Marc through the open door and into the front courtyard.

Marc grabbed him by the scruff of the neck and ground his taut fist into his father's throat, crushing his trachea until he could take no more breaths. He seethed with relentless fury and hissed with revengeful anger like a bull raging in reaction to the piercing stabs of the picador's spikes.

"You might have been able to beat up my mother and slap me around when I was smaller, but you will never do that again." He continued to squeeze his father's neck. He repeatedly smashed the back of his head into the rock border along the walkway more times than he cared to remember. He dropped his father's limp body in the earthen passage. Blood oozed into the ground from the multiple open gashes to the back of his head, which lay wedged awkwardly between two larger border rocks. His motionless eyes stared up at what appeared to be a confused yet vacant recollection.

Marc then turned and calmly walked back into the house where he retrieved a burlap bag which had been stashed years ago in a recess in the stucco wall behind a cabinet. He returned to the courtyard where he stared down at his father's lifeless body. He spat in his face as a final gesture of defiance before strolling into the street where he was immediately confronted by the birthmother of his two daughters.

"More domestic troubles, Santiago?" Elana mocked. "Still

having trouble controlling your temper?" She felt a twinge of regret for the sharpness in her delivery, which exposed her to his seething wrath. His white knuckles gripped the burlap bag. The muscles in his rigid fist and forearm bulged as his entire arm shook with seemingly uncontrollable tremors as did his jaw as he clenched his teeth.

He squinted as he glared through her not pausing to perceive her but instead defying her. "I don't have time for you right now and never will again. Get out of my way," he commanded. He deliberately raised the burlap sack with his left hand and slowly slid his right hand inside. His fingers wrapped around the pistol grip, his finger on the trigger.

A mountainous man stepped forward, flanking Elana. "Need any help?" he asked in a heavy Slavic accent.

"We should talk, Santiago," Elana suggested calmly as she gently reached forward and touched his shoulder.

Her communiqué and gesture left him feeling compliant but perplexed. For whatever reason unknown to him at this moment, he concluded that he had little choice but to obey her. He pulled back. He changed his mind as if a short circuit had altered the instruction. *First Alexandra, then my father, now she is demeaning me*, his thoughts were barely coherent as they raced through his muddled mind. His rage continued to fume under the veneer of his momentary waning restraint, like Mount Vesuvius on the verge of another cataclysmic eruption. Neither Elana nor her bodyguard noted the tremors forewarning of the impending ferocity. His first impulse was to lash out in retaliation. In the shadow of her overbearing bodyguard, he held his temper in check, waiting for an appropriate moment.

"What's in the bag?" the Slav enforcer growled. His eyes widened. His nostrils flared. His breaths became tense as his chest expanded.

"My lunch. Want to share?" Marc replied with a smirk as he

confidently pulled on his index finger while tightening his grip on the Russian Makarov PB pistol.

The silencer protruding from the barrel muffled the noise of the gunshot. The burlap filtered the residue of the exploding cartridge. Like David's slingshot rock, his single bullet felled the Slavic Goliath in a single action. A lethargic dog resting in the shade of a cork tree took little notice. Such sounds were not uncommon in the neighbourhood and posed no threat to those who posed no threat, even mangy mongrels. It lazily closed its surveying eyes but kept his ears raised and alert.

Elana had witnessed the cold glare in Marc's expressionless face on other occasions when he had squeezed the same trigger. She dutifully became the subservient invisible accomplice, if only temporarily, until he returned to the reality of the moment as Marc Bolibar or Santiago López, or someone else. She wasn't certain. She could remember at least three personalities none of which were endearing, all of which had killed. His pupils remained dilated, his breath still short in his tightening chest. She held the door open to his father's courtyard as he dragged the corpse of the Slav inside, dropping it unceremoniously alongside his previous victim.

Marc went back into his father's house and walked down a staircase into a root cellar, where he crawled out through a delivery hatch into the adjacent street. Elana was left behind to fend for herself. She took a few deliberate slow breaths. She had evaded the Grim Reaper's call once again. Next time, she might not be so lucky. The thought of a next time stuck in her craw like a burr in a saddle.

There was something in his demeanour that caused an icy shiver to run the length of her spine. It was something she had never detected before – an ominous tone, a vacant distance, a desolate stare. He had invaded her presence yet was not present. Would the next time be the last time for her, for him, for both?

CHAPTER 20

"Hands up! Stand still! Hands up!" the Spanish police yelled at Elana as she stood in stunned silence, still mesmerized at what had just transpired. The muffled sound of the silencer on Marc's Russian Makarov PB pistol triggered flashbacks she could not supress despite her best endeavours. They were no longer conditioned responses like Pavlov's drooling dog; instead, involuntary survival skills adopted for when the beast was unshackled. Marc was still her perfect warrior trained to exacting KGB and subsequent FSB standards, now gone rogue. She relaxed as she let out a sigh of relief. She still had breath to exhale, unlike the two deceased laying in the courtyard.

Twice he had the opportunity yet chose not to kill me, she ruminated. *Were there other occasions when he had not squeezed the trigger with me in the aiming sights? But why?*

The airwaves crackled. "He has strangled his father, fatally shot one other, and escaped. Elana has been detained for questioning. However, there is insufficient conclusive evidence at this juncture to charge her with murder or being an accessory to any other offence."

Alexandra monitored Alicia's muted reaction as they listened to the real-time intelligence. She looked from Alicia to Daan and Lucas, then back to Alicia who stood in muted silence processing the events. She had endured the temper of Marc Bolibar but never the out of control rage of Santiago López or whoever he was.

"I never was able to maintain long-term relationships with men," Alicia sarcastically muttered. She felt her comment was inappropriate but continued nonetheless. "Marc's rage, which transitioned into the violent murder of his father and calculated execution of Elana's Slavic bodyguard may resolve one issue: a court battle with Marc for custody of Camilla and Sophia. I doubt any Western court will side with a sociopathic murderer. Perhaps in the Middle East under the tenants of Sharia law. But this is the European Union where the rule of law is applied more impartially."

Alexandra acknowledged Alicia's calculated speculation with a supportive nod.

"There are two outstanding matters," Alicia suggested. "First, how to deal with the wild card, Elana. Second, how to explain all this to Camilla and Sophia?"

"We don't have to deal with custody questions or explanations at this moment, Alicia," Alexandra assured her. "Camilla and Sophia are safe and that is all that's important right now."

"We will double the surveillance at the Liechtenstein entry points and at the hotel, in addition to increased facial recognition software with CCTV," Daan advised.

Alicia thought for a moment before transferring her attention to Daan. "I would like to meet with Yolina at the gates to Fort de Queuleu. I need to make peace with my past in order to proceed. Can you arrange that?"

"Certainly," he confirmed. "I am aware she makes a pilgrimage each year around this time."

"'I need to deal with this," Alicia muttered. *She is the senior matriarch. Where she goes, the others follow. If she declares the ground to be defiled, none will return.*

※ ※

AS ALICIA AND YOLINA STOOD IN THE first gathering yard of Fort de Queuleu in front of the bridge leading under the arch and into the holding cells, Yolina spoke with unwavering determination. "Members of my family were betrayed by the Vichy government along with many other Jews in what was supposed to have been

Free France. They were shipped here in cattle cars and held under deplorable conditions pending onward cartage to Dachau and the Final Solution. Just before the Gestapo raided our home, my mother escaped with the help of neighbours with me in her arms," she elaborated calmly.

"Most of my family were from Metz, actually Moulins-lès-Metz," Alicia clarified. "Some may have met your relatives during those perilous times. Regardless, their prescribed fate was the same. My father's life was overshadowed by those events, which prompted his decision to work in intelligence and espionage. Keeping close-lipped about all facts, especially his heritage, seemed fitting and was not questioned. It is in my DNA and, as a result, has defined my secret life and influenced my decisions and behaviour until now. I am convinced it swayed my decisions when selecting Jacques and Marc as intimate partners. That has been the *species elephantidae* – the elephant in my room –since I was conceived. I leave it here today and move on as a stronger and more independent woman for the experience," she vowed.

Yolina acknowledged her declaration of independence with a reverent bow. She shook Alicia's hand as an equal, not accompanied by a mother-daughter embrace like their previous goodbyes. Nothing more needed to be said. They turned and walked out of the compound, a defining part of their respective family histories.

The vestiges of her heritage, like illusionary phantoms, had been reconciled as had the ethos of her spirituality. She was her father's daughter but now her own person, compatible with the character she had consciously adopted.

※ ※

ELANA, ALICIA'S SELF-DECLARED FOE, WAS ABOUT TO enter a tournament of mental métiers. Her opponent would be a forensic psychologist who had bested sociopathic adversaries far more practiced.

Alicia's place was with her fellow legionnaires. Her challenge was to study Elana, whom she knew she would confront sooner rather than later. That was a given. Her mission from the onset had been to identify who had tried to assassinate her, and what their motivation was. The who had been exposed: Elana. Or was there more than one? The motivation remained shrouded in either the supposed Basque unrest entwined with the rationale behind the file her father had squirrelled away in a tunnel.

Who had blown up Jane's house and why? The latter was more than likely linked to the missing MI6 file, perhaps connected to the Basque file given the urgency of Jane's demand to meet. If neither, Alicia considered another option that had been dogging her thoughts – wholly an MI6 initiative, separate from but linked to her father. The ghosts of Kim Philby and the Cambridge Five. Elana appeared to be a common denominator, more so with a Basque connection, less so an MI6 affiliation, but still a possibility. Both met the criteria of a fuzzy dot in a fog bank as Lucas had initially described the potential proposition.

CHAPTER 21

"As you may be aware, we interviewed Marc Bolibar, whom you know from your childhood days as Santiago López," Alexandra announced to Elana. "He told us about your relationship as intimate partners and co-conspirators in the Basque separatist movement."

"If he told you everything you need to know, why do you want to speak to me?" Elana replied as she shrugged indifferently.

"I would like to hear your version of events starting from when you joined the movement for Basque Country independence. I would also like you to tell me where he would likely go after the murders of his father and your bodyguard, which you witnessed."

Elana hesitated and considered her response. "What do I get out of it?"

"What do you need?" Alexandra replied without hesitation.

"Protection."

"Protection from what? From whom? As long as you are here, you can rest assured you will come to no harm. However, you will be on your own after you are released. You have a varied background with international affiliations. So, you know the sequence of events that might transpire. Others who have a vested interest will be free to have extended conversations with you, especially about what they believe you may have told me regarding your mutual activities which might implicate them."

"I need immediate protection from Santiago," she pleaded disingenuously.

"Talk to me first. I can't guarantee anything right now. Where would he go?"

"More than likely he will return to Casa de las Hermanas

Sagradas in Pamplona to be with his mother. He refuses to believe his mother died three years ago from a vicious beating at the fists of his father. Now that he has killed his father and after he has visited his mother's former home, he will come after me with just one thing on his mind."

"Why is that?"

"Let me go back to when we were idealistic teenagers and joined the Basque movement for recognition of our land rights."

"When you first joined as an individual or as an agent of Moscow?"

Elana stared at Alexandra with raised eyebrows, both curious and cautious about her line of questioning in addition to her depth of background knowledge regarding details she thought were known only to herself and her Moscow controller.

Alexandra held her gaze, not wanting her to stall for time in order to fabricate a response. "Carry on or I throw you out to the wolves gathering at the door."

"We joined as naïve kids. Once in, I was recruited by a Russian agent who paid me to enlist others who could be trained and armed as insurgent Basque fighters. Initially, the Russians provided us with handguns and rifles and some cash, not much but enough to keep our interest and maintain our tenuous loyalty."

"Initially?" Alexandra repeated.

"Yes, because later the Chinese pushed their way in with promises of marginally more money and better weapons to advance our cause. *Their* cause as I figured out later! I subsequently learned it was much more violent, more in line with the philosophy of the Chinese Communist Party. That was when Moscow trained me as a Russian agent. I was to report on all Chinese activities in addition to recruiting candidates for Moscow. My compensation fell more in line with my increased responsibilities."

"What was Santiago's role?" Alexandra asked. "If the two of you were partners, he must have been recruiting too."

"Let me again step back. Santiago was the ideal candidate to be recruited by Moscow because his father never supported him. Instead, he endured his father's brutality and witnessed the regular abuse of his mother. The Basque movement was the family Santiago never had. It also validated his talent to be violent, and to kill without remorse. Each time he pulled the trigger, he said he would someday do the same to his father. Moscow honed these skills. I was trained to activate him on command like Pavlov's drooling dog. But he disappeared for three years. Because I wasn't controlling him, he went rogue. Being back here has triggered his violence. He is now a rogue psychopath, a robot, out of control."

"Can you get him back?"

"I don't think so. It's been too long."

Alexandra paused while she listened to Daan, Alicia and Lucas providing feedback through the receiver in her ear.

Alicia was the first to comment. "She hasn't once mentioned the girls, not even alluding to their existence, let alone their welfare."

Lucas added. "She has an ulterior motive. It's not that she wants the children or doesn't want them. The girls are a means to an end. That end is evidently clear. She doesn't want Alicia to have them. I'm convinced she would attempt to kill Alicia again, given the opportunity. She is as much the mentally disturbed agent out of control and gone rogue as Marc/Santiago may be. He is her star assassin whom she supposedly can no longer control."

"Hold that thought," Daan chimed in. "Ask her about her relationship with Jacques. What were they doing in Egypt, in Giza? Who were they meeting and why? She mentioned that the Chinese were increasing the ante with more money and more powerful armaments."

Alexandra re-focused her attention. "What were you and Jacques doing in Giza? Who were you meeting?"

Elana again raised her eyebrows. "He did tell you a lot," she muttered, suddenly more curious about where this line of questioning was going. She wanted to implicate Marc while presenting herself as the innocent victim. She would dispatch her adversaries on a wild goose chase after Marc/Santiago while she walked away free to carry out her primary mission unencumbered.

Alexandra pressed for clarity, not letting go of the momentum. She sensed Elana was negotiating for time while she adjusted her own strategy.

"It was an arms deal – the meeting in Giza. Jacques' Middle East contact had made arrangements to meet a Chinese supplier. I went along to help him. In reality, I was gathering intelligence on Chinese activities for my Russian controller. Jacques didn't want me to come along but I convinced him. He liked the ladies so he was easy prey."

"How did Santiago react? Or do you prefer to call him Marc?"

Elana reconsidered her strategy for a brief moment, debating whether she should challenge her interrogator's increasingly antagonistic approach. "Santiago wasn't happy with the arrangement. We argued and he threatened to take off with the girls. I really didn't care one way or the other. I always remembered his threat to run away with the girls. I became convinced that they were his Achilles heel that I could manipulate. When Jacques and I returned, Santiago went berserk. He was completely out of control. When he started to beat me up, Jacques tried to stop him. That's when Santiago shot him."

"What's the psychological trigger you mentioned? How do you control him?"

"He needs to be in charge. Turn the tables and he will kill. If you talk to him again, he will kill you unless you let him think he is in control. Threaten him physically or emotionally then you see the cold vacant glare in the eyes of his other personality. I used to be able to bring Santiago back by being sweet, intimate and complimenting him. It had to sound real or he would become violent again."

"He didn't seem to respond to you after he strangled his father and shot your bodyguard."

"You're correct. After he killed them, Santiago did not relax. By the way, I think he never strangled anyone before. He always used the Russian Makarov PB pistol. The Soviet psychologist who programmed him told me if killing became a personal issue, like strangling, he would remain in murderous personality mode. To stop him, you have to kill him. That is why I am convinced he will come after me like the accomplished murderer he has become. He now knows his mother and father are dead. Next is me."

"Another point," Alexandra asked. "What about an ex-KGB agent named Dmitri who lived in Valencia, the one who drew the caricatures?"

"I don't know if Santiago knew him. He hadn't met him, I'm sure," she replied hesitantly. "Where did you get that information? From Santiago?"

Alexandra watched as Elana leaned back and disengaged. She urgently needed to regain control of the interview. "You are correct," Alexandra confirmed. "He hadn't met him but he overheard you talking about him. Whatever you said caused Santiago to become exceedingly jealous, protective of you."

With that explanation, Elana's disposition changed from neutral withdrawal to re-engaged curiosity.

Alexandra instantly followed up. "He told me he was going to find Dmitri and shoot him, like the others who he thought were putting the move on you."

"How interesting! I knew Santiago became jealous if other men looked at me. But to kill them? Some men were murdered, found with a single bullet in the back of their heads, execution style. We did not know what had happened. Dmitri was an affiliate. I think he was killed by a Chinese sniper." She shrugged her shoulders with a false façade of indifference. "Maybe it was Santiago after all," she suggested.

Alexandra surmised Elana was lying, trying to distract Alexandra with non- or partial-truths. "Why did you blow up his house in Victoria?"

"I didn't," she replied nonchalantly.

"You didn't?" Alexandra rebutted. "Santiago said you did as a threat to get him to bring the girls back to Basque Country."

"That's what I just said, I didn't blow up the house. I asked Moscow to do it. They sent a sleeper cell agent. He waited for Santiago to leave with the girls. The agent was supposed to kill his supposed wife, Alicia. Bonus. Moscow would say Santiago killed her, and connect him to ISIS and other Middle East insurgents so he would not be able to return. He would have to remain in hiding in Basque Country knowing that there was a warrant out for his arrest. He would hide out in Basque Country where I could control him. I just wanted the bitch dead. Simple."

"What about the other house? Why was it blown up?"

"I don't know. Moscow had another person under surveillance, wanted them out of the picture. Convenient to do both at the same time."

"Thank you for being candid. You are free to go," Alexandra said, sensing Elana was continuing with her lying tactic.

"What do you mean, free to go? He'll kill me. I know he will. You said you would protect me," Elana protested this time in earnest. Alexandra sensed that she was sincerely fearful for her life, different from when she began her interview. She surmised that mentioning little known details had convinced Elana that secrets from her past were no longer secret. Thus, she could no longer trust those she once considered as confidants including, perhaps, her Moscow controller and Beijing contacts. Who else had played the role of Judas Iscariot and betrayed her for a meagre thirty pieces of silver?

Daan's voice crackled in Alexandra's ear speaker. "Suggest to her you will have someone follow her. If Santiago tries to kill her, this person will do their best to protect her. Perhaps she could contact her Russian colleagues and Chinese affiliates. We will keep her under close physical surveillance and photograph anyone with whom she makes contact. Europol will be working with us. Our ultimate objective is to take down both Santiago and Elana, and ultimately as many other conspirators as possible."

"If Santiago gets to her first, so be it," Alicia speculated unsympathetically. She was processing the callousness of Elana's attitude toward Camilla and Sophia, and her indifference in being a co-conspirator in the attempted assassination of herself.

"Or vice versa," Lucas countered. "There are still too many unknown rogue players in the sandbox."

Alexandra responded to Elana's protest for freedom. "You know this region like the back of your hand so you will be better able to evade Santiago. We will put a tail on you and try to protect you as best we can. You can also ask your Russian and Chinese friends to assist."

Elana rose to leave, then sat down again, slouching in her chair. "Not good enough," she yelled in protest. "One person cannot protect me. I need three of your best people at minimum, on round the clock, eight-hour shifts."

Daan's voice again crackled in her earpiece, "Agree with her request. Then ask her about Camilla and Sophia."

"OK, I can do that," Alexandra replied to her request.

Elana adopted a more confident pose, believing she held the

upper hand. "Thank you," she replied with a vacant smile, devoid of emotion.

"One last question," Alexandra asked as if an afterthought. Her strategy was to get Elana to lower her guard. "Do you know where Marc's girls are?"

"I have no idea. In their house where he left them," she laughed indifferently.

"Aren't they yours? Aren't you their mother?"

"Not mine. Don't know. Don't care," she blurted out, shrugging her shoulders. "Why do you think that?"

"But you gave birth to them."

"Bad move on my part to get pregnant. I was tied down for a long time. I could have worked. Santiago wanted babies, not me. After the second baby, I made sure I couldn't get pregnant again."

"Why did you threaten to take them to Moscow?"

Elana laughed. "I wanted to get back at him for what he had done to me. After Santiago disappeared, Moscow threatened me because I lost control over their prized asset. They sent an enforcer to punish me. He was a mean man. I have scars to show his abusiveness. It was retribution on my part. I got Santiago back and they left me alone for the most part. Their enforcer continued to knock on my door to remind me that I could not hide. Santiago at his worse was not as violent as this Russian enforcer."

"As we did with Marc, we will release Elana and keep her under electronic and personal surveillance. I'm convinced more than ever she will lead us to the weapons, which is our top priority," Daan directed.

I wanted to get back at him for what he did to me, Elana's words dragged Alicia back to the moment when she accepted Marc's proposal to marry and, more germane, to her reaction and response. Marc had explained that the girl's mother had been killed in a boating accident on the Spanish Riviera. Alicia could not recall Marc ever using her name – Elana. Perhaps it was too painful for him to do so, she conceded. She had not pressed him at that moment. But she did have second thoughts. If she was the girls' mother and Marc just disappeared with their children, how would she feel? She recalled thinking she would want to get back at him for what he had done. She had not been completely honest with him regarding her background. But that was somehow different. Thus, she justified her response not to pursue the matter with him.

For a fleeting moment, Alicia felt a tinge of compassion for Elana as a mother being denied her daughters. On the eve of her marriage to Marc, Alicia's view of her world was more didactic, black and white. There were the good guys wearing white hats and bad guys wearing black hats like in the Hollywood black and white western movies. You knew in the end the white hats would prevail. Today, her view was more pragmatic. Elana was a sociopath who did not refer to the girls by their names like Marc had not uttered Elana's name. Elana deserved no compassion when she was with Marc. Elana deserved less compassion at this moment.

"I agree with Daan, release her." Alicia spoke with a matter-of-fact tone. ... *Into Caesar's colosseum with the ravenous lions and other predatory beasts,* she mused.

CHAPTER 22

"Thoughts on the interview?" Daan gestured to Alexandra. "By no means was she telling the truth all the time. Instead, she was manipulating what facts may have been based on truth but only those which were to her advantage. I suggest she is more of the rogue sociopath than Santiago. Common denial and projection behaviours. Regarding her described relationship with Camilla and Sophia, classic psychotic symptoms."

Daan looked at Alicia. "You said your motivation to re-join the EUI Unit was to find out why you had become the target of assassination after three years. You now know."

Alicia sat silently. *Marc and Elana make a good pair,* she surmised. "Now I know why and who was involved." An uneasy calm settled over her. *Now what?* she thought. *Just knowing wasn't enough. It didn't fill the gap. Instead, it merely widened the crevice.*

"You know Santiago as Marc. Is he as Elana described him?" Daan asked.

Alicia pursed her lips and methodically moved her head from side to side in a slow deliberate motion as if intuitively scanning for other implicit intimations stubbornly remaining elusive on the periphery of her speculative mind. *What would the resident of 221B Baker Street have considered,* she mused with an inward chuckle. *Perhaps not so elementary, my dear Watson.*

She refocused on Daan's question. "I agree with Alexandra, Elana was swaying the facts for her own benefit, whatever that might be. The Marc I knew was deceitful but he was not the marauding out-of-control murderer she would have us believe. Yes, he had a temper and barked at the girls and me, more so in the past several weeks than previously, as stress was building up. His aggression was verbal with an emotional element, never physical. I suspect the source of the agitation was Elana pressuring him. To that extent, she had an influence over his state of mind. Control, I can't comment. I'm really worried for the girls. I'm convinced she would kill them as easily as purchase an ice cream cone for them. She has no emotional attachment." She allowed her final assessment to hang for a moment. "I'm not certain that emotion plays any part in her personality."

"What would she have had over Marc? How could she have controlled him? Was it as she described?" Daan questioned, looking for the essence of Elana's motivation. He had his own suspicions. He shut his eyes for a moment in an attempt to cull the truth from the facts, both honest and distorted. There was one truth. It just came with many labels and interpretations, consistent with the culture of the purveyor.

Alexandra provided a clinical response. "The KGB and FSB were renowned for hypnotizing people and being able to awaken them on command. That ability does not completely abate from the subconscious over time, certainly not in the short term – three years. More than likely, Elana was his controller. Distance does not always make the heart grow fonder. The more important question is who is *her* controller?"

Alicia added. "No doubt he strangled his father. No doubt he shot Elana's bodyguard. But that was not the Marc I knew. Something triggered his behaviour. I am thinking that when Elana and Marc were in their hotel with Camilla and Sophia just around the corner from Place Gutenberg in Strasbourg, she would have had ample opportunity to reprogram him. Alternatively, the FSB psychologist who initially programmed him could have met them there and reprogrammed him. That could explain why I never noticed this propensity for extreme violence when we lived together in Victoria."

Alexandra nodded in agreement. "That is a viable explanation. If so, he is currently under that influence, triggered to kill again."

Daan focused on those undeniable truths. He lowered his head until he was eye to eye with Alexandra whereupon he posed his speculation. "I'm convinced Elana would murder Camilla and Sophia, and Alicia given the opportunity."

Alexandra weighed the possibility and conceded, "I agree. Anything is possible."

Alicia interjected, "I need to confront Marc on what he was thinking. I'm convinced he will confide in me. Only then will I be able to distinguish between the Marc I know and lived with for two years and the Santiago now influenced by Elana."

Daan analyzed the parameters of her candid response. Such a meeting might reveal facts only long-term partners might disclose. He glanced at Alexandra, seeking her opinion.

"Elana suggested she could control Marc simply by becoming either aggressive or passive. Having just interviewed her, I am confident her control is more comprehensive. If I re-interview Marc before and after he speaks with Alicia, I could hypnotize him and explore the possibility that Elana can control his mind and his behaviour so easily."

Daan monitored his email and slowly looked up. "We will never get that opportunity. Santiago is dead. Elana just shot him. Apparently, she accused him of being a traitor to the Basque cause as his father had suggested. Reference to Basque Country or some related statement may well be the trigger to control him. Santiago attempted to draw his pistol but Elana had the advantage and shot first. Knowing she was under our surveillance, she set him up to make it look like she shot in self-defence. Worse yet, our surveillance people have lost her. One step forward and two steps back."

Confounded, Alicia sat in silence, her mind racing as she tried to make sense of what had happened. The assassin with whom she had shared her bed, the bigamist in common law if not in the eyes of God, the husband, the murderer of her fiancé, the father of her adopted daughters, the Basque separatist whom she had observed walking away from an interview in which she had participated indirectly, was dead. His killer, her stalker, was very much alive. Her Pemberton Estate world was in another universe. *If you miss the train I'm on, you will know that I am gone, you can hear the whistle blow, a hundred miles* ... the voice of Joan Baez echoed in her mind.

Lucas held her gaze in solemn support.

Alicia quietly repeated, "He was deceitful but on his own he was not the marauding murderer Elana described. I'm convinced more than ever that Elana remains the unpredictable wild card, his controller, the conspirator and a murderer without remorse."

Daan's cellphone buzzed with another incoming message: "Ballistics show the bullets recovered from the heads of the unidentified men killed years ago is not a match with the bullet recovered from Elana's bodyguard. The bullet that killed Jacques has been confirmed as coming from Santiago's Makarov PB pistol. There is a high degree of probability that Marc/Santiago did not shoot the other males. He did kill Jacques."

"We may never really know why," Alicia muttered, still in a daze as she attempted to put her thoughts in some semblance of order. Semblance was the operative word. Full comprehension might remain eternally elusive.

"All the other unidentified men were shot with the same weapon, but whose?" Lucas questioned. He glanced at his partner who was present yet distant. Her expression was faint yet resolute. He moved closer to Alicia while maintaining eye contact.

She refocused, acknowledging the increasing closeness of his presence.

"All good?" he whispered.

"All good," she replied quietly. Her distant gaze mirrored the depth and breadth of her deliberation. One less elephant in the room, yet the odor remained.

He was getting to recognize and, more importantly, to trust her modus operandi of patterned analysis. He had partnered with some academic colleagues on research papers only to discover that he had written the majority of the research analysis. If presented at a conference, he also ended up taking on the lion's share of the work. In retrospect, he had been the academic senior with the first name on the paper. That was the protocol in the academic arena of publish or perish. Was his relationship with Alicia different?

From the beginning of their relationship, he and Alicia were equal partners, not in competition for top billing. Instead, they were figuring out how to maximize each other's strengths. Lucas sensed that Alicia was uncomfortable when he spoke about his family background, especially when emotions were involved like his relationship with his wife – how they met, how they grew apart, and the circumstances surrounding their divorce. She had entered into two intimate relationships both of which had ended for different reasons. Both unsuccessful nonetheless. He perceived his divorce as personal growth. Alicia perceived her separation as an Achilles heel. She knew it – one elephant down, the odor of the other elephant remained in her room. As partners, the latter was an elephant in the room they both occupied. Together, they would jointly banish the *deformis elephanti* – the ugly elephant.

"Ballistics are currently being conducted on the bullet that was just recovered from Marc/Santiago," Daan announced. "I will not be surprised if it is a match to the bullets that killed all the unidentified males. If so, we will be able to confirm our suspicion – Elana had been that shooter or at least her pistol had been used in all cases."

CHAPTER 23

"A big unknown," Lucas speculated. "Are we dealing with one case involving armaments being supplied to a select group of supposed Basque insurgents connected to a mysterious MI6 file allegedly hidden in a tunnel? Or are these two separate cases only connected by coincidence, yet linked to Alicia via her father and a list of other players, including Jane and the Moroccan, and perhaps others yet to be identified?"

Daan reconfirmed, "Our mandate focuses only on European Union-related threats and only within EU borders. Evidence gathered thus far strongly suggests armaments are being supplied to a select group of assumed Basques separatists by Moscow, and Beijing via the Middle East. More than likely there is a Tehran association. Moscow has been meddling in the Middle East for reasons of economics and security according to unconfirmed sources. That begs the question: why now? Why are we being fed this information at this time? I can only conclude that we are getting close to something, which is making some feel uncomfortable. But what? Moscow is interfering with these Chinese shipments because they think the EU is in their front yard and not the domain of Beijing. We can safely assume we are not just dealing with a few Russian small arms possibly being supplied by Beijing or another player. The motivation is to distract us into believing Moscow is the primary perpetrator."

"Like Elana suggesting, Santiago was the sole sociopathic shooter?" Alicia reiterated. "She is the one player thus far who is the most nervous about our enquiries and attempting to distract us. That suggests she may be the common denominator."

"Correct," Daan confirmed. "Could she be the leader of this

supposed Basque separatist movement? I say supposed because there has to be more to this case. We know that Moscow is involved and has been for several years, decades according to Marc and Elana. Likewise, Beijing has been a player for approximately the same length of time. Only more recently has Tehran been seen in the arena. I understand Moscow and Beijing but why Tehran? What do they have to gain, if they are involved? Russia and China are major players. Iran is not in their league. Is the mention of Tehran a false lead, a purposeful distraction, or a new intervening variable with its own agenda, a link between the Middle East and North Africa?"

"But there is some evidence suggesting Beijing is supplying major armaments including stolen Russian surface-to-surface and surface-to-air missiles. If this is also correct, what is the strategic intent?" Lucas asked.

"Let's hold that thought," said Daan. "What if the Basque file is not separate but is connected to the hidden MI6 file Alicia's father worked on with the Moroccan, and possibly Jane? Is the Moroccan the link or the key to the link? This scenario could have significant geo-political implications, potentially global in nature and, as such, beyond the EU."

"How significant is any one's guess," Alicia conjectured. "From my relatively brief experience with MI6, and from what little I learned from my father and Jane, I can say it would have to have been a major threat specifically to the UK and broadly to global stability. MI6 does not allocate resources to minor unsubstantiated rumours. If my father believed it was necessary to hide facts, the repercussions must have been truly sinister and far-reaching."

"Surface-to-air missiles suggest the strategic intent would be global instability. That is consistent with the Leninist legacy of disruption," Daan proposed.

Alicia wore an ominous frown. "Regional war that could catapult into global Armageddon."

"Another alarming factor," Daan offered. "Moscow activated a Cold War sleeper cell and Beijing called on two Chinese agents to pose as tourists to follow Santiago. That is a lot of heavy armour deployed just to follow a relatively low-level allegedly outdated ex-Basque separatist, if that's all Marc/Santiago was. This suggests we are dealing with much more than a minor Basque land claim. We need to delve into your father's hidden file, Alicia. I have asked two semi-retired colleagues, Tatyana and Yusuf, to look for this mysterious file in the tunnel between your house and the garden shed. She has KGB and FSB affiliations and he previously served with Turkish Military Intelligence. Any suggestions where they might begin?"

Alicia pondered the possibilities. *An ex-Russian KGB/FSB agent and an ex-Turkish Military Intelligence officer duo. Very strange bedfellows.*

Daan patiently awaited her reply.

"I have spent some time looking but found no traces of the file in that tunnel. So, I can't suggest anything. Fresh eyes from a different perspective might find where a seasoned MI6 agent would hide it. I did look, but to no avail. Having said that, I'm the first to admit knowing my father might have been a disadvantage."

"Or an advantage," Lucas suggested. "What if your father suggested the tunnel as a ruse to protect it? To protect you? And if so, from whom?"

"Only Jane and I supposedly knew of it. The operative word here is supposedly. Was Jane a confederate? I have often wondered why she relocated to Victoria to retire when she had no previous ties to Canada and specifically the Canadian west coast. Why was she followed to Colmar and killed by the Asian suicide assassin?

Why did Moscow have her under surveillance as Elana suggested and why did they activate a sleeper cell agent to assassinate her?"

"Who would not have wanted her to meet with you?" Lucas countered. "And would have been so adamant as to use such extreme means? It was an Asian who pulled the trigger and then blew himself up. Was it Beijing? Or was it Moscow trying to make it look like Beijing? They have both been pointing the finger at each other, more so since the Cold War has hypothetically warmed. The vacuum allowed Beijing to step in."

Daan's text message confirmed his earlier suspicions: "Ballistics confirmed bullets that killed the unidentified males match the bullet taken from Santiago's body. Elana's pistol fired all. High probability she is the shooter. Just emailed Delta team and Commandant Parent to proceed with extreme caution when approaching Elana."

※ ※

ALICIA LEANED OVER AND MURMURED TO LUCAS, "Thanks for the lifeline, for checking in on me."

He looked at her curiously.

"For asking if all was good," she clarified.

"Comes with the turf," he replied. "I'm confident you would do the same if the shoe was on the other foot."

"In every adversity, there are the seeds of its opposite. When I first met Daan in Metz and he updated me about Marc a.k.a. Santiago, the revelation left me stunned, speechless, gasping for breath. Daan provided me with collegial and fatherly support. Yolina and Alexandra have done the same and you also, several times since we started working together, and again just now." She paused momentarily. "Looking back, in all the time Marc and I were together, I cannot recall one time when he provided even a hint of emotional support. He never once asked if all was good. Hearing that Elana had just shot him, killed him, left me objectively sorting out the details in my mind. There was no emotion left to fog the facts."

Lucas acknowledged her revelation. "To be honest with you, although I believe my wife loved me and did thoughtful things for me, she was not there in the same way that members of the EUI Unit family have been. Deep down inside, I knew her loyalty was just not there. Perhaps it had never been there and I had been kidding myself thinking it would somehow evolve. That was the main reason I didn't pursue the option to reconcile our marriage. You are quite right. In every adversity, there are the seeds of its opposite. My divorce process was stressful, of course. But each day after, my inner peace increased as my domestic tensions diminished. Now you know more about me than my ex ever did."

Alicia bumped against his shoulder in a jovial manner. "Let's get back at it, Lucas. We have a case to solve."

"Perhaps two."

She grinned. "I agree. If not two separate unrelated cases, then two separate cases intertwined by high-level strategic intentions or broad geo-political motivations. Either way, those involved benefit, based on their own perceived needs. At a high level, that means power. With power comes influence and vice versa. It's ego. Money just gets you more of both which inflates the ego. At a low level, when you have nothing, it's all about an additional few dollars and more cents. The basics put food on the table. We need to find the source and follow the money trail."

"I agree. That is how the Chinese have short-circuited the Russian monopoly. They offered marginally better weapons and slightly more money at relatively no cost to them given the potential outcome."

CHAPTER 24

"You have been more thoughtful than I have ever seen you since Daan asked where his colleagues, Tatyana and Yusuf, might start looking for the file in the tunnel," Lucas commented. "Talk to me, Alicia. Is there another elephant in the room?"

"No, not at all. It was something he mentioned that caught my attention. If Marc/Santiago was such a low-level outdated Basque separatist, why did Moscow and Beijing activate such high-level resources to follow him? Was it him or someone else, or something connected to him?"

"A valid question. Anything else connected?"

"His observation also tweaked something odd. I played the game of What-If-And-Why with my father. What if the file isn't in the tunnel between my house and the garden shed? If so, why would my father have suggested that it was?"

"And what did you come up with?"

"As a child, my father would also play the game of I-Spy-With-My-Little-Eye with me. I learned that if he suggested something, it was more than likely a red herring, a false lead to distract me. He would tell me I should look in another direction, the opposite direction if I heard anything. So, what if he suggested the file was in the tunnel under our backyard as a distraction to someone else, not me?"

"Who could the other person be?" Lucas continued to urge her as he had done so many times with students learning the art and science of research. It was mostly about the process, not the end state.

Alicia recited with a jocular expression:

"Would you tell me, please, which way I ought to go from here?

That depends a good deal on where you want to get to, said the cat.

I don't much care where – said Alice.

Then it doesn't matter which way you go, said the cat.

So long as you get somewhere, Alice added as an explanation.

Oh, you're sure to do that, said the cat, if you only walk long enough."

"Lewis Carroll in *Alice's Adventures in Wonderland*," Lucas replied, with a similar sentiment. He tilted his head in jest as much as a cue for Alicia to consider. On more than one occasion, he had cited lines of poetry or text not knowing why, only to realize in retrospect the words were clues to information he sought yet hibernating in the deep recesses of his mind.

"The only other person to know that the tunnel might be the location was our neighbour and my father's ex-colleague from MI6, Jane. She told me she had never been successful in locating the file. Why would she tell me that? Most important, why was she assassinated by the Asian in Colmar? I was left with the impression she was a relatively low-level now-outdated analyst, like Santiago. Yet she warranted that level of attention by an Asian who committed suicide. An extreme response! There are too many inconsistencies."

Lucas agreed. "As Daan suggested, this case goes well beyond a few alleged Basque separatists, wanting to raise the attention of the public over land claims, yet more than likely spurred on by outside agitators with ulterior motives. Should someone be talking to MI6?"

"Not until we know what is in that file. If MI6 received an anonymous tip about a mysterious missing file from an unknown or perhaps unreliable source, they would not react. Mix in my father, myself, Jane and the Moroccan and you have an entirely different scenario. If my misgivings about Jane are founded, we need to find out what her confederacy was."

"I am thinking a chat with Daan over cognac to map out strategies and consequences is in order," Lucas responded. "No doubt he will want Yolina involved because of the political implications which go well beyond EU borders. And there is Elana, the wary wild card, as you have aptly described her, and the primary focus of our own efforts at this juncture."

Alicia nodded in agreement yet she remained perplexed.

※ ※

"First," said Yolina, "our immediate priority is finding Elana. She is a live link to the importation of missiles and other armaments into the EU. In addition, she is an immediate threat to Alicia and the girls. Jane may be a confederate link to the missiles, so we keep her in mind while we search for Elana. Second, without the file, we are just in rumour mode. If it does exist, the implications could be international. I agree we need more concrete facts before we consider contacting MI6."

Daan followed up. "I have asked Tatyana and Yusuf to comb through the tunnel between your home and the gardening shed. Let's wait to hear back from them. In the interim, Alicia, think about other hiding places your father might have used. The implications of not turning over every stone may be too grave, especially if it is a link to the whereabouts of the missiles."

Lucas gazed at Alicia. "Two possible scenarios. First, if the tunnel between your house and the garden shed is a ruse, as you suggest, where is the rooster? Second, if the tunnel is not a complete ploy, is it a clue, a hint, akin to a compass bearing to the actual cache? You know your father better than anyone else."

Alicia paused, searching for the most probable response. "When playing I-Spy-With-My-Little-Eye with my father, he would often repeat that it is obviously hidden. Sometimes he said 'obviously hidden' could mean just that. It should be obvious to me it is hidden, not to confuse me but to help me look more carefully. He also said 'obviously hidden' could mean I needed to look in obvious places but not so obvious it could be easily found by people who should not have access."

"And…" Lucas continued, playing the role of the esteemed Professor Peeters from the University of Leuven.

"And, I'm thinking beyond Victoria," Alicia replied with increased confidence. "But where, I'm not yet certain."

"Where were you when you played I-Spy-With-My-Little-Eye with your father? Knowing that, might jog your recall."

She reflected. "In our home in Weymouth on the south coast of England, mostly along the sea wall where we would walk and talk. It had become my classroom for more than one lecture."

"A good place to start?" he suggested.

"As good as any I suppose," she said tentatively. "I need to ponder like Pooh Bear over a pot of honey or, better still, a bottle of Côtes du Rhône."

"Let's go for a stroll. I find walking helps me to think."

Alicia looked up. "This is as frustrating as trying to solve a crossword puzzle without the key."

"Another tidbit of grist for the cognitive mill as you and Lucas amble," Daan added. "I sent copies of the Moroccan's photos of Jacques, Marc and Elana to Tatyana and Yusuf. Yusuf recognized Jacques and Elana and confirmed Giza was the location. He suggested Giza has often been used as a venue for agents of different stripes to meet because it had the reputation of being a temporary safe haven, a no-shoot zone as it were. Even arch enemies sometimes need neutral ground to converse."

Lucas added grist to the mill. "Interesting. The British have had a keen interest in the region around Giza since Nelson's victory at the Nile in 1798, not just because of the economic and geo-political aspect of the Suez Canal built fifty years later, but because it was strategically situated along the ancient trade route between the Middle East and North Africa, particularly Algeria and Morocco. A fact often forgotten is the British army camped in the shadow of the pyramids in the 1930s. Archeologists attached to the military apparently conducted research. Less known was the fact officers of Section Six of military intelligence which later melded into MI6 had been slotted into the regiments. It was rumoured a few of these spooky folks exchanged military uniforms for civilian dress and remained in Giza posing as archeologists after the regiments had been re-deployed elsewhere. Some would merge back into regiments on redeployment."

Alicia stared with renewed curiosity. "My father had a photograph of the Royal Warwickshire Regiment camped on the plateau next to the pyramids in 1934. That photo hung in his office in tribute to his Uncle George who served with that unit as a commissioned officer, eventually commanding the 6th Battalion in World War Two. There was a glass display case in the office with some old Roman coins and other Egyptian artifacts his uncle had found in the sand in the shadow of the pyramids."

Lucas sat up, alert. One of his academic colleagues from Cairo had told similar tales. They had submitted a joint proposal for an inter-collegial research grant to exhume evidence of foreign occupiers in the region from Alexander the Great and Caesar to Napoleon and Hitler. Before them, the Knights of Rhodes, later vested as the Knights of Malta by the King of Spain, had roamed the shifting sand dunes. What hiding places had they crafted? A thought entered his mind. Yusuf, the Knight-errant, the Knight of Malta. Coincidental or consequential?

Alicia dwelt on the possibilities. "Is it merely happenstance or is there a connection between your comment about British military regiments camped in Giza and the photo on my father's wall? And the photo of Jacques in the fedora standing by the Sphinx? Let's go for that walk," she suggested. "The photograph and the coins in the display case may hold the key to where the file is obviously hidden… obviously."

"Before you leave, two final points," Daan added. "The Russian sleeper cell that followed Santiago has gone back to sleep. Perhaps more interesting, the Asian tourists have dispersed. One has gone to Cairo and a select few locations south along the Nile including Giza, Asyut and Luxor. The other has moved on to Algiers. They remain under close surveillance."

"Motion in the backfield," Alicia suggested. "Perhaps it's an indication that another phase in another strategic plan may have moved into operational mode. Or it could be a ploy to ascertain if they are being followed. If so, they could be trying to throw their tails in the on-going game of spy-on-spy."

Daan nodded. "We can check off one more item on our search list. Tatyana and Yusuf found nothing in the tunnel under your backyard. Given their background, it is highly improbable the file is there. Go for your walk. Take as long as you need. Come up with a Plan B." His face suggested that as-long-as-you-need really meant sooner-rather-than-later.

Alicia reflected on the ex-KGB/FSB agent, and an ex-Turkish Military Intelligence officer, a namesake knight, both with *noms de guerre*, as bedfellows. *What if they found the file and decided not to disclose their discovery? I trust Daan. But.*

"What are you thinking?" Lucas queried.

"What do you know about Tatyana and Yusuf?"

"They worked with Daan, and Alexandra and her partner, Paul, on a previous EUI Unit case. Tatyana was wounded and another person was killed. I suggest you speak with Alexandra if you want additional information."

"Have you ever worked with them?"

"Never. Haven't met them before they were introduced at the hotel in Liechtenstein, so can't provide any sense of their loyalty, even as research subjects let alone informants."

"Thanks. I may do that, speak with Alexandra," Alicia replied, slightly less cautious but marginally more curious.

Lucas stopped walking abruptly, leaving Alicia to take a few steps further. She turned and looked back at him.

"I'm acutely aware you dislike unknowns as much as I do, perhaps even more." He watched her puzzled response with the gravity of a wolverine assessing a twitching strand of tall grass as either threatening or benign, or better yet a meal. "Every predator can be prey to another predator higher up the food chain."

"I am not endeared to that expression. In fact, it grates me when used in the context of people as it speaks to bullying and unconscionable abuse, racism and genocide," Alicia murmured as she ambled back to where he had stopped. Images of Fort de Queuleu, Dachau and Auschwitz momentarily grabbed her consciousness. She caught herself and altered the course of her tangential trajectory.

"At one point, there may be too many coincidences," Lucas agreed. "Perhaps not, but worth mulling over if they are distractions. You asked about Tatyana. Certainly, speak with Alexandra. The other pea in that pod is Yusuf. He has the nickname of the Knight-errant because of his lineage as a Knight of Malta, one of several groups who travelled to the Pyrénées region in the sixteenth century, what today is the undefined Basque Country. King Charles I of Spain is said to have employed these Knights of Malta as quasi-intelligence and security service agents for the Spanish realm."

Alicia had a second thought. "Is it mere coincidence or is there a more tangible link?"

"Could be either. Perchance one too many coincidences in this cauldron. But we run the risk of essential information being lost if we do not consider the hidden potential of every aspect of the detail. My preference would be to examine each individually and then conduct a comparative analysis. Regardless, it is worth bearing in mind as we meander down this stony path seeking a mysterious document in a yet-to-be detected tunnel. I would like to have met your father to learn how he strategized. For now, we can only work together, with you explaining and me responding with questions. There is more truth in story than detail in fact. So, tell me stories about your father."

Alicia nodded. Her immediate response would have been to relate some but not all of the details. She was surprised that her father's voice was not reminding her of the need to be cautious. She had been baptised as a Christian in the Anglican Church of England. That was all people needed to know. She had memorized many of the verses from the Bible, in addition to the Anglican communion service in the traditional common book of prayer, which began on page sixty-seven. She had memorized such prodigious details on the insistence of her father and reinforced by his Uncle George on the occasion of her confirmation.

CHAPTER 25

"My father's Uncle George was his only surviving relative. After the Second World War, George left the British Army and became an Anglican minister in Warwick. I recall him saying in the first half of his life he tried to kill everyone as a soldier. In the second half, he tried to save everyone as a minister. He lamented he was never terribly successful at either but found more inner peace administering the gospel. I'm confident he died a happier soul although still troubled by events in his past, some of which I never knew about and still don't. I can only ponder and speculate."

"Besides Uncle George's Roman coins and Egyptian artifacts which your father kept in the glass display case, did he have anything else that meant a great deal to him, that would have influenced the way he thought? Knowing more might help to suggest where he concealed the MI6 file. Anything may provide a clue for us to follow."

"He had Uncle George's military decorations but donated them to the Regimental Museum in Warwick. Uncle George wanted his Bible given to St. Nicholas Warwick Anglican Parish Church. I accompanied my father to Warwick on that occasion and was present when he presented the Bible to the presiding minister. It was a solemn, peaceful occasion, and more so because my father and Uncle George used to spend many hours there sitting in the choir pew just talking. My father wanted to be cremated and have his ashes laid beside Uncle George's grave."

"Talk to me about other places your father found to be peaceful or special," Lucas prompted. "Where would he go just to sit and think or perhaps stroll in solitude?

"I can't recall any other. Certainly, none he spoke about with reverence. You need to understand my father was a very private person."

"I can appreciate that," Lucas commented. "It comes with the territory. I don't talk about what I do. I suspect you never told Marc or the girls about your previous career choices."

"The most secret of all secrets," Alicia mumbled. She was her father's daughter. Her father and Uncle George had often reminded her that never is a very long time but she was never to reveal the secret of her heritage. Only the three of them knew and now there was just one. *The secret was sealed when Uncle George baptised me as a Christian in St. Nicholas Anglican church*, she mused solemnly.

"The secret of all secrets," Lucas repeated. He sensed she had drifted into another deeper realm, one that only she had access to and no other would be invited.

"What?" Alicia asked.

"You said the secret of all secrets."

"The most secret of all *secret* places," she replied. *"Not the most secret of all secrets,"* she reflected *privately*. "But where would that place be? Where would he hide a file?" She repeated out loud in an effort to divert his trajectory of enquiry. She wasn't hiding evidence, instead clandestinely suggesting another route of access.

"Curiouser and curiouser," Lucas replied.

"Well, I've often seen a cat without a grin, but a grin without a cat is the most curious thing I ever saw," Alicia countered with a jester's smile.

"You are also a connoisseur of Lewis Carroll's Alice's *Adventures in Wonderland*?" Lucas queried with a chuckle. Therein, there may be additional clues as to the identity of the tunnel and the missing file, he conjectured. In the absence of other evidence, any possibility was a viable option.

"My father was, as am I. He used to take me to Brighton for holidays. He once showed me Consort House where there is a down-the-rabbit-hole-style tunnel that allows residents of the house to walk to the beachfront through a tunnel under the coastal road. After seeing it, Lewis Carroll is purported to have written about the white rabbit tunnel in his Alice in Wonderland story."

"I didn't know that," Lucas admitted.

Alicia pondered, triggered by that recollection. "My father might not have taken the chance and packed the file with his personal belongings when he moved to Victoria after he retired from MI6. He mentioned a tunnel, not necessarily the tunnel in the Pemberton Estate backyard. Just a tunnel. We saw the inside of the Consort House tunnel in Brighton because the owner of the property was one of my father's friends, not an agent so to speak but an affiliate. Obviously hidden, obviously." For a brief moment, she smiled like a child on Christmas morning eying what Father Christmas had left.

Lucas cast an inquisitive glance, a prompting question without a question.

"A thought!" she exclaimed.

"Care to share it?"

"I need to fill in a few more details first. Are you up to taking the Eurostar from Paris Gare du Nord to London, Saint Pancras station?"

"And a connecting train to Warwick?" Lucas enquired.

"Not necessarily but it could be a Plan B. First to Brighton."

"That's Scotland Yard and MI5 turf," he responded cautiously.

"True. We just mention the trip to Daan for now to keep him informed. The UK is part of the EU, therefore technically within our mandate. We'll have to covertly acquire some pounds sterling."

"Curiouser and curiouser." His own Cheshire Cat grin reflected his slightly mischievous enthusiasm for her proposed yet still open-ended itinerary.

"You are absolutely correct. I need to do a bit of real estate research before I fill you in. You may be brilliant, Professor Peeters. Then again, I may be as mad as the Mad Hatter and you as crazy as the dormouse for following me down the rabbit hole."

With a chuckle, Lucas uttered the words of Lewis Carroll, "But I don't want to go among the mad people. Oh, you can't help that, said the cat: we're all mad here."

※ ※

"A DELICATE ONE," DAAN COMMENTED. "IF YOU find nothing, you are just a couple of tourists, Lewis Carroll fans. If it is there, MI5, MI6, the British Foreign Office, the Prime Minister, in addition to a hoard of other politicians and senior bureaucrats will be all over Yolina and the European Council in Brussels and us, just to remind you."

"But only if they find out where we found this most secret of secret files. If the hiding place never becomes known, political Armageddon will never occur," Lucas speculated.

"Be careful playing in this sandbox." Daan's tight smile re-emphasized the possible ramifications if all did not go as planned. "Best if you perfect your exit strategy with a myriad of contingencies before you set sail. Let me know immediately if I need to call Yolina. If I do not hear from you, I will surmise that no news is good news."

"Without divulging who we are and why we are there, we need to convince the current owners of Consort House to allow us to snoop in the tunnel for a file that may not be present. But if it is, it could have sinister consequences. Up for the challenge, Professor?"

He had gained exponentially more confidence in her ability to plan strategically and, in doing so, eliminate unnecessary intervening variables in advance. He still held a preference for additional details consistent with the increasing level of risk.

"Always up for a challenge. But would you care to fill me in on the last bit of research you had to complete?"

"I needed to confirm the identity of the current owner and, more importantly, the identity of the current occupants of Consort House."

Lucas felt his smile widen. He had always enjoyed having the freedom to head out on short notice following a provisional plan and adapting as circumstances dictated. Had his wife been more like Alicia, he might not be divorced. Then again, he might have been divorced for different reasons. His ex was a sedentary soul, content staying at home tending to the house and her garden. Although they had vacationed around the Mediterranean, she tended to strike off the days on the calendar until they returned to their cottage near the University of Leuven. In contrast, he counted the days to the next conference and research sabbatical along the north African coast of the Mediterranean. In the last few years of marriage, the lure to travel and the desire to get away from their cottage were in equal balance. Today, it was clearly the itchy feet and a yearning for adventure that motivated him. *Professors, especially those on sabbatical, are invariably inflicted with itchy, conducting research*, even down tunnels in pursuit of white rabbits, he concluded. *A self-inflicted hazard of the academic profession.*

CHAPTER 26

"Brighton and Warwick will have to wait," Daan advised. "Facial recognition software identified Elana at the Zürich Airport. She is awaiting a connecting flight to the San Sebastián Regional Airport in Basque Country."

Another female passenger waiting for the same flight brushed against Elana who snarled at her in response to the physical intrusion. *Two can play this game,* the accompanying passenger reflected with a sphinx-like smile.

Daan's text to Alicia, Lucas, Alexandra and Paul: "Be prepared to proceed to San Sebastián airport. Our helijet will take you to Paris Charles de Gaul International Airport. There you will meet Commandant Parent's Counterterrorism Force and other members of our Delta team. The Police nationale jet will arrive at San Sebastián Regional Airport ahead of Elana's scheduled connecting flight."

※ ※

NO SOONER HAD DAAN PRESSED THE SEND key when Benoit Parent's incoming call caught his attention as it lit up the screen.

"Daan. Benoit. Are you sitting down?"

"Could be," Daan replied.

"Long story short. I have an old colleague living in Andorra, Andorra La Vella to be exact. He left the world of policing to run his family import / export business when his father died unexpectedly. Andorra, being off the main routes, gained the reputation for being an in-between location for smugglers. An advantage during the war because many allied pilots who had been shot down were smuggled away from the Nazis into Spain via Andorra. Although my colleague is as honest as the day is long, some of his business associates are less so. To our advantage, he is hearing of weapons and other such related contraband moving across the French-Spanish border. Pamplona was mentioned as a location of interest in addition to Donostia-San Sebastián on the Bay of Biscay and possibly Perpignan closer to the French Riviera."

"Donostia-San Sebastián. Very timely and perhaps worrying intelligence with our forces en route as they pursue Elana," Daan replied.

"That may be the least of our concerns," Benoit followed up. "On a few occasions, my Andorra contact has suggested that there is a mole in Spanish Security and Intelligence on more than one salary. This mole is currently en route to Pamplona from Donostia-San Sebastián. My friend did not believe his intent was to participate in the running of the bulls! As a result of this leak, I have not informed my Spanish counterpart of our mission. That puts us in conflict with the memorandum of understanding we agreed to, to share information. I have been in contact with Yolina at the EU Commission. She will speak with the Spanish representative to the EU and nonchalantly mention that the EUI Unit is following up on some yet to be verified information. If found to have substance, Yolina will confirm with the Spanish representative. In the interim, we need to brief our people to be extra vigilant."

※ ※

I*T NEVER RAINS BUT IT POURS.* DAAN reacted with revulsion as he read an urgent text message from Alexandra. His heart sank. He slowly took a deep breath. No amount of training or experience could have prepared him as a leader or colleague to find the right time and balance of words. He would need to lean on Alexandra as never before.

Camilla and Sophia were found dead in their room. The smell

of bitter almonds permeated their breathless faces. An investigation revealed that one of the part-time chambermaids who was an international student at the University of Liechtenstein in Vaduz had naïvely loaned Camilla her older-model cellphone. In exchange for accepting her as a friend on Camilla's Facebook and Twitter, she had allowed Camilla to use her internet provider and helped her to recover her original account and profile. Camilla immediately posted her location to all her friends.

Elana's Facebook and Twitter accounts announced Camilla's enthusiastic messages. One of Elana's Beijing collaborators also acknowledged her request. They had played on Camilla's narcissistic addiction and figured that she would reappear online sooner rather than later. The trap had been set. The mouse had found the cheese. The spring had snapped shut with fatal consequences.

This virtual pretender had contacted the chambermaid explaining he was also a student at the university and a good friend of Camilla. He knew Camilla missed another of her addictions, high-test caffeine soft drinks so he gave the maid a bottle laced with cyanide as a gift. The maid in turn presented it to Camilla who shared it with Sophia. The perceived innocuous gift sealed their fate.

Daan texted Lucas: "How is she?" He suffered the silence of the interlude.

"When Alicia received the news from Alexandra, her physical body sagged ever so slightly as her eyes darkened in intensity. Her face changed but there was no perceptible transition. There was just a faint flicker of palpable emotion in a pronounced crease on her forehead. A chill seemed to consume her, like the miasma of a plague thinly veiled over the landscape. It was as if something inside her, a candle, had been extinguished yet a distant tinge of light lingered. She had a stronger connection to Sophia but now regretted the fact she had not spent more time with Camilla. She lamented the many lost opportunities but seemed unable to appreciate the effect the girls' deaths would have on her own life. The profound emotions of loss are yet to surface. Like a she-wolf who has lost her cubs, it will take a while for the full effect to play out. Right now, her residual radar is only tuned to justice."

She had not fully dealt with the loss of her parents. Their images laying in their open coffins consumed her memories along with those of Jacques and Marc, the latter blurred with the unsettled reflections like fog banks churned by erratic winds created by the vortex from the congruence of all compass bearings. She could perceive the confluence yet they were eerily silent and beyond her control. She knew what she had to do but seemed powerless as if mired in quicksand.

"Alicia asked Alexandra if she could arrange to have their remains cremated," Daan said. "She explained she was too numbed at this time to make any final decisions regarding interment."

"Thanks for telling me that," Lucas acknowledged. "Understandably, her response is strained. I conclude she is in a state of self-imposed calm. I can assure you she remains focused on catching Elana for justice, not vengeance, although the differentiation between the two has narrowed. God help anyone who crosses the she-wolf."

Daan added, "Interesting you say she-wolf. In the Basque language, the female name Otsanda means she-wolf. Stay close and keep me informed."

"Rest assured," Lucas confirmed. "One final point worth noting. Both her parents are dead and so is her only blood relative, Uncle George. She has no siblings. Both Jacques and Marc are dead and now so are Camilla and Sophia. We can add her enigmatic friend, Jane, to the list. You and I are her only close contacts. She has no one else. She did mention that she holds you in the highest regard. A boss, yes, but I'm sensing a familial father figure."

"Hadn't thought of that. A sobering realization," Daan replied, his voice somber and compassionate.

"For her sake, stay healthy, my friend," Lucas concluded encouragingly.

"And the same to you. Speaking of which, how are you doing?"

"I remain her steadfast partner. She is pensive, analyzing the implications of variables operating in the environment. We are a cohesive team, feeding off each other. The deaths of Camilla and Sophia will increase the bond between us as we work through the healing process."

"Just landed. Be there in ten minutes," read Elana's text message to an associate.

"Engines warmed up" appeared on her screen.

Surveillance cameras recorded the driver and the licence number as Elana got into a Mercedes E Class at the exit gate of the air terminal at the San Sebastián Regional Airport. Within minutes, she had left the vehicle and boarded a yacht tied up to a wharf at the north end of the runway.

"Where to?" the captain asked.

"Port de Caneta just south of Hendaye, captain," Elana directed. Her demeanour was distant and cold. From the ice in her voice, the captain knew better than to engage her in idle chatter. Best to leave her to her own thoughts and only follow orders.

The EUI Unit helijet lifted off with a full complement of armed agents en route to Port de Caneta. Two Basque dockworkers sitting on the wharf were detained and replaced with counterterrorism agents.

As soon as the yacht docked, Elana jumped onto the concrete wharf and swiftly walked to a group of non-descript buildings. The dockworkers followed close behind. She unlocked the door of an otherwise non-descript warehouse and stepped inside. "Carry the wooden crate to the yacht," she barked at the men. They followed her direction without a word or other acknowledgement and promptly exited the warehouse without her.

Other counterterrorism personnel hidden behind the side wall of the warehouse raced inside followed by Alexandra and Paul. Alicia and Lucas trailed the dockworkers onto the yacht with additional counterterrorism agents providing protection and surveillance. Shots echoed from inside the warehouse that was all but empty. A single shaft of light shone through an additional side door to the left of the main entrance.

"She has escaped through an adjacent door," Alexandra shouted into her brooch microphone.

"Elana appears to be stationary in the warehouse according to our GPS signal," E-surveillance immediately countered.

"Yet she has disappeared," Paul advised. He then quickly followed up, "She found the tracking device and microphone bug, and conveniently left them on the table by the side door as a snub to us. We have lost this slippery eel once again."

Local French police cordoned off the immediate area, but to no avail. The surrounding streets were eerily abandoned. Windows had been covertly curtained.

CHAPTER 27

As the dockworkers were securing the crate, the captain stared up at guns pointed in his direction. He assessed his immediate surroundings. An escape by land was blocked by a man and a woman with weapons drawn. Escape by water was blocked by the dockworkers who had loaded the crate onboard. They now stood directly behind him. Options were minimal and dwindling fast. He had a pistol in the wheelhouse in a map drawer and another in the galley under the table. It would take tactical maneuvering on his part in order to access them.

Alicia gestured to the captain with her pistol to step down into the galley. Her manner was cordial under the circumstances. Her expression was not. Her demeanour even less so. She shouldered the weapon into her holster in a disciplined fluid motion. The male accompanying her kept his handgun trained on him. Her stare was direct, not shy. He should have known, at least suspected. She extended her hand as if to shake the captain's. Instead, she grabbed his baby finger and ratcheted it back, breaking it at the knuckle. As he bent over in pain, she drove her knee into his face, fracturing his nose. A cocktail of blood and saliva spewed over the immediate area. He stared up at Alicia in disbelief of her prowess and the condition in which he found himself. Except for his own moans of pain, he only heard the faint sounds of water lapping up against the bow. His situation was surreal. Anonymous words of sage advice reverberated in his mind: *control your environment or it will control you.*

"Who is she?" Alicia demanded.

"I don't know," the captain cried over the slur of his impaired reply. He spat out more blood and saliva this time mixed with teeth.

His watering eyes blurred his vision. The jarring impact of her knee on his chin and nose had left him dizzy. He reached out for whatever was within his grasp in order to steady his balance. All that was available was the table. His injured hand was paralyzed and could only provide limited stability. He could see the pistol holstered under the table but could not grasp it. Even if he could, he would not be able to draw back the slide to seat the round in the chamber. He now had no options.

Alicia grabbed his ring finger and ratcheted it back, breaking it at the knuckle. "Wrong answer," she informed him in a calm yet deliberate voice. "Two down, six more fingers and two thumbs to go. I have no sense of humour today. So, best try again."

"Her name is Elana," he slurred, this time even less coherently.

Alicia squeezed his disfigured fingers. "That's better. Now what's her real name?"

He screamed back in anguish, "Elana."

Alicia grabbed his middle finger and wrenched it back, breaking it at the knuckle. "What's her real Basque name? Next to go will be your index finger, and then we start on the other hand."

"She is known as Sapphire. She is the head of the Basque separatist movement," he screamed. His voice trembled. Tears flowed down his cheeks diluting the coagulating blood. His vision blurred from the tears of excruciating pain.

"What's in the crate?"

He paused. Alicia reached for his lone index finger now standing erect.

"No, no, please no," he pleaded. "There is a Russian shoulder-fired surface-to-air missile in the crate."

"Where are the other missiles?"

"I don't know exactly, somewhere around Donostia-San Sebastián."

"Why don't you know?"

"I only know of this one because I helped to deliver it here."

"Where are you supposed to deliver this one?"

"Just to the wharf at the north end of the San Sebastián airport runway. The dock we departed from."

"Why move it now?"

The captain hesitated. "I can't tell you. Sapphire will kill me if I do."

Alicia grabbed his thumb and yanked it back. "You can take your chances with her or I may just break the rest of your fingers and thumbs right now. Your choice. Deal with the known pain if you can stand any more or the unknown outcome with Sapphire."

"No, no more. Please. I'll tell you. We will meet a van that will take it to a location just south of the Pamplona Airport."

"Why?" Alicia pressed.

"I don't know. I swear I don't know," he whimpered.

Alicia grabbed all of his broken fingers.

"No! I don't know. I swear I don't know," he cried out with a stream of tears running down his cheeks, mixing with fresh blood that continued to flow freely from his disjointed nose.

Alicia applied more pressure to his hand.

"Please no, no more. It's to be used to shoot down an airplane. I swear I don't know any more. Sapphire didn't tell me."

"She took off from the warehouse. Where would she go?" Alicia pressed.

"I swear I don't know. This is her backyard. She could be anywhere."

Alicia squeezed a little harder. "Think."

"I swear I don't know," he bellowed in agony. "This is Basque Country and Basque people protect their own from all outsiders, like you. Some of the local police are Basque. They help to hide her."

Alicia nodded. "I suppose so." She let go of his disfigured hand. "Thank you for your cooperation, captain."

Alicia tapped her index finger several times on his mangled swollen hand. "We may need to talk some more so keep yourself available. Just as a reminder, if you have not been totally truthful with me, I will re-interview you but I won't be so nice."

He gingerly pulled his hand back, gently cradling it in his lap. The throbbing pain reminding him of his mortality. "I'll be in the hospital for the next while," he blurted.

Alicia smiled as she looked at Lucas. "Do you have any questions of the captain?"

"None."

"One last point, captain, when I next meet up with Elana, and rest assured there will be a next time, I will mention how helpful and cooperative you were."

Her direct declaration conjured a raft of dreaded reactions the captain had not anticipated. The throbbing pain in his hand took a back seat to the fear he felt at the thought of Elana's retaliation once she found out he had betrayed her confidence.

"LET'S COORDINATE WITH ALEXANDRA AND PAUL," ALICIA suggested to Lucas as they stepped back onto the wharf, leaving the Delta team to secure the cargo and tend to the captain.

"Your interview tactics were a bit intense," Lucas commented, "not judging in a subjective sense, but remarking objectively." There was a time and a place where engaging in conversations that matter would be appropriate. The captain did not appear to be an intellectual, nor was he unintelligent. Lucas was not a novice to such techniques. He simply didn't realize Alicia was practiced in such interviewing competencies. The she-wolf had unfurled her colours. His forehead furrowed. "I will agree they were effective in getting the necessary intelligence by the quickest means."

Alicia stared back blankly. "The urgency of the situation

dictated that we needed to use a more direct approach. As you say, it was effective, not vindictive. Nothing personal. I am confident that the captain will pass the word along to his colleagues telling them it would be appropriate to respond to the lady's questions quickly and honestly. No doubt, Elana/Sapphire will be made aware. I am confident that she will reassess her strategy when she considers her next engagement with her demure surrogate competition. She is on notice." Alicia gave a curt nod as they entered the warehouse.

Lucas agreed. He acknowledged time was of the essence. The consequences of not having real-time intelligence were too dire, especially with Elana on the run once again, free to rally additional forces in pursuit of her cause.

"Furthermore," Alicia stated, "rules of engagement as declared in the Geneva Convention of 1949 were premised on the conduct of soldiers in the Second World War, not cyber warriors operating in a borderless battle space where the fog of war is a constant. The consequences of an attack by multiple surface-to-air missiles regardless of other armaments disproportionately outweigh someone's hurt feelings or fractured fingers. Those inflictions are temporary. The captain will recover although he will more than likely be reminded of his mortality in his December years when arthritis sets in. He will be alive to reflect, to perhaps tell stories to his grandchildren. Camilla, Sophia and Jane, in addition to others, will not have that luxury."

Alicia paused in deep thought as she often did at junction points like this. She would conduct comparative analysis. She wasn't cold or indifferent to the feelings of others. Instead, she found solace in solitude. It provided a quiet time to reflect. Had she achieved what she set out to do? Could she have done better? For the moment, she felt content.

CHAPTER 28

"No sight of Elana," Paul reported, "but we did find traces of fresh blood so we can safely assume she was wounded in the exchange of gunfire." From his own experience of being shot, he was well aware what goes through the mind of a wounded warrior. How the body rests and heals, how the mind reflects on successful and failed coping strategies, and how the soul responds to post-traumatic stress. With all aspects re-aligned, clarity is once again brought to bear on mission success with the discipline of a sniper's steady aim. Readiness to re-engage would be signalled when dreams were no longer dominated by distortions of repeated images in the form of frenzied nightmares. For some, they never go away.

"Lesson learned," Alexandra added. "When next we take her on, and there will be a next time, we maximize our use of all resources." She paused and looked at Alicia. "What did the captain have to say?"

Alicia provided her with a summary of the essence of the interrogation and the captain's eventual answers to her questions. Her expression was neither stone-faced nor Sunday-schooled. Instead, it showed a determined strength and resolve. Her attention was on the task at hand – negating the imminent threat to the safety and security of the European Union.

Alexandra nodded. "There is a certain psychological element to reverse pain therapy. The captain must be breathing more calmly and with assurance of safety now the interrogation is over. Assuming he has told the truth, he will calm to nurse his wounds."

Daan agreed with their proposed strategy. They would permanently disarm the missile-firing mechanism and accompany it to the Pamplona Airport. Delta 1 would immediately replace the van driver and passenger escort before Elana/Sapphire could warn them. Deltas 4 and 2 would provide air and ground escort to the van. Others would proceed directly to Pamplona via the helijet to conduct reconnaissance and wait for the van and its now-benign cargo. Daan anticipated they might get lucky and find the other truant missiles. High on his priority list would be to call Benoit's colleague in Andorra to confirm the reliability of his intelligence, specifically the links to Donastia-San Sebastián and Pamplona. The police responsible for Hendaye on the French side of the Pyrénées would be investigated for disloyalty within its ranks.

"We will continue the search for Elana with Commandant Parent's counterterrorism people," Paul added. "She can't be that far away. She has to come up for air. In the interim, the Counterterrorism Cyber Unit will expand its e-monitoring with emphasis on Basque Country on both sides of the Pyrénées and the Pamplona region."

"I doubt the captain will be willing or able to navigate his return voyage on his own. He might get lost and we couldn't have that. So best we have Deltas 1 and 3 assist him," Alicia recommended, seemingly indifferent to the captain's circumstances and need for medical attention.

"Well done," Daan's text read. Yolina advised that the EU Defence Ministers were planning a strategy meeting in Pamplona. No doubt a missile attack would have caused havoc. The scheduled meeting will continue as planned but will then be moved to another venue at the last minute, announced internally for logistical reasons.

Daan was dumbfounded. How did Elana know so far in advance when to plan and execute a pre-emptive attack? Meetings of defence ministers would carry the highest security designation. Where was the leak? He had posed that question to Yolina in his initial encryption of the text. She had not responded. That was unlike her not to at least confirm his misgiving. Too many lives had been lost to assumption. For that reason, the final line item in any mission text message was ACK – acknowledge receipt of all. If not asked for, it was understood, incumbent on all to confirm receipt and understanding of all details. He would employ alternate means of secure messaging to verify Yolina was aware of his concerns.

"This hiatus because of Elana's disappearance should give us an opportunity to find additional armaments if any other missiles are being deployed to the Pamplona Airport," Lucas noted.

"For your information," Daan announced, "Tatyana confirmed that several Russian shoulder-fired surface-to-air missiles, rocket-propelled grenade launchers and other unspecified armaments had been taken from a Russian armoury on its eastern border with China. Most alarming were Russkiy Sokol mini drones taken in the heist. Not surprisingly, Moscow has not openly acknowledged the theft. All armaments were subsequently transported via cargo ship to Mogadishu. There they were immediately transferred to a Somalian freighter with Panamanian registration which sailed into the Mediterranean via the Suez Canal. An unknown number of hand-held surface-to-air missiles, drones and rocket-propelled grenade launchers were dropped off in Tobruk. The balance was offloaded in Istanbul, under the nose of the rightful owner. This movement was confirmed by Yusuf who said one missile was rumoured to be in Iran, exact whereabouts unknown. From Tobruk, the shipment was moved to Barcelona where a supposed Basque cell picked it up. I say supposed because intelligence suggests those who are in receipt are foreign insurgents posing as Basque revolutionaries. Just the mention of the word 'revolutionaries' suggests early twentieth century Leninist or Maoist doctrine used in communist Russia or China. The armaments were subsequently transported overland to Donostia-Don Sebastián and to an unknown location across the border in the French shadow of the Pyrénées."

※ ※

"Do you have a moment?" Alicia asked Alexandra, gesturing that she would like to speak alone.

"Certainly."

Looking directly at Alexandra, Alicia asked, "What is the link between Tatyana and Yusuf and the EUI Unit?"

"Why do you ask?"

"Covering all my bases."

Alexandra replied, "Are you asking whether I trust them?"

"I'm asking if I can trust them," Alicia responded, mildly defensive. "No offence intended." She sensed a slight hesitation in Alexandra's voice. She knew from experience her abrupt nature could elicit such a response. She was also aware she could disarm such a response with a less assertive explanation.

"No offence taken. It is always good to be careful," Alexandra replied. "The Russians have an expression, *doveryay i proveryay*."

"Trust and verify," Alicia translated.

Alexandra nodded. "You speak Russian?"

"Enough to get by."

"Well, to put your mind at rest, Paul and I worked closely with them on a previous EUI case. Tatyana put her life on the line for us, as did Yusuf. I can say unequivocally that I trust both of them." She allowed her reply to sit for a few moments. "You will have to make up your own mind regarding your sense of their trustworthiness."

"Thanks," Alicia replied, smiling. She reflected on the concerns Lucas had expressed regarding the Knight-errant's lineage to the Knights of Malta, and their employment relationship with sixteenth-century Spanish royalty. Marc had also mentioned his own supposed affiliation with the olden Spanish hierarchy. Life must have been simpler in the Court of King Charles I. Certainly, individual surface-to-surface armaments were limited primarily to slings, long bows and arrows.

As a student, her life had been simple, Alicia recalled. There had been virtually no stress even as she approached graduation and had to think about career options. There was no pressure to follow in her father's footsteps, certainly not from him. In retrospect, she acknowledged she had grown up protected from the seedier side of life and, as a result, had approached decisions naïvely. Now she was the target of assassination. Her life had become complicated. Her deceitful fiancé and duplicitous husband had been murdered. Through direct association, Jane had been killed. Unintentional association with Camilla and Sophia had contributed to their deaths. Recently, she had broken the fingers of someone for whom she had held no direct malice and did so without a second thought. The she-wolf within had been born out of circumstance. Her stress had increased exponentially with a perceived conflict of ethics.

Did my sense of morality die with Jacques and Marc and Jane, and Camilla and Sophie? And with the renunciation of my Jewish faith and baptism into the Christian Church? And my acceptance of the fate of my ancestors at the gates of Fort de Queuleu? Was acknowledging the same as remembering? Where is my consciousness, my moral compass with two faiths, neither chosen with free will or personally affirmed? Am I simply numbed by it all? Her eyes that once talked and laughed were now muted. Her face that once communicated her innermost feelings now impassive. Her motivation, now a determination devoid of clearly defined parameters.

CHAPTER 29

"And?" Lucas prompted, tilting his head in a gesture of inquisitiveness, which had come to define his character. He doubted his former wife would recognize him or approve of his choice of working associates. Then again, Alicia's former fiancé or husband would not recognize the she-wolf.

"And what?" Alicia returned his volley. His prompt was a rhetorical probe for her benefit. She took no offence by it. Instead, she interpreted it for what it was, a gentle whack on the back of her head, a prompt for her to lead as equals.

"And what is occupying your mind? You seem distant once again."

"In debate with myself," she muttered in a jest of emotional re-engagement. They were partners and she needed to step up to the challenge.

"Queensberry rules? Any knockout punches?"

"No rules, no TKOs. Instead, just thoughts that go back to my MI6 days. Jane once said I would make a great analyst but not a field agent because I didn't have the Cold War objective fortitude to extract the intelligence from enemy agents or dispose of them as circumstance dictated. I was not yet a feral feline who could survive as an equal in the land of ill-tempered canines. The potential was there but I wasn't." She lingered in the space of the moment. "Jane was absolutely correct – I wasn't wholly committed to the cause. I was my father's daughter following in his footsteps, not my own person climatized to the arcane art of espionage and intelligence gathering. Today, it remains a masculine world for the most part, but for women it has an advantage for those who are astute and determined enough like wolverines born with the instincts and attuned to the proficiency of the hunt."

"And?" Lucas repeated the prompt, appreciating Alicia's impartial candour as she felt was needed to keep the conversation alive and productivity ongoing. They were feeding off each other as polished and disciplined partners.

"I have found my *raison d'être*. Camilla and Sophia were not mine, but they were more mine than Elana's. She is not just a threat to the EU. She is devoid of decency and integrity. She needs to meet her maker sooner rather than later. You keep prompting, 'And.' Well, I need to ensure that objective is achieved, out of neither vindictiveness nor vengeance but from a sense of duty, justice, atonement."

"Well then, we had better get on with our mission," Lucas replied. "Thoughts on our next move? Do we need to travel to Warwick or Brighton or both?"

"A couple of priority unknowns are nagging at me. First, who was Jane – a friend and neighbour and colleague, or an adversary, an agent of Moscow or Beijing or Tehran or elsewhere? Was she assassinated to stop her talking about my father's file or something else germane to this Basque case? She felt a sense of urgency in coming to Colmar to speak to me, personally, perhaps irrespective of loyalty."

"I think your conversation was purposely cut short. She had more to disclose or ask. I'm confident of that. Else, why would she have come all that distance? The violence of the attack and destruction of her house in Victoria, independently or in combination with your Pemberton Estate triggered the need to meet face-to-face. Else, she could have communicated with you from the relative safety of Victoria. The key is the need to meet in person."

"Was she purposely leading the Asian assassin to his real target, me? If so, what had I done or said that prompted such an urgent response?"

"We have been working together a relatively short time yet long enough to start thinking alike. I agree with your analysis. Were you the intended target all along?"

Alicia pondered whether she had inadvertently told Jane about the tunnel and garden shed? Was the bombing of Jane's house merely coincidental, connected to the current Basque case or her father's missing MI6 file? Or both? Or something else independent? "Elana had stated when interrogated by Alexandra that the Russians had blown up Jane's house for another reason. But was there more? Jane had promised my father she would watch over me. Watch over, or spy on me?" Alicia pondered out loud seeking input.

Lucas waited, silent yet expectant.

"Elana has gone to ground. She will surface after she has licked her wounds, established a new strategy and rallied new followers to storm the bastions of the European Union with the aid of her Russian controller or more recent Chinese contacts. I'm convinced her loyalty is to Moscow, not Beijing. Both are playing select Basque people to achieve their own political ends. We need to take advantage of this lull in order to find my father's file, which I am sure has a connection to both Jane and Elana, and the Basque factor. The Moroccan as much as confirmed the latter."

"Where do we pick up the trail?" Lucas probed.

Her response was immediate and deliberate. "Brighton, the Consort tunnel. I am convinced there is a link." She dwelt on the thought before continuing. "Somehow."

※ ※

As they approached Consort House on Lewes Crescent, Lucas

commented, "Not just a beach house but an elegant estate. I'm impressed by your taste in acquaintances."

"Not mine. My father's. That is why I am convinced that the answer or another clue is hidden, connected to the tunnel somehow. Otherwise, why would my father have brought me here. It was part of his game he taught me – I-Spy-With-My-Little-Eye."

"Was his friend MI6 also? You said he had introduced him as an associate."

"Yes. Just a convenient associate with close connections to some rather influential people who maneuvered on the periphery. My father knew me well and was confident that I would follow in his footsteps one way or another. Leaving clues like Hansel and Gretel's bread crumbs, he knew that I could not resist the challenge. I had the intellect and intelligence. I just needed the focused motivation. That is why he played those mind games with me."

A distinguished lady answered the door. "Philippa," Alicia stated confidently.

"Yes, and who are you?"

"Alicia Dupuis. You may remember me accompanying my father when he came to see your father many years ago. They were colleagues."

Philippa paused more for effect than a need for recollection. She prudently scanned the woman at her door. "Ah, yes. I was home from college. You were much younger. Please come in. And is this your husband, if I may be so bold as to enquire?"

"This is Dr. Lucas Peeters, a university research colleague." She felt awkward with the suggestion of a marital status or intimate relationship. It was a natural assumption but uncomfortable nonetheless, another elephant peering into the room.

Philippa smiled at Lucas as she shook his hand. "Nice to meet you. How can I help?"

Lucas experienced a tinge of hesitancy at the cordial yet terse introduction. It was as if he had just been physically frisked, mentally interrogated and emotionally evaluated. He surmised that Philippa was not a naïve fashionable society lady born into privilege.

"I remember being in the tunnel. I hid an envelope when I was playing, as Alice in Wonderland might have done. It contained a short story I had written. I was wondering if I could try and find it."

"We can look but I very much doubt if it will be there. I had the tunnel refurbished so now it has new walls, walkway and ceiling. The only original structure is the door from the house leading into the tunnel itself."

"How sad to have had to replace the original structure and door that opened to the beach," Alicia sighed. "From a child's eyes, they were intriguing and wonderfully mysterious. From a historical and cultural perspective, they were what motivated Lewis Carroll to write about the White Rabbit in *Alice in Wonderland*. I shall not bother you then."

"Yes, indeed sad. But it was a safety issue. It became a matter of either closing off the tunnel altogether or renovating it completely. Would you care to stay for tea?"

"Thank you for your kind offer but we must leave for London."

Philippa pondered, *if she allocated time to search the tunnel, why would she not have time for tea? Who is this Alicia and what is her true motivation along with her supposed university research partner?*

As they walked up the hill to the Brighton Railway Station, Alicia muttered, "We may never know. I really thought there might be something, some clue there. A longer shot is Warwick and St. Nicholas Anglican Church. I'm not hopeful but we need to follow up on all possibilities, however far-fetched."

As soon as her company departed, Philippa scanned the bookshelf in the study, running her index finger lightly across the spines of books which had not been touched for longer than she cared to remember and preferred to forget. She stopped on an 1883 first American edition of *The Tales of Robin Hood* by Howard Pyle. Immediately under the cover, she retrieved a delicate sheet of tissue paper. She read a faint pencilled inscription of a name and telephone number. She carefully dialled.

"Yes," a timeless, unremarkable voice greeted her.

"Maid Marion, please?" Philippa asked.

"You have the wrong number."

"Kilo-kilo-two-zero-five-two-one-one," Philippa recited.

After a momentary lull, the voice advised, "Please wait."

The line clicked. She was on hold.

Moments later, it clicked a second time and a male voice said, "Maid Marion no longer resides here. If you would like to leave a message, I will pass it along should Maid Marion enquire."

Philippa hesitated. This was not a response that gave her confidence. There had been set protocols to follow. Any deviation was an assured signal that there had been a security breach. "I must only speak with Maid Marion."

"You could leave your name and number if that would be more convenient," the voice explained. This response, like the first, was a violation of protocol to her reiteration of the coded request for confirmation.

Again, Philippa felt uneasy. "No, thank you," she replied politely. She hung up immediately. Had her call been too short to trace? The past, her past occupied her present. Hopefully, not her future. She gauged the potential severity of the violation of the protocol. Like Pandora's box, there would be a plague released that could once more define her present and future. This was not her first choice but a condition to which she had committed on her informal retirement in the not-so-distant past. Like George Smiley in John le Carré's novel, there was no such concept as complete retirement in the lexicon of the intelligence tradecraft if one wanted to continue to receive the modest pension and tenuous benefits for service to God, Country and King.

Philippa ran a full security check of all CCTV circuits and cameras. She double checked the electronic and manual locking mechanism for the doors from her house into the tunnel and from the tunnel to the beach. She then confirmed the status of all the motion detectors. Their installation had been an integral part of the tunnel upgrade.

She remembered Alicia's father and the conversations he had had with her own father behind closed doors in the study where she now sat. She reached under the desk and withdrew a Beretta 93R pistol. She confirmed its readiness. In years since their first meeting, she had become aware of the suspicious circumstances under which Alicia's father had retired. Although she had never worked directly with Alicia or her father, she was aware of her brief tenure with MI6 and her relationship with Jane which she had sanctioned. Jane's semi-retirement was a cover for her ongoing unofficial surveillance of Alicia but mostly her father.

But why was Alicia knocking on her door after all these years with Dr. Peeters under the pretext of research? She would need to follow-up.

CHAPTER 30

From the Warwick Railway Station, they meandered down the hill and into the medieval town. Alicia recognized St. John's House that housed the Museum of the Royal Regiment of Fusiliers, Royal Warwickshire Regiment, where her father had donated Uncle George's military medals and decorations. From there, it was a short stroll to St. Nicholas Parish Church where he had donated his Bible.

Before entering, she strolled through the cemetery, a community of the deceased souls and voices of the incarnate. She stopped and gazed at the headstones of Uncle George and her father. Lucas waited at a respectful distance, scanning the grounds for living souls whose sole purpose was not reminiscence. His vigilance may have been piqued by the tacit whispers of the residents or the ominous absence of songbirds singing, the latter more telling because they were accustomed to those earthly decedents who visited to leave flowers in respect. Alicia's confidence that clues were present somewhere and Philippa's suspicious greeting like a premonition sensed but not seen continued to haunt him. There was a *je ne sais quoi* about Philippa's demeanour, her essence that lingered like an acid reflux after an unpleasant meal.

Alicia lamented the fact she had no siblings, unlike Camilla and Sophia who at least had each other. She had been their mother for two years, at a period in their lives when maternal guidance was so important. Her own mother had been absent from her life because of the battle with cancer which curtailed her involvement. The deadly disease took her life shortly after they had moved into their Pemberton Estate in Victoria. Alicia had visited her grave in the Ross Bay Cemetery, a relatively short walk from their house, to pay her respects just as she found herself now reading the brief epitaph on her father's gravestone and that of his Uncle George.

They acted as tourists when entering the church. Alicia scanned a plaque mounted of the wall with the names of previous parish clergy. An inscription read: Colonel the Reverend George A. Dupuis. Memories of the day he presided over her first Communion held her attention. After the ceremony, both her father and Uncle George reminded her of the necessity to publicly embrace her new faith and privately remember her old. A contradiction in religious oaths of allegiances. Pointing to the name, she whispered to Lucas, "that is my father's Uncle George." Lucas picked up on a sense of uneasy conundrum in her voice.

"Can I help you?" a voice echoed from the solitary doorway leading from the centuries-old chancel adjoining the altar and nave.

"I am Alicia Dupuis. My great-uncle was Reverend Dupuis. As I am visiting from Canada, I wanted to look around as it will probably be the last time I'll be able to do so."

"Ah, yes, I know about your uncle. I see you have found his name on the Nominal Roll of serving clergy. Please take all the time you need."

"As a child, we often sat in the back row of the choir pews. May I sit there one last time and reminisce?"

"Certainly. Be my guest."

Alicia leaned closer to Lucas. "Can you distract the minister while I search around the choir pews?" Her voice was a murmur that only Lucas could hear. "It's a long shot I know but I don't have any other ideas beyond intuition and instinct."

While Lucas and the minister chatted, she searched for any indication of hiding places. Seeing and sensing nothing, she felt under the back pews. Her fingers floated across what felt like the remnants of old adhesive tape, now brittle like dried leaves which had fallen into a crevice years before. The torn edge of an envelope fell into her hand. Printed in the left corner were the faded but still visible letters OH. She bowed her head in reverence and in acknowledgement of why God had bestowed this gift upon her even if it was just a mere candle flame flickering in the distance beckoning her to follow.

As they left the church, she showed it to Lucas.

"OH?" he queried, with an expression of I'm-not-following-you.

"OH, the first two letters of OHMS as in On Her Majesty's Service," Alicia replied with a tinge of excitement. Finely a tangible clue. "The Foreign Office and other government agencies used these envelopes for everyday correspondence, certainly not for anything that might be classified. My father had some of the envelopes at home. They were discontinued many years ago."

"OK, so we struck out on Brighton Consort House where we thought there might have been something. Warwick St. Nicholas Parish Church was a faint possibility," Lucas acknowledged. He perceived the din of ominous silence, the illumination of darkness, the clarity of vagueness behind the spiritual essence of the tacit communiqué. As they walked, he detected minute details not noted when they had approached the church, the flutter of a leaf, the drooping of a flower petal. Invisible yet perceived shadows seemed to float, drifting around ill-defined fringes.

Alicia stared back with a frustrated frown. It was her turn to prompt: "And?" but she chose instead to maintain a distant alertness, to await the manifestation of his thoughts as her father had mentored her to do so many times, and again at this moment as if reverberating from his gravestone and encouraged by his Uncle George.

With a nod, Lucas refocused on a previous conversation with her hoping to connect undefined dots now prompted by St. Nicholas Anglican Church. "What is your interpretation of Philippa?" he asked. Perhaps Alicia had sensed a similar misgiving or lingering suspicion.

"Distanced," Alicia replied after a moment of contemplation. His question seemed open-ended more so than specific in nature and scope as if he was seeking validation for fuzzy content within undefined context. "Why do you ask?"

"I felt like I was being interrogated without questions, almost as if she and I had met before or, at minimum, she knew me or knew of me. Had you ever crossed paths with her elsewhere, not Consort House?" Lucas asked, not certain where his question came from or where a reply might lead to.

"I don't think so. I certainly would have remembered."

"What about your suspicions that Jane might have been a confederate with ties to Moscow, Beijing or Tehran, or elsewhere? I agree with your assessment. It seems suspicious that Beijing or whoever sent the suicide bomber to Colmar did not want Jane talking to you, if that was their true intent rather than simply killing her for another reason. That is excessive force for a single-use resource compared with how you describe Jane as a low-level has-been MI6 analyst. They were clearly following her for some reason. If they just wanted to eliminate her, they could have acted at any point before she arrived at the safehouse in Colmar." Lucas dwelt on his conjecture as he squinted. "Another matter perhaps related, maybe not. Did Philippa have an alternative motivation for inviting us in for tea, but not following up after you declined her hospitable invitation?"

"As well as the two Asians who were activated to follow Marc," Alicia added. "I'm confident there is something there, something connected to the missing file. Elana/ Sapphire has not yet surfaced so we still have time to follow up."

"A long shot," Lucas probed. "Would MI6 kill their own people or contract others to pull the trigger? Would the Asian who killed

Jane in Colmar have done so on orders of MI6 or some rogue agent alone within that organization?"

"Never heard of it first-hand but strongly suspect it has occurred," Alicia speculated.

"Another unrelated question. Would Jane have known Philippa?" Lucas followed up.

Alicia raised her shoulders and eyebrows, adding, "I don't know." She turned around and stared at the graveyard. With a pensive reflection, she carefully added to her response. "My father never mentioned anything that I can recall. But that doesn't mean they hadn't known each other on a first-name basis or only known of each other. I don't think I ever knew what Philippa did for a living, nor did I have a reason to suspect anything untoward. Perhaps her father left her money. Likewise, I don't remember meeting any of her siblings or her mother for that matter." She reflected again on tangential options based more on intuition rather than objective fact. Rightly or wrongly, I assumed she was a student when we met. "You seem to be bothered."

"Not sure," Lucas replied. "Maybe nothing. Just an itch that needs to be scratched. Speaking of different names, does the word *Otsanda* mean anything to you?"

"Why do you ask?" Alicia responded, nonchalantly but curious.

"Daan used the term and said it was a Basque woman's name."

His explanation caused Alicia to reflect for a brief moment. "Marc called me that once. When I was doggedly pursuing something, he said I was like Otsanda, a she-wolf. He knew enough to get out of my way or suffer the domestic consequences."

"Curiouser and curiouser, like Lewis Carroll's White Rabbit tunnel at Consort House in Brighton." Lucas rubbed his nose.

Alicia stared at her screensaver of the girls posing in the garden shed. "I keep coming back to the tunnel. A clue might not be about what may be there but a clue to another clue, a tunnel within a tunnel like the Russian dolls. In times like this, I find my father's games beyond frustrating."

"So, what do we know for certain?" Lucas pondered out loud.

"Daan had previously asked Tatyana to make enquiries. Her reply suggested there could be some truth in my suspicion that Jane might have been a confederate, not completely forthcoming. But Tatyana's source had no hard evidence of a direct Russian connection. The Moroccan said nothing that suggested confederate but he never did speak fondly of her." Alicia shook her head slowly as her mind traced elliptical circuits through her memory. "Absence does not mean nothing. It just means an absence for now."

"OK, but we are here to gather intelligence, not necessarily evidence. Intelligence is not always evidence, although it could be. The end states are different, gaining knowledge to solve problems, to answer questions."

"Let's not be too quick to dismiss Tatyana's reply," Alicia suggested, circling back to her initial suspicion. "Tatyana's communiqué indicated not Moscow-directed but Moscow-related. She has used that nuanced expression before. That's different from just suspicion or denial of association. Likewise, not MI6-directed could still mean MI6-related."

"I agree," said Lucas. "We need to look beyond the old Cold War mentality of East versus West. Russian agents were active around the political globe, as were other agents of varying stripes. I suggest we ask Daan to clarify with Tatyana what she meant by not Moscow-directed but Moscow-related. In addition, we need to have Yusuf poke the Middle East bear for a reaction, flinging a wider net around Istanbul, Mogadishu and Tobruk. That is where intelligence suggests some Russian surface-to-air missiles and possibly some drones left their footprints."

Alicia was thoughtful. "We are back to the Beijing connection which has a big monetary and political presence in East Africa with tentacles in traditional North African trade routes. Today's Cold War battle lines have been drawn down the center of Africa with the U.S. and West European influence on the west half of the continent, although less influential than it had been by the early 1960s and 1970s. The Moroccan didn't mention anything – because there wasn't anything, or there was and he chose not to pass it along. He answered our questions. Perhaps we didn't ask the right questions."

Lucas attempted to envision the future and to discern facts from rumour, or worse, fiction. "The Moroccan held you in high regard because of his association with your father. Had there been something there, I'm confident he would have mentioned it. He would not have knowingly put the daughter of Friar Tuck in harm's way. If there is nothing untoward taking place, the HUMINT, the human intelligence network, would be silent. If there are a lot of armaments, contraband moving, it would be reasonable to expect more chatter on both the e-net and the café net. There is the old adage, loose lips sink ships. I can only conclude if there is a major shipment en route, it hasn't arrived yet."

Alicia relaxed at this analysis. She recalled her initial assessment of Lucas when they met at the hotel in Liechtenstein, the professional robustness, not to be crossed. She would amend that evaluation to include dependable as in a reliable professional partner yet with some tension perhaps brought about by her own frustration. Emotions were contagious.

As they climbed the hill back to the railway station, she muttered, "not Royal Warwickshire Regiment-directed but perhaps Royal Warwickshire Regiment-related. Related as in Uncle George, the Regiment camped in Giza under the surveillance of the Sphynx and the Pharaohs."

Lucas eyed her with encouragement. "And related as in the torn envelope with the initials OH in the upper left-hand corner, all linked to your father's supposed secret file. I too am becoming increasingly frustrated with all the unknowns we are having to contend with. Can I suggest we not look at them as obstacles but instead as clues? The more clues we have the higher the probability we will be able to solve the unknowns. You just said that absence does not mean nothing. It just means an absence for now, a pattern."

"Agreed," Alicia replied. "We need to analyze all unknowns as a whole, as a map. We have found a trace of a government envelope with the letters OH in the upper left-hand corner. That confirms the presence of a written communiqué, possibly the missing MI6 file. Find the tunnel and we locate the whole envelope and its content. Its existence is less likely to be a ruse, a riddle."

CHAPTER 31

Without preamble, Yolina suggested with some trepidation, "Let's go for a walk, Daan."

"Had I known you were in town, I would have put on the teapot with a dash of chamomile and ginger." He tilted his head in response to her wary invitation and somber grin. Her request for walkies meant only one thing. He patiently waited for her executive summary as a ship's captain would wait for high tide in a shallow harbour entrance.

"It's better we chat face-to-face than use electronic means to respond to your initial message regarding Elana's knowledge of the defence minister's strategic planning conference in Pamplona." Daan knew there was more to follow and it would not be good. "You are correct in your suspicions. There is a leak," she confirmed.

Her rationalization shocked Daan. Like Dorothy in *The Wizard of Oz*, he concluded that he wasn't in Kansas anymore not that he ever was. "I don't like the sound of that nor the thought of the implications to our current investigation. Compromised intelligence would be devastating at this juncture. Threats to the safety and security of any agents would be unconscionable."

"A mask is a face telling a story more comprehensively than individual words ever can. Please tell me you know the identity of the person behind the mask," Daan pleaded. His immediate priority was to assess potential damage already done and to immediately implement risk management strategies to counter this threat for decisions on the cusp of execution.

Alicia's expressed concern regarding Jane's motives made him stand up a little more erect. If not the actual leak, could Jane have been a link, the chink in the European Union intelligence armour? Could she have indirectly breached the bastions?

"We believe we have the suspect," Yolina confirmed. "She has been mobile throughout her life and career, mostly in previous Soviet bloc countries some of which are more recent additions to the European Union. She also spent a few years as an exchange student in Southeast Asia. We've given her the code name Waterloo."

Any suggestion that the European Union Intelligence Unit had been infiltrated through the back door of the European Council raised serious concern. Daan's breathing tightened as he waited for the full revelation. This boded ill for a perfect-storm scenario, given the known players in the Basque file, primarily Russian and Chinese but also some suspected Middle East and northern Africa players. He seriously considered replacing his stained portable mug of tepid coffee with a bone china cup of steaming hot chamomile tea.

"This is why I did not get back to you posthaste when I received your text," Yolina explained. "I apologize if I caused you any grief. We were at the height of the investigation and I didn't want to alert the suspect about our investigation. We didn't know the breadth and depth of her network. Nor were we aware of the identity of her controller. We are still in the dark regarding some aspects of the investigation."

Daan cleared his throat. "How long has this person been an employee of the European Council?"

"Three years but only five months in her current position, which unfortunately has allowed her access to classified information. Before that, she was a receptionist. Worst-case scenario in this initial position, she would have been able to identify new employees and verify other senior employees as they came and went from the European Council chamber. She would have had intimate knowledge of their appointments because one of her functions was to maintain their e-calendars." She stopped and stared at Daan long enough to allow his acid reflux to cause him to grimace. He reached into his pocket for his prescription antacid medication. It had been years since regular across the counter remedies stopped having a mitigating affect. Perhaps it was time to consider retirement.

She then said the words that he dreaded the most: "Including my calendar."

"Two questions," Daan posed. "First, how do you and I communicate regarding the Basque file during our ongoing investigation? Second, how do we mitigate any damage already done?"

Yolina handed him a new cellphone. "The answer to question one: this has the latest technology for encoding plaintext into ciphertext. Your second question: we mitigate by still using our older cellphones. It is essential that we keep up with the volume and pace of messages to avoid giving Waterloo any indication we are on to her. Our technology folks have scripted a series of communiqués for us to use on our old phones. Each contains bits of coded information for them to easily track. Once we have identified all her contacts, we spring the trap. In the interim, it's e-business as usual."

"What's an estimate of how long it will take?" Daan pressed her for clarification and operational planning purposes.

"Four to six weeks. I will advise you of any major changes to that time estimate."

"Given our progress with the Basque file, I would like to advise my team in addition to Commandant Parent of the Police Nationale Counterterrorism Unit."

"Yes, advise your team. I will speak with Commandant Parent. Please note that only a select few of the Europol members will be informed for obvious reasons. Between us, I don't have confidence in all member state representatives of the European Council any more than I trust all members of Interpol and Europol."

"And Spain?" Daan asked.

"Not on the list to be advised, at least not for now. Their Europol representative has ties through marriage to some Basque people. Even more problematic, he previously served on Spain's Counterterrorism Unit. And he has been tapped on the shoulder for advanced promotion to their executive level. Until such time as we can confirm no one from Spain is in the spy net with Waterloo, we cannot include anyone. I am aware Commandant Parent is working closely with the Spanish Counterterrorism Unit. That relationship must be maintained for appearances and the sake of our Basque file. For that reason, I will speak directly with him. All e-communiqués between Benoit and his Spanish counterpart will be benign."

Daan thought about his own security clearance procedures. Jacques had eased into the inner sanctum of the European Union Intelligence Unit without anyone knowing he had spent time in Giza. It wasn't speculation. There was the photo the Moroccan had given Alicia and Lucas. Who else had a copy or knew he had been employed as an agent with the EUI Unit? The Moroccan had once been an MI6 informant for Alicia's father. Was he currently an informant for another MI6 agent? Had he passed along information regarding Jacques to this new MI6 agent?

Yolina held Daan's gaze that was grave if grave could be classified as empty of expression. "I know that you have complete confidence in all your people. Given the limited identity of Waterloo and the lack of knowledge regarding the full extent of her network, it would be appropriate to conduct complete security checks on everyone. Suffice it to say, your file has undergone a thorough review as has mine. I appreciate the clearance for Tatyana and Yusuf may be more of a challenge given their previous employers. But we are not seeking Top Secret status for them, just an enhanced integrity clearance. We need to know on which side of the fence their loyalties fall."

"Consider it done," Daan replied without hesitation.

Perhaps it was opportune that Alicia and Lucas wereing up on the truant MI6 file in Brighton and Warwick b e-traffic to and from them had been minimal and then only cryptic in nature informing me of their whereabouts, Daan reflected. He would debrief them in person.

CHAPTER 32

The Counterterrorism Cyber Team had detected an increase in the volume and frequency of encrypted e-traffic referring to Sapphire, particularly on the French side of the Pyrénées. This intelligence suggested Elana/Sapphire was more than likely still in the Hendaye region possibly convalescing from her gunshot injuries. The Cyber Team were able to decode some transmissions which suggested a pending meeting. The time and location would be advised via other means of communications suggesting the meeting was high-level and the agenda most secret.

There were six known recipients on the distribution list. The Cyber Unit had recognized at least one profile from an Asian chat net. This signal currently emanated from central North Africa, more than likely Tunisia. Yet it had been highly mobile in the Mediterranean region, recently Turkey, Egypt and Libya. This entity had previously entered the EU several times by stowing onboard a fishing boat with questionable registration and mingling with the French and Spanish fleets.

A newly encrypted text from Daan to Alicia and Lucas read: "Elana could surface sooner rather than later. While waiting for clarification from Tatyana and Yusuf on Jane's status, head back to Basque Country and work with the proprietors of the vacation villa."

By the time they met Alexandra and Paul in Donostia-San Sebastián, the Counterintelligence Cyber Unit had broken the Basque code. They were confident Elana was unaware because there had not been a noticeable change in the content, frequency or volume of Basque e-traffic. But that was the tactic Yolina had advised Daan to adopt regarding Waterloo, the recently identified spy at the EU Council in Brussels. Those operating the Basque network could be employing the same strategy. Likewise, the Chinese affiliate in Tunisia hadn't altered the format of any messaging structure. With this breakthrough, the Cyber Unit reviewed all previous e-traffic. They speculated the Chinese entity was not just a passive affiliate of Elana's but was influencing operations. That revelation was sufficient evidence for Daan to join the EUI Unit in Donostia-San Sebastián. His presence would also reduce the amount of e-traffic among himself, his EUI Unit agents and Commandant Parent.

Alicia had gained respect for code breakers after her introduction to the realm of covert cryptographs and encryptions in MI6. Technology had advanced exponentially since then. The EUI Unit's cyber warriors were a force unto themselves, having once again proven themselves indispensable. Alicia was determined to learn more about this cryptic electronic world after this case concluded. Would she remain with the EUI Unit or return to Victoria to rebuild her house and the sedentary life that once was, but without the burden and false façade of an integral family that never actually existed?

※ ※

"CAN YOU GIVE US A PSYCHOLOGICAL PROFILE of Elana and what she might do next?" Daan asked Alexandra.

"Sapphire, as she likes to be referred to, is very confident when in Basque Country. She's not arrogant, not careless, but cunning. It's her own backyard after all. In her sociopathic mind, she sees herself as a strategic force. When away from Basque Country, her confidence wanes. This chink in her psychological armour became readily apparent when we first interviewed her. Outwardly, she didn't appear to be intimidated in the slightest. To the contrary, it increased her sense of bravado. That invariably became a weakness for many a modern-day narcissistic martinet. We play that attribute of her character to our advantage. Her worst-case scenario isn't being cornered but being caught. Each time she evades capture like a slippery eel, she believes she is increasingly invincible. That is her Achilles heel, which we can also exploit. My recommendation is to get her out of Basque Country."

"How do we accomplish that? What would draw her out of her sanctuary and into our snare?" Daan countered.

Without hesitation, Alexandra responded, "Irresistible bait."

"Bait!" Daan retorted.

"The only reliable bait would be Alicia. Alicia is her nemesis, with whom she is obsessed. If her network is as comprehensive as we suspect, she will know that Camilla and Sophia are dead. She will have quietly gloated. We suspect, to some degree of accuracy, she didn't so much want the girls as she did not want Alicia to have them. They were pawns in her game. What she wants now is the *coup de gr*âce, Alicia's head on a proverbial silver platter like the sub-King Herald of Galilee ordering John the Baptist's head presented to him on a platter."

"What you are saying is that her obsession with Alicia is her Achilles heel?" Daan conjectured.

"That's correct," Alexandra acknowledged. "Logic and critical analysis dictate people will do what they perceive they must do. Obsession is neither logical nor rational. But in Elana's sociopathic state, it is. That makes it her Achilles heel, her greatest weakness."

"No way will we expose Alicia to that level of danger!" Lucas uttered.

"Yes, I will go," Alicia rebutted. "I'm not obsessed. Instead, I'm committed. I'm not cavalier. Instead, I'm confident. That is the difference between Sapphire and Otsanda. The she-wolf meticulously plans the fate of her prey, all senses alert. Not careless revenge but strategic planning with backup from the best team of professionals."

Lucas's face communicated his continued strong objection to his partner's response. Yet, like Marc, he knew better than to stand in the way of Otsanda, the she-wolf, on the hunt. He had been clear in his protest after weighing options, threats and risk mitigation strategies. But now he had to support her decision.

"That begs the question: how do we entice Elana/Sapphire out of the security of Basque Country," Daan reiterated, "especially if she is still nursing wounds from her recent encounter?" He reconsidered his own question. "The task may be easier than we think. She must have ruminated over details of her ambush at the warehouse in Hendaye and concluded that Alicia was present, even may have fired the bullet that wounded her."

"That would infuriate her, send her over the top so to speak," Alexandra suggested. "If she is truly fixated on Alicia, which I surmise she is, then the ultimate revenge will be a second and final rematch. She will not delegate to incompetent Moscow sleeper cell agents but complete the job herself. She will not assign this assassination to anyone else. To our advantage, we can conclude that she will carry the weapon, more than likely a hand gun. She will want to see, need to witness firsthand Alicia fall victim to her personal actions."

"I texted the head of the Cyber Unit with that question," Paul declared. "Because his team has broken the Basque code, he could send Sapphire a message, posing as the Chinese agent, suggesting Elana ask for a meeting with Alicia – her target."

"I like the idea," Daan acknowledged, "but we need to come up with another means of communicating with Elana which would not disclose the fact we have broken the code."

"The captain could be persuaded," Alicia offered. "Given our recent relationship, I'm confident a personal visit by me would be sufficiently persuasive for him to relay my request for a one-on-one meeting with Elana. Thereafter, we keep the captain *incommunicado* so he can't warn her off."

Daan considered Alicia's interviewing technique with the captain. He reflected on another time and place when he took similar actions to elicit intelligence that was integral to resolving a situation of higher priority that otherwise would have remained unsolved. There were other occasions when the urgency of time dictated similar tactics. *We have all sinned*, he acknowledged, *and I will not judge lest I be judged.*

Daan solicited feedback on Alicia's proposal. "Thoughts?" His relaxed smile and open question masked what he wished to keep hidden.

Alexandra replied, "Let me reiterate. It would meet her ego needs to be perceived as being the preeminent goddess, akin to a Gallic tribal emissary travelling to Rome to bow before Caesar, or in this case travelling to Egypt to bow before Cleopatra or once again return to Giza to bow before an entombed Pharaoh. I have no doubt she would respond to this request favourably if for no other reason than to communicate her authority to the Chinese agent in Tunis. The Cyber Unit will monitor the subsequent e-traffic. A bonus to us, each time she communicates by whatever means, we learn a bit more about her personality to add to her profile."

"I agree fully," Daan confirmed. "If Elana commits to the meeting and conveys this to the Chinese agent, she will have to agree with our – Alicia's – location outside Basque Country for fear of losing face. Our choice of location would be the hotel in Strasbourg. She should be comfortable with this locale because that was where she was with Marc and the girls."

"It might also provide her with added motivation because that was where Alicia snatched Camilla and Sophia from under her nose," Lucas added. "Like Hitler taking the surrender from General

Foch in 1940 in the same railway car, the Wagon of Compiègne, in which the Armistice had been signed in 1918. Elana will gloat in the same way as the megalomaniac Führer."

Daan grinned. "An analogy to a dent in the Kaiser's spiked helmet. I like it! The hotel will be easy for us to staff and secure."

※ ※

"Elana has taken the bait," Daan announced. "She wants to meet with Alicia and has agreed to the hotel in Strasbourg as the location. As predicted, she sent a coded message to the Chinese agent in Tunis who didn't just acknowledge it but granted permission. That suggests the actual controller of Sapphire and the Basque separatist cell is this Asian agent and not Elana. She is the subordinate, number two in the Asian hierarchy at best."

The Chinese agent directed Elana to rendezvous with him at the fishing port of Les Oursinières, east of Toulon, prior to the Strasbourg meeting. His fishing boat would be monitored by one of the French counterterrorism high-speed armed attack vessels, from the moment it leaves Tunis and surreptitiously infiltrates the French fishing fleet. Its camouflage fishing nets could be jettisoned if need be. This water-born French resource would be reinforced by armed air support.

Daan concluded, "We will fly into Toulon-Hyères Airport. From there, additional tactical air support will be on standby ready to deploy. The French Naval Fleet in Toulon will provide marine support while the counterterrorism personnel seal off all roads into the port."

Alexandra smiled, knowing that her recommendation to maximize resources when next they engaged with Elana/Sapphire had been taken seriously. Short of installing a permanent satellite tracking device, every possible contingency had been factored into their operational plan. Elana would not evade capture a second time with a minor wound.

Alexandra looked forward to a subsequent interview. In her previous career as a forensic psychologist, she had interviewed sociopaths and psychopaths, successfully eliciting confessions to some of the most heinous crimes. Each interview although exhausting was invigorating, although challenging was gratifying. Alexandra would have the advantage of first-hand experience. To her disadvantage, Elana would be even more arrogant believing she held the high ground. Alexandra would focus on her arrogance, her Achilles heel.

CHAPTER 33

A freighter flying a Panamanian flag and with a declared cargo of Turkish domestic goods passed by the Tower of Leandros having left behind the Bosporus Bridge that connected the continents of Asia and Europe. Its destination was the North Atlantic.

It traversed the Sea of Marmara and was entering the Dardanelles by the time the Russians became aware that it could be carrying their stolen hypersonic surface-to-air missile, other handheld missiles, Russkiy Sokol mini drones and a sundry of other armaments, in addition to an undisclosed quantity of high explosives. The Russian Black Sea Navy gave chase with a Yasen-class attack submarine on manoeuvres north of the mouth of the Bosporus. It surfaced immediately for passage through the Bosporus Straits because of the relatively shallow depth and treacherous undercurrents. Much to the chagrin of the Turkish authorities, the submarine commander gave very short prior notification consistent with the terms of the 1936 Montreux Convention. Upon entering the Aegean Sea, the Russian submarine commander closed in on the freighter at less than maximum speed, concerned both for the heavily congested shipping traffic of the Mirtoo Pelagos and the unknown motivation of the freighter captain who might transfer some or all of his cargo to a third party, ship-to-ship or ship-to-shore.

A Russian Grigorovich-class guided missile frigate, with an assault transport helicopter capable of carrying sixteen highly trained naval infantry was on exercise south of Sevastopol when the order was given to also deploy in pursuit. It headed for the Bosporus Straits at maximum speed, also giving very short notice to the Turkish authority. Turkey immediately filed a complaint with the Russian Fleet Commander on the heels of a prior incident only days before in which a Kilo-class boat had not given any notification. The Russians rebuffed the complaint stating that it was headed to the Baltic for repairs in the drydock where it had been built, all consistent with the Montreux Convention.

Communication between the Russian Navy and the Turkish authority could at best be described as a conversational gambit. It indicated the Russian intolerance of any conditions that attempted to curtail their declaration of a Soviet right to unfettered passage. The Turkish authorities were well aware that their own complaints would fall on deaf ears. They were also aware the best they could hope for would be international embarrassment. If enough complaints were raised, the ultimate level of retaliation would be a threat to blockade all access to the Strait of Istanbul and the Black Sea. International embarrassment elevated to an international marine incident could involve NATO allies. Neither Moscow nor Ankara wanted to advance beyond a tango of words.

The American 6th Fleet Headquarters NSAN – Naval Support Activity Naples – was not aware of reasons why the Russians had deployed two of their newest and fastest naval resources on such short notice. In response, they immediately deployed two Arleigh Burke-class destroyers and one Task Force 69 nuclear-powered SSN fast attack submarine to follow. Additional land, sea and air resources were placed on alert. The Turkish authorities would be smiling. The Americans would be frowning. The Russians would be expressing hubris intolerance for now.

Having entered the Mediterranean, the freighter hugged the west coast of Italy and the French and Spanish Rivieras, in a futile attempt to seek protection from its sub-surface and surface pursuers. A decision was made by the Russian commander not to intercept until it passed through the international Straits of Gibraltar for offshore Atlantic waters. The Russian concern was the unknown cargo. If the freighter was carrying quantities of high explosives, there would be the probability of monumental casualties in addition to damage to civilian infrastructure should it explode close to shore near concentrated civilian populations in coastal communities. That would result in sanctions against Russia, including denial of access to the Dardanelles and Bosporus Straits if only temporary – an international incident of the highest magnitude.

Having crossed through the Straits of Gibraltar, the Russians became impatient, not wanting to wait for the freighter to enter deeper Atlantic waters. Instead, they closed in and hailed the captain to prepare for boarding. Simultaneously, the assault transport helicopter lifted off the Russian frigate with its full complement of armed boarding party naval infantry. The freighter turned ninety degrees to starboard and stopped all engines, as if in compliance with the Russian demands. The crew of the freighter promptly boarded lifeboats which were launched, all curiously monitored by the U.S. vessels.

Massive explosions cracked the hull of the freighter on the port bow below the waterline, and the stern immediately below the propeller shaft. The freighter began to keel over to port when a third explosion, larger than the first two combined, ripped through the midship. The helicopter veered sharply to the starboard to avoid shrapnel and the impact of the explosions. White trails of explosive material shot into the sky like celebration fireworks above bellowing acrid black smoke and flames. The freighter sank in multiple sections before the Russian navy infantry could board, taking with her its captain, who had not abandoned ship in time. The Russian helicopter pilot could only report a black oil slick and floating debris on the surface where the freighter had left its profile on the horizon moments before. With confirmed notification of the explosion, the U.S. NSAN fleet commander ordered additional surface and sub-surface, in addition to air, resources to deploy.

No confirmation could be established that the purported

surface-to-air missiles, rocket launchers, drones and other armaments were on board. Initially a ship with a questionable cargo, it was now a sunken ship with a dubious cargo. A subsequent submersible examination of the remains resting on the deep ocean floor might disclose the truth. From the characteristic signature of the explosions, it was evident that there had been large quantities of undeclared high explosives, including white phosphorous, in clear violation of the Law of the Seas agreed to by all seafaring nations, including Panama. All crew denied knowledge. The only witness to the true identity of the cargo, its captain, had gone down with the ship.

The Russian assault transport helicopter continued to fly search grids over the ocean surface for the better part of an hour while its frigate patrolled the edge of the search pattern. With its naval infantry back on board, the Russian frigate and the attack submarine set course for the Mediterranean and the Bosporus en route to their Black Sea home port. There was no incident with the Turkish authorities as they slowly passed by Istanbul and under the Bosporus Bridge. The American destroyers and nuclear-powered SSN fast attack submarine shadowed them back to Çanakkale at the southern entrance of the Dardanelles. Tensions subsided as both continued on to their respective Mediterranean and Black Sea home ports without further incident in their wake.

CHAPTER 34

Elana scanned the café out of habit. Her eyes lingered on vague silhouettes. Images from the past both provoked and plagued her. Other familiar patrons sat pursuing memories from their youth, never considering they might find themselves one day living in the orbit of a stealthy life swirling around them, one step ahead of the shadowed players. That day had arrived, unbeknown to them. Elana had arranged for her emissary to meet the Chinese agent on the dock and escort him to their rendezvous.

"I have eyes on her," Lucas announced. "She is on the dock, walking toward the fishing boat just coming alongside. We have her blocked in unless she elects to jump off the wharf into the water in which case she will be confronted by French navy divers. Other personnel are disguised as fishermen on the pier and posing as crew from other craft tied up."

A French naval vessel moved into position, sealing off the entrance to the harbour. Their boarding party was poised to engage, the high-speed attack launch held back in support. Their crew got into position to jettison the camouflage fishing nets.

"I'm not certain that the female meeting the fishing boat is Elana unless she is wearing a disguise. She very well could be," Alicia countered. "I suspect she is probably skittish so it would not be out of character for her to do so." Alicia had modified her own identity at the safe house in Victoria before she departed, and again in Metz upon arrival.

"Hands up! Get on the ground! Hands Up! Get on the ground!" Repeated commands rang out from behind, from both sides and in front of the Chinese agent and Elana's emissary who were walking quickly along the wharf from the fishing boat. Everywhere they looked, counterterrorism agents were approaching in a pincer movement with automatic weapons at the ready, pointed directly at them. Before they could assess their situation, the agents forced them onto the concrete deck of the wharf. Other counterterrorism personnel boarded and seized the fishing boat, taking the crew into custody. The two agents sitting on the pier had replaced their fishing rods with automatic weapons which were aimed at the vessel.

Alicia stared down in astonishment at the two cuffed suspects. "It's not her!" she exclaimed. "It's not Elana! She isn't here."

Daan's response to Alicia's announcement was immediate and clear to all personnel. "Hold your positions on all roads and pedestrian walkways. Detain all suspected females and immediately forward e-pictures."

Counterterrorism personnel began door-to-door searches. The French naval blockade of the harbour was reinforced with additional patrol vessels. The high-speed launch repositioned itself for maximum surveillance off the coast both east and west of the port, reinforced by additional French naval vessels. Its camouflage fishing nets had been removed and securely stored on deck. Its crew manned 30-calibre deck-mounted machine guns on the bow and stern. A counterterrorism surveillance helijet now augmented by a French naval boarding helicopter stood by. Another helicopter hovered over the town. Despite Alexandra's insistence on maximum resources being made available, Elana seemed to have evaded capture once again.

The Counterterrorism Cyber Crime team quickly broke into the Chinese agent's cellphone, confirming that he was Elana's contact and unofficial leader of the Basque separatist cell. His Peoples Republic of China diplomatic passport identified him as Liu Chang.

"I am agricultural attaché with Chinese embassy in Tunis. I object to being harassed and abused like common criminal. I demand to be released immediately. Demand apology from your president!" he protested.

"Your embassy documents and passport indicate that you are a supposed diplomat in Tunisia, not France," Daan replied. "Your status as an illegal immigrant in France will stand for now until such time as the Chinese Ambassador in Paris verifies your status to the contrary. In the interim, you have some questions to answer."

"Nothing to say. Will say nothing. You have no authority to detain me. I demand release immediately," he insisted again. He paused before modifying his demand. "Not report you if you release me immediately."

Daan remained stoic in his response. *I don't think a diplomat would enter France on a fishing boat with no fish in its hold or attempt to negotiate such a deal*, he reflected. He continued to glare at the diminutive detainee who had averted his eyes from the French authority towering over him. He felt insecure, looking straight ahead into the clip holding the knotted necktie 30 centimeters below his captor's piercing eyes. His façade and composure seemed to wither in the face of the challenge to his own perceived authority.

It was another tactic by the Chinese Communist Party confirming they have engaged in undeclared war against the West, Daan considered. *This style of unorthodox diplomacy is more rapacious than any declared battlefield engagement. Something just doesn't seem right*, he concluded. His immediate priority was the capture of Elana, not debating political dogma with someone of dubious Asian character.

The interview with Elana's emissary was less officious and more productive. Facing terrorism-related charges, the emissary was in no position to negotiate terms in exchange for information related to her association with a suspected Chinese official, Basque terrorists and Elana.

"Where were you scheduled to meet with Sapphire?" Alicia demanded. Her glare emphasized the potential consequences of evading a misleading or altogether false response. The emissary became acutely aware she was alone, left abandoned by Elana to fend for herself.

"In Le Café de Port. But she would have been watching and, if suspicious, she would have vacated the café immediately. She is long gone by now."

"Where would you meet her in the event Plan A was aborted?" Alicia asked in a tone that left no room for ambiguous debate.

"There was no Plan B. Instead, Sapphire would email me and the Chinese man. The alternate meeting location could be here in Les Oursinières or elsewhere. When disruptions in plans like this occur, it's anyone's guess when and where the subsequent meeting might take place. I can confirm alternate plans have been consistently inconsistent. That has always been her strategy."

"Elana could be anywhere," Daan announced to all personnel. "Suspect that she is hiding in a house or business establishment adjacent to Le Café de Port. Interview everyone."

Lucas provided a status report. "We did find a half cup of cappuccino on a table in the café. With all the excitement, the owner said he couldn't remember who the lone client had been. It seems the long arm of Basque influence reaches beyond Basque Country. We have taken him into custody on charges of aiding and abetting a known terrorist. I anticipate that he will become more cooperative once he realizes the consequences of his lapse in memory. Life in prison and a press release to that effect for the benefit of all his family, relatives and neighbours is not an attractive option. For now, he will remain in custody. Alexandra will follow up on the interview."

"We may have to give Elana another nom de guerre, *lubricam cel* – slippery eel," Daan quipped. His expression fell midway between amusement and annoyance. He enjoyed a challenge but Elana's escape had moved beyond the realm of the magic that Houdini had mastered.

An e-picture appeared on Daan's cellphone which made him frown. He immediately forwarded the picture to Alicia and Lucas for confirmation of identification. Elana's luck appeared to have run its course. She had eluded her greatest fear: of being captured.

"That's Elana," Alicia promptly replied. She seemed more like an elusive enigma than a tangible foe. Alicia stared at Lucas. "Perhaps poetic justice. I can only imagine what she might have revealed to me, mother to mother. A myriad of unknowns will forever remain concealed behind the veil of death, the fourth of the Four Horsemen of the Apocalypse riding in pale green, representing death accompanied by Hades. Elana will now face the final judgement on her own. All those she has killed will bear witness, including Camilla and Sophia."

Lucas maintained eye contact with Alicia in support of her denouncement of Elana, her tone both sincere and uncertain, tranquil and disturbed. He searched with a haunted look for clues which might provide some clarification as to what it all meant.

Alicia mirrored the annoyance of the she-wolf, Otsanda, betrayed, forever denied the confirmation of the death rattle, now without the trace of the final breath of her prey and scent of her blood to forever linger as the anti-climax.

She continued to stare at the e-picture of Elana, absorbed in silent fleeting reflections flashing before her. The image merged into reality. She would never know for certain who had murdered Camilla and Sophia, poisoned in cold blood. She called to mind conversations with her own father about how to process circumstance of both place and time by which ultimate deaths took front stage. How many things had she wanted to say to Marc and the girls that were now left unanswered?

"What we don't say haunts us more than anything else. Was it fate?" she muttered, more in reflection for the benefit of her own analysis than as a prompt for Lucas to fill the mental space.

"Not sure," Lucas replied. "Fate is a simple single syllable word like truth with a multitude of meanings each with their own connotations. Perhaps it's just a path that provides immunity for those who wish to walk in solitude along it."

"The duality of fate and fortitude," Alicia slowly uttered as she gazed at the normalcy that seemed to be returning to the residents of Les Oursinières, themselves oblivious to the global implications churning in their midst. The voice of Joan Baez resonated in her soul with the lyrics of 'Farewell Angelina': *and friends nail time bombs to the hands of the clock.*

Elana's corpse was found face down in a back alley, her own Russian Makarov PB pistol with the silencer attached lying beside her head, with the fresh scent of cordite lingering. Blood oozed from a bullet hole at the base of her skull, staining the collar of her white blouse. The high velocity round had exited through her throat like a mushroom into the gravel that bore witness to the lethal assault. A cryptic handwritten note had been stabbed onto her collar with a pin warning of an imminent missile attack on unstipulated targets in the EU.

Daan was unsure if the alleged manifest of armaments on the sunken freighter were destined to be deployed in this cryptic declaration of war. But the seizure of the shoulder-fired surface-to-air missile at the Pamplona Airport suggested the threat pinned onto Elana's blouse was real and imminent.

His text to Yolina at the EU in Brussels on his upgraded security cellphone was received with the same level of heightened concern. News of Elana's death conjured mixed emotions, a sense of relief and angst at what might follow – the unknown, unimaginable aftermath of an ambiguous declaration of civil war within the European Union. There were no specific targets identified. Thus, there was no possibility of implementing an evacuation plan. Any mention of an attack would leave EU residents feeling fearful. Worse, confidence in the EU hierarchy and security apparatus would be irrevocably eroded. Panic would erupt. It was better to say nothing and deal with the inevitable aftermath, should it unfold.

Yolina's reply was explicit: "As per my previous communiqué, you have carte blanche. Activate all contingencies. Deploy all resources. Use all tactics. You have complete support from the EU Council."

"Complete support for carte blanche" caused Daan to contemplate the horrors of potential Armageddon. Contingencies had been drafted for such a scenario, a normal strategy for all field commanders. He doubted the initial epicenter of an attack would be Basque land. More than likely it would be Belgium and the EU headquarters in Brussels, in addition to the region of Lorraine closest to Strasbourg and the European Union Parliament. A secondary target might be Geneva and the United Nations complex.

He followed protocols as outlined in the preliminary contingency plan. It would be up to Yolina and the EU Council to advise all member states. In the interim, he and Yolina would be linked at the hip, communicating almost hourly. With the spy identified by Yolina as Waterloo tapping into all communications, his options would have to be reviewed with the upmost scrutiny.

Contacting Commandant Benoit Parent was his first priority. Requesting that Waterloo be taken into custody as soon as possible was his second. Third priority would be briefing his personnel currently working on the Basque file. Benoit would do the same with his counter-terrorism personnel. They were in the eleventh hour and rapidly approaching the fifty-ninth minute. Locating and, most importantly, neutralizing the weapons that posed the greatest threat – the surface-to-surface and surface-to-air missiles, and Russkiy Sokol mini drones with their capability to fire their armaments with pin-point accuracy was his sole mission.

CHAPTER 35

"If not a Beijing agent, then who assassinated Elana?" Lucas asked. "Was Liu Chang being set up or had he set up Elana? Perhaps he was to be the target for Elana's gun. Alternately, both Elana and Liu were being set up conveniently sitting together at the same table in Le Café de Port. Too easy for a third-party assassin. If so, who would gain and who would lose from a double assassination? Beijing? Moscow? Basque Country? Another unknown?"

"Alexandra, can you interview Liu Chang?" Daan asked. "Tell him outright that Sapphire was fatally shot and the assassin had orders to murder him also. Gauge his reaction and response. Also, ask him about the stolen Russian armaments. Our number one priority is the imminent threat of attack on the European Union."

"I demand asylum, protection," Liu Chang pleaded as soon as Alexandra entered the makeshift interview room. He glared straight at her with crystalline dark eyes as if he wanted to pierce through her to establish control. Instead, he divulged the wide chink in his fragile armour that instantly betrayed him.

Her stare irked him. He was the first to falter. She shrugged her shoulders and grimaced. "Protection from whom? If you really are a Chinese diplomat, from whom would you need protection? Once we have verified your identity, we will release you to a representative of the Chinese embassy in Paris."

His pseudo-consular manner crumbled as it had done under Daan's domineering presence. His shoulders slumped mirroring his deflating self-image. "No. Please no. Not them. They kill me. You must protect me." His pleas for safety were pathetic.

"Why would your own people want to kill you?" she pressed.

"Not diplomat. Passport not correct, just false front to make necessary transactions."

"What kind of transactions?" Alexandra demanded.

"I do business."

"What kind of business?"

"Import/export business."

"Stop playing games with me," Alexandra barked sharply. Her scowl showed her contempt for his pathetic charade. "I don't have time for your nonsense. Talk fast or I will kick your cowardly butt out the door and advise anyone interested that you have betrayed everyone who has ever done business with you including your Basque business partners."

Her abrupt challenge shattered what remained of his fabricated bravado. "Please no do that," he begged. His eyes dropped. His hands shook. Beads of perspiration covered his forehead. He drew his soiled sleeve across his face. "I tell you." His voice quivered. "I do import/export – guns, munitions, explosives, armament, contraband on black market. Whatever anyone wants, I get."

"Who are you getting them from and selling to, and what types of armaments are you handling?"

"I buy from anyone, sell to anyone. I sell at inflated price and buy back same guns at lower price when market becomes too hot. Many transactions in African countries like Mali, Somalia, Sudan. Make good money. Russian missiles and other weapons from Asian business associate."

"An Asian business associate?" Alexandra yelled, now leaning into his personal space which he was unable to protect from disrespectful foreign intruders. She sensed he held females in contempt yet was powerless to defend against. He felt violated and Alexandra knew it. She would play the uneven battlefield to her advantage.

Liu reeled backward, intimidated by her full-frontal assault on his deception and fragile façade. "Chinese Mafia pay me sell to highest bidder, Basque sep'tists. I no know where they get money. Don't care. Sapphire is contact, report to me. Those people who got me weapons want money. I no have money. That why I meet with her. She pay me for final shipment." He lingered momentarily as he formulated his final self-magnified importance. "She betray me." He hesitated again. His eyes blinked uncontrollably. Froth foamed at the corners of his mouth. "She pay for deceit," he seethed angrily at the mere mention of her name. His concentration was elsewhere. A thin smirk then fleetingly replaced the mien of his fury, which did not go unnoticed by his interrogator.

"What final shipment?" Alexandra demanded. Her intent was to keep Liu off-balance and on the defensive. She was now his worst nightmare.

"Reported on freighter but sank. Captain of freighter Russian double agent. Killed him, he sabotage freighter. Only trick. No weapons on board, only limited high explosives in otherwise empty cargo hold."

"Where are the weapons now?" Alexandra pressed, curious about others who might have been in on the planning and execution of the maritime deception.

His eyes seemed to scan two realities, one elsewhere and one present. He focused on Alexandra and the quandary he found himself in. "I no know where weapons are."

"What do you mean, you don't know? Every weapon is a dollar owed by you to your Chinese Mafia debt collectors and another to go into your pocket. I find it difficult to believe that a businessman as experienced as you would not have tight control over your inventory, and your financial transactions."

"Not on freighter. I said. In warehouse east Istanbul. Someone found weapons and took to place I no know. Man told Russians weapons were on freighter. Russians follow after freighter, weapons not there." He chuckled to himself as he sat back gleeful with the realization he had out-maneuvered Moscow and whoever had betrayed him, more than likely another Asian or Middle East arms dealer.

You are one pathetic hoax, she deduced. "What were the Basque separatists going to do with them?"

"Want to hold EU hostage to get land back. Attack some places, show they strong. Power."

"You said this was supposed to be the final shipment. What have you already delivered?"

With an air of bravado, he proudly declared, "First delivery Chinese, Russian small arms, semi-automatic rifles, pistols, hand grenades. Second, hand-held surface-to-surface and surface-to-air missiles, rocket launchers, grenade launchers."

"The now-missing third shipment. What is it made up of?" Alexandra followed up immediately before he could second-guess the implications of his self-indulging betrayal.

"Bigger more powerful weapons, missiles. I no know. No see manifesto."

"You had better elaborate with details and numbers if you want our protection. Else, you are out the door," Alexandra growled more forcefully as she leaned further into his deflating sweaty face.

He twitched. "One hypersonic surface-to-air missile, six hand-held surface-to-air and six more surface-to-surface missiles, ten rocket launchers, two crates anti-personnel land mines. High explosives, fuses, detonation cord. Best price, ten unmanned Russkiy Sokol mini drones."

"And now you want my help?" Alexandra replied with a sarcastic growl.

His arrogant bravado became completely deflated. The whimper of a little boy replied, "Yes. Russians want me, and Chinese, and people who stole them. You must protect me."

"If you live by the sword, then you die by the sword," Alexandra muttered in a mocking tone for Liu's sake. "You just wait here while I present your case to my colleagues. In the interim, you had better think about what you haven't told me and what you have to offer in exchange for our cooperation and protection. If you don't, I will personally fling you out of here by the scruff of your scrawny neck. And I'm the nice one. Rest assured, you do not want to meet my friends."

Liu stared at his feet crossed under the table as if he was in another world, another dimension, another space, safe from the onslaught of malevolent intruders undeserving to be in his presence.

"The motherload," Daan declared with a broad smile. The doomsday clock had been turned back a few precious minutes. He would immediately share the news with Yolina.

The mention of Russkiy Sokol mini drones brought horror to the already alarming scenario. This Russian class of unmanned aerial armament was vastly superior to the American Predator and Raptor drone systems in range, speed and advanced guidance systems. Interesting, it would take considerable knowledge and training in aeronautics to operate them. Such expertise could not be learned from streaming internet video games.

He beamed at Alexandra in complete admiration. "You read his treachery correctly. Congratulations. I owe you another all-expense paid vacation at our favorite vacation spa in Lichtenstein. I know the proprietors personally!"

CHAPTER 36

"Yes, but…" Lucas interjected, "if the Russian pursuit on the high seas was all a ruse, a purposeful distraction, then where are the armaments and explosives? More importantly, who has possession and control of them? Drones launched from anywhere in the Mediterranean region could reach any destination in the European Union. Amid the havoc caused by their deployment, surface-to-air and surface-to-surface missiles could hit their intended targets with a high degree of accuracy including civilian commercial airlines. The death toll would be unimaginable. The global economic impact would be equally as devastating."

Alicia sighed. The threat had the trappings of Armageddon. "The note pinned to Elana's corpse warned of an international confrontation not seen in Europe and the Middle East since the Second World War. The ever-present nagging unknown to consider, is that also a ruse? If it is, what is the actual destination of the armaments? Either Basque Country or another location, or both Basque Country and somewhere else. Regardless, I am not convinced the Basque people are involved. Instead, there is a third party using the Basque as a decoy like Moscow blaming Beijing and vice versa. The purpose remains the same, to hold the EU hostage but for what reason?"

Daan looked up trying to grasp the magnitude of the repercussions, not just the one factor that commanded his attention most of all – the not yet accounted for Russkiy Sokol mini drones. A launch and flight path anywhere near Russia would result in the deployment of an equivalent counter-threat by Moscow. We witnessed the American response of one-upmanship in the case of the

Russian Black Sea submarine and frigate tailing the freighter into the Mediterranean and ultimately the Atlantic.

"I've seen that look before," Lucas observed. "Care to share your thoughts with the team?"

"The safest place for these armaments is in an inaccessible location cut into innumerable tiny pieces. If that isn't an option, perhaps they would be safest in the possession of the rightful owner, the Russians. I think that quiet détente may be in order. Better relations between East and West at our operational level would be an added bonus. I need to speak with Brussels, and then Tatyana if we get the go-ahead. In the interim, we dedicate all resources to finding the armaments already in the hands of the supposed Basque separatists. I say supposed because I agree with Alicia. I am convinced now more than ever that the intended recipients are not the Basques. It takes sophisticated knowledge and technical skills to operate missile systems of this calibre. The Basques do not have that level of expertise. Only technically savvy foreign insurgents inserted into Basque Country would possess that technical knowledge. This may be the worst of worst-case scenarios because we do not know who they are or where they are located."

"On a brighter note, there will be less resistance now Elana is out of the Basque chain of command," Alicia suggested. "With Liu Chang in our custody and motivated to cooperate in order to save his own cowardly rump, we have more influence. So, we should be better able to round up what weapons have been delivered already."

Lucas watched Alicia's eyes widen as she scanned the screen on her cellphone. She took a slow deep breath as she showed him the message from the Moroccan: "You were interested in a seaside house in Brighton with private tunnel from house to beach. This house will be coming on real estate market as estate sale. The owner's body was found floating in water under the Brighton Palace Pier. The British authorities are reporting the death was as a result of drowning. My source says MI5 has taken over from the Brighton Bobbies. Robin Hood does not hold the Sheriff of Nottingham in good stead." His warning to Friar Tuck's daughter was undeniably clear.

"Daan, you will want a copy of this text for your record. Another body added to the heap. I sense we must be getting close to something sensitive but to exactly what, I'm not certain." Lucas summarized. "We haven't found any weapons yet. We haven't found the truant MI6 file yet. We are running out of time."

Numbed by the deaths, Alicia gazed at mental images of Jacques, Marc, Camilla and Sophie, Jane and now Philippa. *You stop searching when you find what you are looking for. Jane was the last of the old school agents perhaps for that reason. She or something close to her must hold the clue, the key to the lock which will reveal the link, the truth, what she was looking for. I accepted Daan's offer to re-enlist in the EUI Unit in order to find out why I had become a target for assassination. What caused the fight to be brought to my front door, literally? Once that unknown had been unveiled, I was confident other truths would be disclosed. I was premature in that assumption. Only additional questions, unknowns have been revealed.*

"Individuals take on different personalities when they communicate in different languages – their mannerisms, their confidence," Lucas suggested. "I noticed that transition in many foreign exchange students when they spoke in their native tongues and when they communicated in Germanic or Latin-based romance dialects including English. The change was even more dramatic, particularly for female students whose traditional culture for their gender was being suppressed or bullied. Let's put this into the context of cultures of all the players associated with this file. From a research perspective, that might shed light on some of the unknowns if we hold all these variables constant."

Alicia frowned as she thought about his proposition. The crucible of creativity would definitely take on different dimensions. She didn't criticize herself for not thinking of that scenario. Instead, she relaxed into their relationship as equal partners feeding off of each other.

"It might be influencing our interpretation of communications from Tatyana and Yusuf, and most recently the Moroccan," Lucas proposed.

With a sly smile, Alicia nodded confidently. "I very much appreciate your line of thinking, Professor Peeters. After two years of living with Marc, I learned that he was influenced by his deep roots in Druid and Celtic culture. It was philosophical and ponderous but most of all meditative, based on communal wisdom. The power of nature and the spirit world played a dominant role in his thinking. Traditional Basques don't make deceitful business deals like Liu has described, especially not for weapons or contraband that would destroy the natural world. It would anger the spirits which were the nucleus of their cultural beliefs. That knowledge is our strength when we speak with Basque people. Liu's weakness is he no longer has Elana/Sapphire as his liaison."

"I am in your backyard," Yolina's text to Daan read. "Put the pot of chamomile tea on. Commandant Parent will be joining us."

"Hold that final thought, Alicia," Daan directed. "Yolina has requested an urgent meeting."

CHAPTER 37

Looking at Daan and Commandant Benoit Parent, Yolina started with a terse introduction. "I need to brief both of you on the latest regarding the security breach at the European Union Council and the suspect code-named Waterloo. Her actual name is Diana Molnár. What I am about to tell you has direct implications on the Basque file and our counterterrorism involvement including our cyber cell."

That prelude commanded Daan's and Benoit's full attention in ways that neither of them wanted to hear at this juncture in the operations. Individually, they were aware the other had previously been briefed by Yolina. Together, they had not discussed the specifics because of the top-secret classification protocols. Nor had they disclosed details to any subordinates.

Daan was the first to respond to this latest revelation. "As you are aware from my most recent text, we are on the eve of implementing the next phase of our search and seizure process for the missing weapons. Do we need to stand down completely or just modify the contingencies?"

"Perhaps the latter," Yolina replied, transferring her attention to Benoit. "But we will have to adjust our strategy in terms of your counterterrorism preparations and to what extent we share some details with Spanish authorities. They are already aware we have been focusing our efforts on Basque Country on both sides of the Pyrénées. They are less aware of our counterterrorism cyber surveillance. Let's keep it that way for the time being."

Benoit reported, "My people are finetuning last-minute tactics as we speak. Best I advise them to pause, pending my return."

Yolina nodded in agreement. "I previously mentioned that

Spain's Europol representative has indirect ties through marriage to some Basque people. That has been downgraded to a lower priority at this juncture. Possibly more problematic is we recently found out the Spanish Europol representative had previously served with Spain's Counterterrorism Unit and continues to maintain close ties with the unit's senior officer currently in charge of operations."

Daan and Benoit exchanged glances before returning their attention to Yolina. Nothing she had revealed so far appeared to be a cause for major concern. Her manner gave nothing away yet they knew she would not come all this way to drink chamomile tea and socialize. But nothing more needed to be disclosed to set the stage.

"Regarding the security breach at the EU Council, more in-depth research into our suspect, Diana Molnár, revealed she has an identical twin sister named Ana Molnár, born in Prague, Czechoslovakia. Today, Ana Molnár is known as Maya Pérez, the wife of Spain's representative to Europol and previous senior member of the Spanish Counterterrorism Unit. They met in Brussels at a conference of EU counterterrorism executives. Her sister, Diana Molnár, code-name Waterloo, arranged a reception at the EU Council where she purposely introduced them. Thereafter, she encouraged the relationship by inviting them to private and other social events. She went so far as to make her apartment available for intimate liaisons. Being identical twins proved to be their shortcoming as one of our security folks working on this current security breach remembered them from their near-identical photo IDs." The Spanish counterterrorism mouse unknowingly went for the seductive Prague cheese.

Daan and Benoit took a deep breath like synchronized swimmers about to execute their next sub-surface manoeuvre. With a sense of foreboding, they awaited Yolina's elaboration of the details regarding the quickly unfolding espionage conspiracy.

Yolina concluded, "Both sisters, while in high school, had been selected as foreign exchange students in Hong Kong. They subsequently attended the University of Rostov in southern Russia under a similar undergraduate exchange program. Their education and living expenses were subsidized, we do not know by whom. Beijing, Moscow, or another entity with deep pockets and strategic perspectives."

Daan interjected, "Two questions. First, when will you be arresting Waterloo? Second, when will you be dealing with the Spanish representative to Europol? Both will have equal impact on our planned operations in Basque Country."

"The coded texts you have been sending me on my original cellphone, and my replies, have identified what we believe to be many if not most of the foreign agents in Waterloo's network," said Yolina. "Our security people in Brussels would prefer to continue the project for another month. However, because of the looming threat to the EU from the stolen weapons and munitions related to the Basque file, they were ordered to terminate the surveillance effective today. The identified agents living in the EU are being rounded up at this time, including Waterloo. The good news is we have broken the ring. The bad news is we do not have them all. It was a balance of priorities. To your second question, the Spanish Europol representative has been recalled to Spain and suspended from duty because his top-secret security clearance has been withdrawn. His wife has been arrested. The current senior operations officer in the Spanish Counterterrorism Unit has been suspended pending further investigation."

"I now have a better appreciation of the immediate impact on our counterterrorism operations in Basque Country," Benoit acknowledged. "I did not inform my superiors after your initial briefing. I need to bring them up to date as soon as possible, specifically my involvement with Daan's people outside French borders. I can envision a scenario where Daan moves into Spain without Spanish support and I have to stop at the border. I do not want to leave him alone should push come to shove. What is your direction?"

"I will speak with your chief," Yolina replied. "For now, we carry on with our plans, with one exception. You are not to share anything with your Spanish counterpart. This continues to be a delicate inter-jurisdictional matter which will have broader implications as you can appreciate. The head of Europol is handling that aspect. For now, Daan will take the lead as director of the EUI Unit with jurisdiction in all EU member states. Benoit, your people technically do not have jurisdiction on the Spanish side of the Pyrénées. To resolve this jurisdictional conflict, Benoit, you and a select few of your best agents will be temporarily seconded to the EUI Unit. That's the best we can do. Adjust your plans accordingly."

"The realm of cyber-crime has no borders, nor does counter-terrorism cyber-security surveillance," Benoit countered, slightly more content with the strategy that provided sufficiently greater latitude to achieve the objective of the mission.

CHAPTER 38

"We have the go-ahead from Brussels," Daan announced with fervour. "However, we will need to monitor the mission very closely. The factor weighing in favour of proceeding was the imminent threat to the EU from the weapons already in the hands of those who present themselves as Basque separatists but may not be. For the true Basque, the motivation for cooperation in the disclosure of the whereabouts of the weapons could be an acknowledgement of historical claims to Basque Country."

"That would be consistent with Marc's interpretation of the Druid/Celtic belief in, and respect for, the power of nature," Alicia added. "We allow for an abbreviated meditative communal decision-making process with the emphasis on an understanding that the weapons will be surrendered soonest. If not armaments alone, then the identification and location of those pretending to be Basque peoples with their knowledge of advanced weapons like the Russkiy Sokol mini drones."

"We play both the carrot and the stick," Daan directed. "I like your proposal. The Druid/Celtic cultural factor is the carrot. If those in the know fail to cooperate, Basque Country will become the focus of intense police action that would apply to all suspected separatists with repercussions on any family members who have aided and abetted the activity. In brief, there would be no clemency for any hostile actors. That would be the stick." Daan paused. "A wary reminder, we could be on the precipice of the first European Union civil war with global ramifications."

Tatyana provided the name of the most discrete détente contact in Moscow. If this endeavour to have the missing armaments and explosives returned to their rightful owners was successful, the contact would be prepared to provide intelligence regarding Jane's status as either a loyal subject on Her Majesty's Secret Service or an MI6 turncoat. There was a codicil. The Moscow contact strongly suggested that the U.S. be kept in the dark as they tend to react negatively to any warming of relations. Peace is bad for the U.S. weapons manufacturing industry. Assuredly, the U.S. National Rifle Association would be twisting arms in Washington to quash any such initiatives to ease East/West tensions because their membership would perceive it to be un-American, an affront to their constitutional right to bear arms and produce additional arms for profit.

The threat of being released from his quasi-protected association with the EUI Unit helped to keep Liu Chang on a short and obedient leash as he took on the role of negotiator between his new keepers and supposed members of the clandestine Basque separatist clan. Initially, some were reticent to trust in any commitment toward recognition for land claims in exchange for arms or identification of insurgents. For centuries, Spain had failed to demonstrate any degree of integrity, at least from the Basque perspective. Instead, they had responded with brutal and lethal retaliation.

Alicia and Lucas agreed that coercion was not a card to be played at these delicate preliminary encounters. It was evident most residents of Basque Country were peaceful. They just wanted an assurance their claim to the land of their forefathers would be acknowledged. Establishing trust was paramount. Presenting herself as the spouse of the Basque, Santiago López, could possibly ease tensions and establish tentative relationships. Although no weapons had been surrendered initially, tacit assurances had been given that the EU was not facing the eleventh hour and fifty-ninth minute, as the note pinned to Elana's blood-stained blouse had forewarned. But it would take just one rogue actor with a nasty attitude and a loaded rocket launcher to undermine the whole deal.

"And…" Lucas commented to Alicia's familiar pensive pauses. Like Pooh Bear pondering over a pot of honey, he was confident the output of her mental wanderings would be productive with a gentle nudge.

"Not one of the supposed Basque separatists we have spoken with thus far was aware of a resupply of armaments. That would suggest the Istanbul armaments allegedly in the hold of the freighter weren't destined for Basque Country but another location if it existed it all. Previous intelligence suggested Tehran. Was Liu playing the part of a less than righteous double-crossing entrepreneur with a higher bidder in Iran? It seems unlikely if Liu was selling to the highest bidder, which he said he was, the Basques could not outbid major players like Iran. My dearly departed father had mentioned to me on several occasions that if I heard a suspicious sound or noticed a curious movement, I should look in another perhaps opposite direction. The Moroccan also alluded to that as a strategy. Have we been too focused on the Iberian Peninsula?"

"When you prostitute yourself for the almighty dollar, you give up your integrity, and the ability to adhere to moral standards. I highly doubt Liu can spell integrity in Mandarin or English, let alone understand the parameters of its interpretation even taking into consideration differences in cultural interpretation. Perhaps we need to address this point with Liu at our next coffee meeting," Lucas suggested.

Alicia nodded. "That chat needs to take place sooner rather than later. On a related note, I've noticed after each meeting with his Basque clients, Liu seemed increasingly nervous and hesitant. It could be he perceives any new or renewed acquaintance as a personal threat. I think he believes there is an increased probability of hostilities aimed directly at him, Russian roulette but not necessarily Russian."

Lucas supported her assessment. His silence echoed occasions when he had considered theoretical propositions to research outcomes. He missed the exchange of ideas in conversations that mattered over fine cognac with academic colleagues at the University of Leuven, especially Daan. Although their time working together had been brief, he found himself looking forward to Alicia's analytical responses to his prompts.

"Another intriguing observation," she followed up. "Are the physical features and behaviours of some of Liu's supposed Basque contacts more North European, certainly less Spanish? In addition, their command of the Spanish language is limited. When they do speak, there is a noticeable accent inconsistent with the region on both sides of the Pyrénées. Their Basque dialect is virtually non-existent."

"I agree with your analysis," Lucas replied. "Curiouser and curiouser cried Alice on her journey with the White Rabbit. But Alicia Dupuis, not Alice in Wonderland, insinuates with uncanny accuracy. You are on to a critical factor. Daan is less convinced the Basque separatists are Basque. I have to agree. I have no doubt there are a few disgruntled Basque entrepreneurs like the captain but they are in the minority. Elana may have been born in Basque Country but Sapphire was Russian in ideology and loyal only unto her narcissistic sociopathic self."

"If we knew who Elana's assassin was," Alicia proposed, "we might be able to allay Liu's concerns. Unfortunately, forensics have come up with a blank slate. All they can say is the bullet was fired from a high-powered handgun fitted with a silencer. It passed through her neck at the C-3 level and exited through her throat. At that angle, she would have had to have been kneeling and the shooter standing behind her, execution-style. The bullet smashed into the stone wall of the foundation, obliterating virtually all the rifling groves."

"Whoever fired the gun wanted to leave only one message:

absolute assurance of death for perceived or actual acts of betrayal. Only God and the perpetrator know who pulled the trigger. It's another discussion item for the agenda at our follow-up coffee discussion with Liu," Lucas added.

Alicia found herself in a quandary attempting to balance her frustration with the absence of definitive facts she could analyze to arrive at the truth, in addition to assurance she was eliminating potential factors she would not have to consider. She recalled one of her professors at Oxford University repeatedly saying in less than academic utterance: when you are up to your ass in alligators, it is difficult to remember that your initial objective was to drain the swamp. She had a better understanding of that adage. Her objective was to find out why she had become the target of an assassin since taking a leave of absence from the European Union Intelligence Unit. Examining sterile case studies in her university classes in statistical analysis failed to take into consideration the degree of human emotions, ever present in the real world, brought to the equation. This reality was further compounded when the analyst was the target in the crosshairs. Emotions fell into the realm of qualitative research not quantitative statistics. She could only conclude with any degree of certainty that people in all cultures were fickle at best.

CHAPTER 39

"Absent the broken knuckles," Lucas prompted. He agreed with her interpretation of the rules of war as articulated in the 1949 Geneva Convention. However, it was a slippery slope, the universal dilemma. War was not ethical under any conditions. Neither was carnage resulting from terrorism. The introduction of unmanned drones operated by technical combatants thousands of miles away to summarily execute individuals in an undefined battlespace with no formal declaration of war had not been considered by the authors of the Convention. That was Plato's argument with his Ring of Gyges, realpolitik based on practical rather than moral criterion. The fog of war, as Alicia suggested. No holds barred as Brussels alluded.

"The captain needed to know who was in charge. Liu already knows and is well aware of the consequences. Having said that, he may need to be reminded. When he said his life was in peril from Moscow, Beijing or his Chinese Mafia affiliates, I think he knows more than he is saying. He just needs to be convinced we are his only option for a longer, relatively healthy but not necessarily prosperous life. Time for another MI6 interrogation technique with a minor modification to Maslow's hierarchy of needs."

"A little Maslow motivation?" Lucas queried. They would need to engage in a conversation that mattered over cognac or Côtes du Rhône, or both, in order to define the parameters of the interrogation. He had not previously considered the topic worthy of debate. Now it was.

Alicia grinned at the thought of Maslow's tacit approval.

※ ※

Liu was escorted to the café by the Delta team for the petit-déjeuner meeting with Alicia and Lucas who were already sitting in a secluded corner. Two of the team sat inside while two others occupied a table outside under the quintessential French red awning.

Alicia welcomed Liu with a sincere yet troubled tone. "We need to chat, Liu," she whispered, wringing her hands and pursing her lips for theatrical effect. "For all we know, an agent may have been sent to put a bullet in your head. That person could be in this café right now or sitting at one of the tables outside. We don't know." She raised her shoulders and eyebrows in an expression of suspicion. Looking inquisitively at Lucas, she asked, "Do you know who this person might be?"

"I don't know," Lucas replied with a whisper in an effort to further heighten Liu's sense of impending doom. Lucas scanned his text messages as if a related e-communiqué had just come in. "No updates. It could be anyone here or someone outside. That is why I asked Liu's escorts to position themselves in both locations."

Alicia had achieved her first objective, to communicate concern to Liu for his immediate safety and security.

"What happen? I need to worry?" Liu quickly replied, clearly on edge. His worrisome eyes scanned the room abruptly moving from patron to patron and finally the waiter serving and owner behind the bar.

"We have received intelligence that suggests we, or rather you, are being followed, stalked. The threat is real and imminent. Whoever it is wants you dead, a fait accompli. The informant suggested the source of the threat could be Russian, Chinese or another entity, more than likely another Asian but possibly Middle Eastern. To keep you safe, we need more information. Of these, who would be the most likely assassin sent to put a bullet in your head like Elana/Sapphire?"

He didn't have to think long. "Chinese Mafia. They missing hundreds of thousands, millions of dollars. Will not forgive."

"Why not the Russians?" Alicia asked, purposely baiting her question to elicit the greatest reaction.

"They don't do that. Don't write messages. Note is too personal. Russians not like that. They just kill."

"Would they have contracted out the assassination of Sapphire or sent one of their own to pull the trigger?"

"Do you know calibre of bullet kill her?" Liu asked.

"A high-powered .357 magnum round. A wound resulting from a lower calibre like a .38 or .32 might not have killed her immediately."

Liu's face became as pasty as Ebenezer Scrooge's complexion in Dickens's 1843 novel when he was visited by the Ghost of Christmas Past. His breathing became short with weak gasps. His pupils dilated as he continued to scan the room. He adjusted his chair so his back would not be to the entrance door.

"Talk to us, Liu," Lucas encouraged with deceptive compassion. "We are your only hope of security. You need to tell us all you know. What was said between you and the other players? More importantly, what was *not* said, just insinuated? Now is not a time to be vague. If you haven't already come to this conclusion, your life depends on it. Even Sapphire's mother would not have been able to identify her. I won't overwhelm you with the details of what the .357 magnum did when it entered the back of her head. But it was horrific, the damage the bullet caused to her face as it exited through her lower jaw. Even as good as Sapphire was, and you have to admit she was good, she could not escape the assassin's bullet."

Liu's complexion turned to a whiter shade of pale. His sweaty hands trembled uncontrollably. His squinting eyes filled with tears.

"Work with us," Lucas repeated in an encouraging, compassionate tone. "We are your only friends, your only hope."

"They have ninth tentacle," Liu stuttered. "Collaborator spy in EU intelligence community. This person not Asian, for sure. Been around long time, ten years, careful. Person hires assassins."

"This ninth tentacle, male or female?" Lucas pressed.

"Could be either. I no know."

"And the shooters, which gender?"

"No know," he snivelled with a desperate child-like plea hoping to evade the inevitable corporal punishment from an abusive parent.

"*La nuit tous les chat sont gris* – all cats are grey at night," Alicia muttered with an air of resignation. At the moment the trigger is squeezed, the identity of the assassin becomes irrelevant to the victim.

"Protect, please, I beg you. Not like Sapphire." Liu's voice cracked as he stared at two new café patrons who entered and sat at a table almost out of the range of his peripheral vision.

"That just doesn't add up, Liu," Alicia replied with a puzzled expression. Her delivery was deliberate and practiced.

"What wrong?" he retorted, pleading for clemency.

"Those who dispatched your assassin seem too compelled for just monetary reasons. There has to be another explanation. I think they feel betrayed regarding a certain matter." Alicia leaned forward within inches of his face which was turning pale once again. She whispered, "There were no weapons on the freighter. Your supposed Basque contact doesn't exist. Elana/Sapphire didn't have any millions of dollars. You made another deal with someone from the Middle East, didn't you?"

Perspiration dimpled on his face. With his opposing thumb and index finger, he rotated a disproportionately large diamond ring on his baby finger in the same nervous manner he had done when evading disclosure of his false Chinese diplomatic identity.

"An Iranian. You made a deal with an Iranian, didn't you?" Alicia insisted.

"No, no me," he choked.

Alicia reached over and grabbed hold of his baby finger as if wanting to admire the ring, but instead she deliberately bent it backward to the point of breaking. "Now, tell me the truth, Liu. If you do not, I will kick you out of this café after breaking your finger. The person sent to assassinate you, the one my source said was very close by, will put a .357 calibre bullet in your head." Alicia pointed her extended index finger at his head with her thumb pointed up replicating a pistol and said forcefully, "Boom!"

Liu gulped with an inhaled breath as he tried in vain to push against the back of the chair with a startled jolt. With Alicia still gripping his ringed finger his attempt to escape was thwarted. Present was only the growing pain.

"You had better be completely honest with her, Liu. She broke all the fingers of the last person who didn't tell the truth, the whole truth, and nothing but the truth," Lucas whispered, suggesting he had neither control over her actions nor the ability to negotiate on Liu's behalf to mitigate the pain now radiating through his hand from Alicia's pressure on his ringed baby finger.

Anguish replaced the muted words he was repressing. His tear-filled eyes were dark yet translucent, insistent yet panicked.

"He seems to have a low tolerance for pain," Lucas commented to Alicia who continued to bend his baby finger to its maximum extension without fracturing. Her facial expression was purposely devoid of emotion, an interrogation tactic for Liu's sake to suggest she couldn't care one way or the other if he was in pain or dead.

"Stop, please," Liu pleaded.

"Talk to me then," Alicia invited in a nonchalant manner. "I am your friend, your only hope," she repeated. "Your choice. It's either me or the assassin outside with the hungry .357 magnum." She paused for continued theatrical effect. "Maybe the assassin isn't outside, instead inside, one or both of the café customers who just entered."

She tilted her head as she glanced at Lucas. "What do you think?"

Lucas looked briefly at the two before transferring his gaze back to Alicia. "Could be," He whispered as he shrugged his shoulders. He then stared at Liu and again recommended with a forceful tone and an abrupt nod, "You had better talk to her, Liu, and be completely honest."

CHAPTER 40

"Weapons moved to warehouse east of Istanbul," Liu repeated. "When Russian looking for freighter, weapons moved again to Ankara. Truck take to small village of Van close to Iranian border. Security from Turkish Emniyet not care. Pay police not to care, not to arrest. Don't say to anyone I tell you this."

"How were you to be paid?" Alicia asked.

Liu hesitated.

Alicia gazed down at his swollen baby finger as she slowly reached forward with the intention to grab his attention.

Lucas stared at Liu with widening eye. He then raised his eyebrows. His non-verbal communication for Liu's sake was abundantly clear.

Liu immediately replied to Alicia's question. "They deposit half into escrow account in Arab Bank of Switzerland, Geneva. Pay balance later when receive shipment. All moved from escrow account to my account when deal done."

"Let's get back to Istanbul," Alicia said. "How and where were they moved?"

"Go from Istanbul to Ankara after freighter leave. After, go by road in truck to Van, followed by another truck with armed guards, some Iranian, some Turkish police, some private police. All watch each other. No one trust the other."

"There had to have been a point man, someone to oversee the movement if for no other reason than for continuity and security," Alicia insisted.

"Captain of freighter, his first mate in on the deal. He go with shipment. He take train from YHT Station at Pendik in east Istanbul to Ankara Gar. From there, he drive in car final leg of route to the town of Van. He had own security guards in car with him and follow in other car."

"What was the first mate's name?" Alicia asked, friendlier and less aggressive. She had withdrawn her outstretched hand.

"Name Mehmet."

"Now that the captain is dead, how will you contact Mehmet, to pay him?"

"No contact him. He contact me," Liu replied. His whining voice dropped an octave.

"So, if something happened to the shipment en route, the Iranians would get their escrowed deposit back and the first mate, Mehmet, would get nothing for his effort. He wouldn't be a happy camper, so to speak. You would have Mehmet hunting for you in addition to the Chinese Mafia and the Russians. You would be a popular guy, Liu. Who do you think would be the first to put the .357 magnum bullet in the back of your head and blow your face into smithereens, like Sapphire?"

"Oh god," he shrieked. "You protect me. Please. Iranians have secret police spy on me. They torture first then shoot if still alive."

Alicia sat back and stared at Liu while collecting her thoughts. She then motioned to Lucas.

"We'll do our best to protect you," Lucas assured him. "Best get some rest. We will have a guard outside your room." Lucas motioned to two inconspicuous men sitting in the corner sipping coffee. They stood up and escorted Liu to his room.

"And…" Lucas gazed inquisitively at his partner, looking forward to the account of her tactics.

"And, occasionally, a mixture of reverse pain psychology and Maslow are needed to prompt the dialogue," she replied with a sly grin. "He's a weak slimy self-serving lizard. I didn't have to break it."

Lucas bowed in response with a reassuring yet slim smile.

"Urgent that we pass along to Daan this intel on the suspected confederate in the EU intelligence community and the movement of the armaments into Iran. The only time and place to intercept would be on the highway between Ankara and Van. Once they cross the border into Iran under Iranian armed escort, it will be virtually impossible to secure them." He quickly keyed in the text. The subject line read: "The Détente URGENT".

After the shuffling of Liu's footsteps faded, Alicia looked at Lucas and posed the inevitable question. "Is he playing with us or being truthful?"

Lucas replied immediately on the heels of her question. "Or both, to varying degrees depending on the circumstances in which he finds himself. In the final analysis, he is only loyal to Liu. I agree, he is a slimy lizard subsisting in an equally slimy swamp. That is where and how he learned to survive. One of these days, a more devious reptile will devour him or leave his diseased corpse for something lower in the food chain to dispose of."

"A chameleon adapting to its environment – one of the first competencies to be mastered by a highly-trained intelligence operator. That might suggest he underwent specialist training by a professional intelligence organization like the Chinese Ministry of State Security."

"Did you note his effeminate voice?" Lucas asked. "I hadn't noticed it with previous conversations, even when he was taken into custody on the wharf or when he admitted his Chinese diplomatic passport was a forgery. His voice changes when he becomes highly stressed."

"First time I picked it up, too. So, is it a part of his well-rehearsed ploy or is it an indication of selfish narcissist grovelling?"

"I'm thinking both," Lucas admitted. "We don't know enough about him. As you say, he could be an exceptionally talented spy sent by the Chinese Ministry of State Security to find the weapons and stir up the pseudo Basque separatists. Or, he could be an amateur Chinese Mafia affiliate solely motivated by personal profit and greed."

"We play all options for now," Alicia acknowledged. "We haven't disclosed all the cards in our hand. From what we have revealed, he wouldn't be able to figure out what we know or don't know. Let's just carry on approaching his Basque contacts."

"In the meantime, we ask Daan to have our forgery folks speed up their analysis of his passport. If he is a Chinese Ministry of State agent, their examination will validate its authenticity. That appears to be inconsistent with his erratic behaviour we have been witnessing. Alternately, if he is an envoy of the Chinese Mafia, it will more than likely be a fake, mirroring the dubious persona we are seeing."

"Hmmm," Alicia murmured as she stared upward into the abyss of possibilities pondering only long enough to analyze the viability and risks associated with each. She then lowered her gaze and looked back at Lucas. She composed her reflective question confident that he would whole-heartedly support the exploratory outcome of her analysis. "Have we been side-tracked by Liu's Asian appearance?"

Lucas held her inquisitive stare, not wanting to run the risk of interrupting her train of thought. He had experienced similar intuitive thinking processes when searching for delicate cognitive concepts not yet fully formulated in the mind. These elusive deliberations were akin to images barely exposed on the margins by a spotlight focused on center stage. They were there but would disappear sometimes forever if the viewer shifted their attention from center stage to this peripheral world. They needed to be left alone to bloom in the fulness of time.

"Are we barking up the wrong tree?" Alicia said as if replying to her own question. "Is his training FSB or KGB and not Chinese Intelligence Services?"

Lucas replied after a reflective pause of his own. "If so, Sir Winston Churchill must have had this association in mind with his assessment of the Russians: a riddle, wrapped in a mystery, inside an enigma. Was Liu this riddle?"

Their cellphones vibrated in unison: "Liu's status as Chinese diplomat bogus. He is an unscrupulous independent arms dealer, works internationally for the highest bidder. Chinese Mafia want their dollars or his head on a plate. Regarding intel on movement of armaments, our détente Moscow colleague dispatched an intercept team. He expressed sincere gratitude, especially the reference to the Russkiy Sokol drones. Worrying – the intel on potential intelligence confederate within the EU. Action being taken as we e-speak."

"You were correct in playing on his fears of lethal retaliation," Lucas acknowledged with a sincere congratulatory bow. "Let's continue with the psychological squeeze, without the thumbscrews. I don't think he needs to be reminded again. With that eventuality hovering over his head, he seems to be talking more, though not always motivated to divulge the truth, the whole truth and nothing but the truth."

"I may be a lousy judge of male amorous intentions, but I am an excellent arbiter of an opponent's objectives and weaknesses," Alicia grinned with growing confidence.

"And you can get intelligence by physical or psychological means," Lucas noted. "Jane would promote you to field agent status, posthaste."

"Thanks. We just have to figure out Jane's intentions as a loyal agent of Her Majesty or double agent with a rogue nom de guerre." That dilemma continued to plague her.

With Elana's murder, there are still too many outstanding unknowns, Alicia ruminated as she retreated into herself. There an image of Sophia appeared, as excited and expressive as ever, jubilantly switching from Spanish to English and back again with a smattering of Basque dialect. It was as if one language was insufficient to express all the thoughts and emotions racing through her youthful mind.

With that image, tears came to her eyes. Alicia realized she would never again experience Sophia's exuberance and her mishmash of words seemingly spilling out ahead of her thoughts. But at least she would always have the cherished memories. Sophia and Camilla were casualties of the war as was their father, Marc, unknown to the girls as Santiago López. The girls died anticipating they would soon be together again with their dad and superwoman. Alicia concluded, unlike those who had passed through the gates of Fort de Queuleu, the names Sophia and Camilla would never be forgotten or their memories blurred by the sheer number of anonymous victims of unfathomable violence. Each time she raised a goblet, she would reverently murmur: To Sophia and Camilla. That would henceforth be her mantra, her battle cry.

Lucas noted she had calmed. He slowly nodded and smiled in acknowledgement. Alicia was making peace with her world. He would await the rhetorical response should it arise. He would also pursue those conversations that mattered regarding moral behaviour in the age of drones as Plato might have proposed in a revised contemporary edition of *The Republic*. It was not a matter of either the discussion or the cognac, but both. In retrospect, he realized he had never engaged in such deep philosophical conversations with his ex-wife, although she had the intellect to do so. She just did not show the interest or motivation.

With his next update, Daan would be comforted to learn of their progress as a team. Certainly, Lucas was confident. Alicia was a worthy warrior who would cover his back should aggression escalate. She had read Liu like a professional psychologist experienced in analyzing sociopathic-like behaviour. Lucas would remain close to her and fully supportive of her decisions. Liu had presented at least two personalities and possibly a third. One was the unscrupulous manipulating chameleon who would betray his mother. A second was the insecure male chauvinist with a distinct dislike of females, whom Liu held in contempt because or despite his repressed effeminate attributes. A third was particularly troubling, the superficial charm and glibness of a psychopath who could dine on his mother, putting Hannibal Lecter to shame. Apparent in all were the restlessness and agitation in addition to the wild swing of mania and depression consistent with pronounced bipolar disorder. Lucas had noted many similar symptoms of psychosis in students who tended to wander in increasing numbers through the hallowed halls of academia at the University of Leuven, seemingly devoid of purpose or vision.

CHAPTER 41

"Beware of Greeks bearing gifts," Yolina announced with a chuckle as she presented Daan with an air-sealed tin of herbal-infused chamomile tea. "I noticed you were getting low after our last social gathering." She extended a welcoming hand to Commandant Parent. "Glad you could join us, Benoit."

"Much appreciated and gleefully accepted as long as it doesn't contain any bugs, electronic or biological," Daan jested. He carefully scrutinized the label, *Chamaemelum Nobile*, the best Roman garden variety sold on the continent only by the most prestigious tea merchants. This one was from Amsterdam in the Amstel district. He was gladdened by Yolina's welcoming smile and jubilant manner. "Do I need to prepare a pot to steep?"

Yolina nodded reluctantly. "Yes, I'm afraid so. I need some time to update both of you on recent revelations. The spy in the EU Council, code-name Waterloo, has been most cooperative in exchange for overtures by our security folks. She explained her nefarious lifestyle had been taking a toll on her health. She wants to get out of the game. Both beneficial and troublesome news. On a positive note and pertinent to our investigation, she identified a few others in her network, one of whom lived in Andorra but has travelled extensively in Catalonia, Navarre and Basque Country in the shadow of the Pyrénées. Waterloo said she rents an upscale home in Valencia overlooking the beach. The registered owner is Maya Pérez, her sister."

"If that is the good news, I sense the bad news is about to cause me heartburn," Daan muttered. Over the span of his career in security and intelligence, he had become all too aware of the double-edged intelligence sword.

Yolina pursed her lips in a drawn-out expression. "Better the devil you know than the devil you don't know. No doubt Waterloo will be replaced with another agent we will have to identify and track."

"Renting a beach home in Valencia, you can't afford that on a government employee's wages. At least I can't," Benoit commented doubtfully. "Where is she acquiring that sort of cash?"

"That was my first thought," Yolina replied. "Waterloo admitted to receiving three paychecks – one from the EU Council, a second from Moscow and the third from Beijing. She has been playing three hands simultaneously."

"Nice work if you can get it," Benoit jested. "I have an appreciation of the extent of her stress level now and desire to get out of that racket before the cross-hairs of an assassin's sniper finds its mark."

"An intelligence entrepreneur?" Daan questioned. "The Moroccan mentioned to Alicia and Lucas there was an ex-KGB agent operating out of Valencia, code-named Dmitri. He portrayed himself as an intelligence entrepreneur in the guise of a caricature sketch artist. Coincidence? The Moroccan insinuated there were other individuals operating around the Mediterranean, particularly along the Spanish and French Rivieras. The exact number and location he didn't know."

Yolina continued, "We have corroborated Waterloo's most recent record as a legitimate employee. Her service with the EU Council was preceded by an approximate one-and-a-half-year stint with the Municipality of Antwerp, for a total of about four years fulltime. There were some part-time, short-term jobs which could not be verified. She was adamant she had only been passing along information to Moscow and Beijing for approximately three years. I think longer, perhaps a decade. Liu told you there was a confederate in the European Union intelligence community who had been active for ten years. We initially thought Waterloo might have been that person. If Liu is correct, and that's questionable given his chameleon-like personality, there is at least one other counterfeit gladiator operating in the European Union arena."

Daan took a long fragrant sip of his tea as he considered Yolina's accounting. "What if Liu is telling the truth? He didn't know if the confederate was male or female. Ten years is long enough for Waterloo to have known Dmitri. She could have seen him from her beach-front house, met him when he was sketching tourists on the Valencia beaches. That could have provided her with the opportunity to create a network of her own. Tatyana verified Dmitri had an active network of agents, both Russian and Chinese, in addition to some plying the traditional North African trade routes. The Moroccan confirmed this. One of Dmitri's own Chinese snipers is supposed to have assassinated him, loyal only to a higher bidder among the unscrupulous slimy swamp dwellers. Can your people question Waterloo? Is it possible she was working in the entrepreneurial arena earning her spurs ten years ago under the tutelage of Dmitri?"

Yolina lingered for a brief moment as she slowly shook her head. Her silence was menacing, suggesting Daan's request was not possible. She blinked and looked down at his bone china teacup as a signal for him to take another sip of his chamomile tea. "Although we had Waterloo in protective custody, someone got to her. A bullet to the back of the head, execution style, from a .357 magnum pistol fitted with a silencer."

"Same calibre and methodology as used on Elana," Daan sighed. "On a positive note, that reduces the pool of regional suspects and suggests a greater probability that the shooter is Chinese or was hired by Beijing."

"It does tell us the Basque file has tentacles reaching into crevices perhaps not previously considered. We need to validate all current sources and intelligence," Yolina reconfirmed with the tone of a battle-hardened field commander. "We also need to cast our nets wider." She looked directly at her colleagues. "That means both electronic, internet and satellite networks, Benoit. Also, the informant café net, Daan," she added. "I appreciate Alexandra has been working part-time. It is opportune to ask her and Paul to cut short their sabbatical in their fairy-tale Liechtenstein Principality and work full-time cultivating human intelligence HUMINT sources."

"A tangential thought…" Daan proposed. "Waterloo's sister, Maya Pérez, lives in Barcelona, not far from Valencia as the Mediterranean espionage crow flies. Could she have been an active member of her sister's network? If so, there would be colossal implications for her husband. What intelligence might he have passed along to his wife, purposely or by accident, while he headed Spain's Counterterrorism Unit, and was Spain's representative with Europol?"

It was Yolina's turn to take a prolonged sip of her tea, hoping the herbal infusion would calm her. "Benoit, for your action with your team, I'll reconfirm with the head of Europol that they are investigating this possible security leak. Review all your current plans to ensure you have contingencies to mitigate any damage from intelligence already leaked. The closer we get to solving this case, the higher the probability those implicated will respond with lethal force as we have witnessed with the recent assassinations of Waterloo and Elana/Sapphire. Let's not forget Camilla and Sophia, Jane and Marc. What is the common denominator?"

Daan nodded. "I'll update Alicia and Lucas as they are about to re-interview Liu."

"Time is of the essence, gentlemen," Yolina added. "One last point, Benoit, we have the authority to temporarily second you and a select number of your best agents to the EUI Unit, as required, to assist Daan in achieving operational objectives – to recover all the truant armaments and explosives, especially the surface-to-air and surface-to-surface missiles and the Russkiy Sokol mini drones which pose the greatest threat. You will retain your position as Head of France's Police Nationale and Counterterrorism Cyber Unit. This new appointment provides you with extraordinary authority to officially cross out of France into other national jurisdictions as an EUI Unit agent under Daan's direction. Tread carefully, mon ami, as I know you will. There is a great deal at stake."

Yolina looked at Daan solemnly in a way he had never seen before. "Keep me informed. As you can appreciate, the European Union Council is on an augmented diet of antacid medications these days. I have a large pot of chamomile tea steeping full-time in my office to accommodate most of my colleagues who traipse in and out on an impromptu frequent basis. Not quite a carte blanche but you have whatever you need." That statement told him he would receive without question everything he would write on his wish list to Father Christmas. But he needed to capture and secure the weapons soonest.

Daan texted Alicia and Lucas to await his update before meeting with Liu. He then contacted Alexandra and Paul who agreed to suspend their sabbatical and return to the fold. In the interim, Benoit briefed his Counterterrorism Cyber Unit. They then re-examined every minute detail of the strategic, operational and tactical plans. Mitigation options at every decision point in the updated plans were drilled. Together, they would brief both teams and practice tactical entrance and exit strategies. They had worked together before on other missions but never at this level of readiness with the consequences of deadly threats to metropolitan centers within the European Union so imminent.

Yolina stared after Benoit and Daan as she had done before not singularly as colleagues in the effort to achieve their joint mandate

– to preserve the economic and political stability of the European Union. Instead, as fellow warriors fighting to preserve victory at all cost over those who conspire against peace and goodness with evil intent. Her annual pilgrimage to Fort de Queuleu was her penitence, her mandate, her mantel, her cross to bear, to always be on guard, to never become complacent as had occurred in the years leading up to 1939 and thereafter. Too many had paid the ultimate price against immoral tyranny, now buried in a few marked but mostly unmarked graves throughout Europe.

She stared up as she wiped away the tears building up in her eyes. Each was a reminder of individual ghosts, including her parents barely known to her, other relatives not known. Just numbers reverently inscribed at the entrance to Fort de Queuleu. She ruminated: *There is no survival without peace. There is no peace without sacrifice.* "I will ensure Gideon's sword will always be held at the ready." She declared. "Always."

CHAPTER 42

The détente contact sent an indebted, veiled communiqué to Daan advising that the chickens were back in the coop and the perimeter fence had been reinforced to ensure the foxes would henceforth be kept at bay. Regarding Jane, Moscow had been following her as a possible link because she had more intimate hands-on knowledge of Beijing than had been released previously. They were aware she had not been just a low-level analyst at MI6 but an active field agent, working the China desk. How Moscow knew this, the détente contact did not elaborate. This shared intelligence shed light on Tatyana's prior reference to Moscow-related but not Moscow-directed. As Lucas had suggested and Alicia had agreed, the parlance on the periphery of espionage determined the context in which the content would be culturally defined.

With this most welcoming update, Yolina turned off the steeping teapot in her office. She had fewer colleagues parading in and out of her office on a sporadic basis. Visits tended to be announced albeit on shorter notice following email or text messages. Those who did chat briefly passed along their sincerest compliments and gratitude for the professionalism of her EUI Unit team members. She was assured that future demands for budget cutbacks would only be token in order to appease other departments also subjected to ongoing financial budget constraints. That level of professionalism and security expertise could not be turned off and turned back on at a whim. The heterogeneity of the expanded member states compared with the six founding countries dictated otherwise.

Daan did not press for further clarification at this early stage of nourishing operational cooperation with the détente contact. Nor did Brussels. Both understood all too well the budding delicacy of post-Cold War trust and relationship building which had been suppressed since Stalin's post-revolutionary dictates almost a century before. There were people on both sides who had benefitted from keeping relations cold. They would kill to protect their interests, mostly financial short-term. Others saw future advantages in warming relations, mostly economic, long-term.

Daan was more troubled by the vague reference to Jane's hands-on knowledge of the inner workings of Beijing. He no longer had sources inside MI6 headquarters at Vauxhall Cross in London to confirm this revelation. The ramifications of the disclosure of the treasonous Kim Philby and his associates, the Cambridge Five, had welded shut virtually all internal doors. Those not sealed had multiple layers of even more secure firewalls. External inter-agency cooperation was still a rarity. He was unsure whether his fledging relationship with the Moscow détente might jeopardize his ability to build an equivalent link in London. Perhaps there was merit in Alicia's intuitive reservations about Jane's loyalty. It was not a priority at this juncture but an item set to simmer like his pot of chamomile tea.

The EUI Unit would be left to identify the ninth tentacle, the mole Liu warned had infiltrated the EU intelligence community. This wasn't the first time such a possibility had come to his attention. Daan had more confidence in the honesty of his personally vetted colleagues selected from the original six EU members. He had less confidence in agents from the EU intelligence community who had joined after the fall of the Berlin Wall in November 1989. Once bitten, twice shy, not to be wholly trusted again.

Daan's immediate attention was on weapons seizures completed and the ongoing interrogation of foreign insurgents already deactivated. Although small in quantity, each demonstrated progress and a willingness to maintain unifying peaceful principles as outlined in the European Union Charter. Immediate de-escalation of armed threats and neutralization of additional foreign activists was the first half of the priority. The second focused on long-term commitment to eliminate all future threats to regional unity and economic prosperity. This caused him the greatest trepidation.

When moving into offensive action, the rules of engagement were clear – never leave enemy in your rear echelon. Daan was directing his team to do exactly that: leave a known-unknown intelligence confederate to roam freely, to mount guerila attacks, to ambush at will with superior weapons. Worse, surprise attacks could be launched on terrain familiar to enemy forces and unknown to friendly forces. To Daan's advantage, real-time satellite imagery would be portrayed on monitors mounted in surveillance and security vehicles. However, once dismounted, that eye would be closed. Alicia, Lucas and the Delta teams would be on their own, relying solely on skills finely honed through hours, days, weeks, months of training and tactical braille, augmented with tacit intuition. Daan had complete confidence in his agents. He was backed up by Benoit and his highly trained counterterrorism team on the ground and the Counterterrorism Cyber Unit monitoring real-time electronic traffic from the e-battle space. Regardless, he could only monitor the progress and pray.

It was a fine line between intelligence gathering, squeezing Liu for information, and operational enforcement, seizing armaments with Delta team personnel providing operational and perimeter security. They were interlacing patterns across these contours like line and pattern weaving there, rich scenes of old romance as E.J. Pratt described in his poem, *Frost*. But there was no romance with any of the fraudulent players, just the weaving of deception and dishonesty of increasingly deadly insurgents maneuvering in the murky shadows of the Pyrénées.

Although it was more comforting to have the Delta teams following as close support at a discrete distance so as not to raise hackles, it left less room for flexibility that came with Liu's oscillating personality and increasingly erratic behaviour. It was another fine line to balance like security guards having to adjust to politicians breaking rehearsed protocol in order to mix with their constituents for reasons of political and financial gain. Delta's silenced helijet would be Daan's Mobile Command Center while providing closed-circuit surveillance and armed tactical air support to his teams.

CHAPTER 43

Alicia and Lucas reviewed a cryptic note anonymously left for them describing the location of a substantial cache of weapons. It said they should not delay their decision to take immediate action or loiter around afterwards. Most residents were not completely supportive of armed efforts by foreign insurgents masquerading as Basques to promote their land claims. Neither were they warm to the thought of having non-Basque intruders in their community. If the seizure of armaments and munitions were to be made public, it would draw unwelcome attention and gawking sightseers. Basque Country was not to be interpreted as a tourist destination. The author of the mysterious message also cautioned them to be careful of Liu whom the source described as having the morals of a gutter rat.

"What about Liu?" Lucas queried. "Would it be more advantageous to keep him with us or leave him here under guard? He could be a detriment if push came to shove."

"Best not to divide our forces at this time. We assign Delta team members to guard him closely, with the emphasis on vigilance," Alicia confirmed. "He can introduce us to more of his Basque contacts. Some new contacts might leave us more anonymous communiqués regarding the whereabouts of additional weapons and insurgents. Don't forget the old adage: keep your friends close and your enemies closer."

Lucas nodded. He asked Liu's guard to escort him to their vehicle without explanation or friendly chatter.

"Liu, think about who on your list of Basque contacts you should introduce us to next," Alicia instructed. "But before that, we have one stop to make."

"Where we going?" Liu enquired uneasily while gingerly rotating the diamond ring on his still swollen and colourfully bruised pinky. He twisted in his seat craning his neck for a better perspective. Yet with each unsuccessful search, his apprehension increased like prey alerted but not yet able to verify its predator who was merely observing, carefully selecting the opportune time and location for the fatal lunge. His comfort zone did not incorporate the realm of the unknown, the unseen, the unexpected. He needed to be in control in an environment that was not within his control.

"Not sure where we are going exactly but we'll know when we see it," Alicia replied. Her vagueness only heightened his wariness. Each successive blind intersection caused his head to flip from side to side in a vain attempt to see through the high stucco walls hiding the residential and business courtyards.

"Who are all these people?" Liu followed up, his eyes darting around.

"Just friends."

"My Basque contacts will not talk to you in the company of all these people," he insisted in a futile effort to gain the upper hand. His obsessive need for control had become phobic, overriding any semblance of rational behaviour. He perceived taking orders from anyone, let alone a woman, as humiliating. He did not tolerate such incursions on his fragile masculinity from Sapphire and certainly would not allow it from Alexandra or Alicia, whom he thought to be contemptible. They needed to have their feet bound and their pathetic voices gagged.

Alicia was terse but not because of her Asian navigator. "Thanks for the advice, Liu." She then focused her attention on the narrow lanes and stucco houses with unwelcoming closed wooden doors. No numbers confirmed addresses to aid those unfamiliar with the narrow lanes in the barrio. Shuttered windows on the street level and windows lined with lace curtains on the upper floors obscured their view. Alicia felt uneasy sensing wary eyes monitoring their careful yet deliberate progress.

Dismissed again by this despicable woman, Liu's internal rage boiled. His mind raced. He seethed. Spittle accumulated at the corners of his mouth. He would retaliate at the first opportunity. He would teach her to be respectful. Lucas, being another strong male, would understand him, support him, follow him, carry out his orders without question. He would recognize the fact Liu was the Chinese Führer, the rightful Emperor of a new dynasty greater than any other, including the Ming. The voices of all previous emperors had unanimously informed him that those were his roots. He had been chosen. It was his destiny.

Daan's helijet silently hovered overhead providing surveillance as they approached a derelict building enclosed by a walled compound topped with razor sharp shale described in the note. "All looks secure," Daan's voice crackled over the airways. Image and infrared cameras mounted in the nose of the helijet provided a 360-degree scan on the monitor in their vehicle. There was no unusual movement close to the compound.

"Perhaps too quiet," Daan said cautiously. "Anything from street level?"

"Nothing," Alicia replied with a wary yet tentative tone.

Lucas signalled to the Delta team to set up perimeter security.

"Why are we stopping? Why are we here? What's going on?" Liu peppered them with questions. His voice went up an octave as the muscles controlling his larynx contracted under the stress.

Alicia signalled to the two Delta team members assigned to remain with Liu. She and Lucas followed the others as they forced their way through both the front and back doors, weapons at the ready.

"Eureka," Lucas called out as they saw several crates of small arms, rocket-propelled grenade launchers and surface-to-air missiles including Russkiy Sokol drones, in addition to semi-automatic rifles all stacked in piles against a wall. He quickly took a series of e-pictures.

"Daan will be pleased to receive this text and attached pics," Alicia advised as the Delta team quickly loaded the cache into their vehicles and promptly departed, all under Daan's watchful eye in the sky. Alicia and Lucas relieved the two Delta team members assigned to guard Liu. Liu's information had proved to be correct. The team members' close presence would impair Alicia and Lucas's ability to cultivate new potential contacts from Liu. It was a balance which they perceived was tenuously in their favor. The tension in the neighbourhood was palpable, however, and could change at a moment's notice.

As they departed the compound, her attention was drawn by sheer curtains moving in an adjacent house. The shadowy image behind the curtains retreated as Alicia looked over. Lucas responded to her whisper, following her scan of other windows and surveillance of unnatural movement on the street.

"We appear to have guests," Alicia announced into her mic.

"Others are approaching your location from adjacent streets," Daan confirmed from the helijet. "Too much irregular movement. Recommend you get out soonest."

The few pedestrians in the lane rapidly sought shelter, scurrying momentarily into alleys only to disappear into doorways. The barrio communication was patent yet implicit.

"Best we vacate," Lucas said to Alicia who was driving while he was sitting closely beside and carefully watching Liu. They continued to scan the environment and the images projected on the monitor in their vehicle console taken from the cameras in the nose of the helijet.

Daan immediately forwarded their announcement and attachment e-photos to Yolina who responded with jubilant congratulations. He recalled the advice of one of his superiors when he was a junior intelligence officer. Keep your boss informed at all times even if the news is bad. It will grease the wheels when you are asking for an increase in your resources. He was confident that Brussels would respond favourably to future requisitions for additional funding for EUI Unit operations which had recently been chipped away because of budget constraints. Despite their recent accolades, politicians tend to suffer from what he referred to as promise dementia. Immediate and frequent reminders were the best antidote for this memory disorder.

The Delta vehicles carrying the armaments and munitions returned to their base of operations with the additional Delta vehicles providing ground security. All were monitored by a second helijet. Alicia and Lucas continued on with the next phase of their mission with Daan providing air surveillance. Commandant Parent would coordinate immediate ground support with his counterterrorism personnel who had held back to cover the Delta force for the first phase of the operation. He and his team would next provide primary support for phase two, with cover for Alicia and Lucas.

"Our Cyber Unit is reporting a significant increase in e-traffic, both voice and digital," Benoit advised. "We appear to have stirred up the bee's nest with this latest seizure."

"Copy that," Daan confirmed. "Keep your eyes open and your radar up."

"Confirmed," Lucas replied as Alicia drove away, initially at an accelerating speed. Once away from the compound, she lowered her speed to a more careful rate that would allow them to scan the buildings enclosing the narrow lanes and the few pedestrians some of whom seemed to be conducting their own surveillance of traffic foreign to the neighbourhood. The guarded shroud that suggested a need for caution around the warehouse where the weapons and armament were seized extended beyond that immediate borough.

"Where is your next location?" Daan voice crackled in their earphones.

"Get back to you soonest," Alicia replied with a wariness in her tone transitioning from tentative to apprehension, communicating more than the ambiguousness inherent in the words too simple, given the purpose and heightening tension of the mission.

"Increase our altitude to allow an expanded 360 degree visual and electronic monitoring of the narrow lanes and enclosed compounds," Daan directed the helicopter pilot.

"Roger," the pilot replied as he rose an additional 100 metres then 200 and finally 300. At each interval, the telescopic lens on the camera in the nose of the helijet zoomed in and out as it focused on all pedestrian and vehicular movement.

"Status report from your cyber surveillance," Daan then asked Benoit.

"Quieter in comparison to when the seizure was made," Benoit's team leader replied. "That could be troublesome."

CHAPTER 44

"OK, Liu, lead us to your next Basque contact," Alicia requested politely. She sensed that he was growing more reluctant and resentful of her since this morning. In addition, he did not want to be a party to the raid and seizure. Perhaps, he was fearful of being identified as a collaborator with those who were stealing from those whom he had initially sold the weapons to at inflated prices.

His attention was elsewhere. His voice had lost its weight, its intensity. His expression was a mute stare. He was the leader. He had asserted control by willing her to ask for directions, follow his edict, his direction to the next contact which he had created and cultivated with the aid of Sapphire. Now, Alicia was his chauffeur. She was learning to obey him. Her punishment would not be death. She could become a concubine, a comfort woman, like his mother and sisters had been. There was a usefulness, not for breeding purposes because she was from an inferior class. Instead, her role was to be merely for his pleasure.

"Not too far, just a few blocks," he replied. Liu was as tense as a deer ready to dart away at the first sound of a twig snapping warning of imminent danger.

Alicia caught Lucas's attention in the rear-view mirror. He became acutely aware of Liu's short breaths and the perspiration again beading on his face. Lucas nodded, subtly confirming her concern for heightened guardedness. They maintained their attention on Liu and the house he had identified as their destination.

"Benoit's counterterrorism personnel are still a few blocks away, three to four minutes," Daan advised. He was not comfortable with the gap in distance.

"Roger that. We will pull over and wait for Benoit's people," Alicia replied to Daan in a low voice, out of audible range of Liu.

Liu corrected his directions as their vehicle came to a stop. "Sorry, this is our next Basque contact." His tone was confident. Yet it was inconsistent with his demeanour that spoke of anxious deceit.

"Correction," Alicia advised Daan in a louder voice. "Liu just confirmed we are here… maximum surveillance… acknowledge."

Daan became acutely aware of the hesitancy in her voice and the underlying guarded message of her communiqué.

Lucas held a firm grip on Liu's trembling arm as he tried to open the side door in order to flee. Despite Lucas's anticipation, Liu bolted from the frying pan into the fire with an exasperated jolt. Lucas was partially dragged away from his seat.

Shots rang out from the windows of an adjacent building on the exposed right side of the vehicle. They had no cover. Alicia returned fire as Lucas and Liu fell to the ground. Liu's lifeless body remained eerily immobile as blood gushed from a gaping wound in his temple and a second in his jaw. His right eye bulged from its socket staring at an awkward angle.

"They are under fire," Daan's voice rang out for the immediate attention of Benoit and his team.

"Have them on our monitor. Two minutes out," the lead from Benoit's counterterrorism team announced.

Lucas gasped, "I'm hit." He staggered to his feet, still returning fire at the windows as he rushed toward the building for cover, drawing fire away from Alicia who had exited from the opposite side. He fell again as he reached the stucco portico which provided temporary cover from the direct line of fire from a gunman in the window directly above the door.

Alicia reloaded before scrambling to the front door in a zigzag motion simultaneously returning rapid fire. The door frame provided partial cover for her also.

"I can't break in another partner," she joked as she pressed her palm against his hand which covered the hole in his shoulder now oozing crimson blood. Oozing was better than pulsating, she concluded, allowing the thought to terminate on its own.

"We will provide you with cover fire," Daan announced. A series of short bursts of machine gun fire from the helijet struck the second floor. "Benoit's people are one minute away. Can you hold on?"

The firing from the building stopped temporarily and a disconcerting short-lived silence filled the narrow street. Small arms fire immediately began to hit the stucco above their heads coming from an adjacent building.

"Under renewed fire," Alicia replied. "Request you focus your gun fire on the closest building."

"Locked on," Daan replied.

The pilot rotated his guns and peppered the target with several short bursts of surprisingly accurate machine gun fire.

Shattering glass and splintering window frames from the machine gun bullets striking the buildings reminded Alicia of her Pemberton Estate home in the immediate aftermath of her SUV exploding in her driveway.

"Can you make it back to our vehicle?" Alicia asked Lucas sharply.

"I'll follow you anywhere," he quipped, grimacing. "I still need to beat you at backgammon."

"You're on," she replied as she held him steady on their return dash to the quasi-cover of their vehicle.

They again came under fire as she heaped him into the back seat. Glass from the shattering side windows showered them with tiny shards.

"You're brilliant, Professor Lucas Peeters," she purred under her breath. "Backgammon! Of course! You are absolutely brilliant." His grimace was a combination of excruciating pain and puzzlement about her compliment. How could getting shot be anything close to brilliant?

Alicia elected not to spend additional time and effort grappling with Liu's dead weight while in the direct line of fire again from another window in the first building. She contemplated the corpse with the same level of professional courtesy as she would extend to road kill. Liu's parting adieu was a blank stare appealing his death sentence *postmortem*. She was on the radio to Daan calling for backup fire from his hovering helijet to cover their exit as she sped away, dodging the continuing gunfire. Images of Jacques, Marc, Jane, Camilla and Sophia haunted her. The final two picture frames were blank. She desperately wanted to keep them that way.

※ ※

LOOKING AT DAAN, ALICIA ASKED, "HOW'S THE patient?"

"Ask him yourself."

They both entered the hospital room.

"Slacking off," Alicia jested. "I sincerely hope you don't expect me to have to cater to your beckoning call."

Lucas smiled. "I suppose you think I owe you one."

"I'll leave the two of you to work out your differences," Daan interjected. He smiled at Alicia. "I'll wait for you in the hall."

"Thanks, pal," Lucas acknowledged. Any gestured movement resulted in a jolt of pain from his shoulder and upper chest. "I may just rest here a moment."

"Now just stay calm," Alicia ordered. "I'll tell you all about it. Benoit's counterterrorism people secured the scene until the local police arrived. They arrested the people in the houses where the shots came from. Surveillance video from the helijet provided a blow-by-blow recording – you'll be able to show your grandchildren one day. They seized a medium cache of hand guns and semi-automatic rifles, in addition to one Russkiy Sokol mini drone. Its existence away from the warehouse was a worrisome reality – redistribution of the armaments had already begun."

The expression on Lucas's face confirmed the serious ramification of such actions on the part of those responsible. Some solace could be gained from the fact the drone was still sealed in its shipping container and none of those arrested seemed to know how to deploy it. As well, no surface-to-air weapons that could have targeted the helijet were found.

Alicia continued with her accounting of the events. "Elana and Liu are dead. Thus, the cell has no apparent leader. Several foreign insurgents have been arrested and most of the armaments and munitions have been seized. We think those left cannot respond aggressively, at least for a while. Talks are on-going with the contacts we had previously established. I hope this will contain the violence long enough to provide an umbrella of calmness for additional negotiations to get underway."

"I think I might adjourn to my favourite fairy-tale castle in Liechtenstein," Lucas confirmed with a resigned smile. "I need to convalesce. I am not ready to return to the classroom just yet."

"All very well for some," Alicia laughed. "I will join you there but first I need to return to Victoria to take care of some domestic chores."

"As we were vacating the shooting gallery, you said I was brilliant. I didn't think that getting shot was such a brilliant move," he conceded with a sheepish grin.

"I'll get back to you on that. Now rest up for our backgammon tournament. *Jusque là* – until then."

Alicia approached Daan as she left the hospital room. "Got a moment?"

He nodded.

"I need to return to Victoria. Apart from my house being in shambles literally and needing immediate repairs, there is one thread I need to follow up on related to the missing MI6 file in the tunnel."

Daan responded, "In light of the message from the Moroccan regarding the drowning of the owner of Consort House in Brighton, I would like to have Alexandra and Paul accompany you. I'm sure they would be more than pleased to become reacquainted with their colleagues, Tatyana and Yusuf."

Alicia bowed approvingly. She had grown comfortable with Lucas by her side since taking on this case, not that she wasn't confident working alone. Working with Alexandra and Paul would allow time to get to know them better.

"Can we expect you back relatively soon?" Daan asked, hoping for a positive reply. He had an ulterior motive asking this question. It would be received as a gracious reinforced invitation to consider working with the EUI Unit full-time.

"Absolutely," she replied without a pause to consider all her options or to suggest she had not taken time to reflect on her future beyond her stated short-term objective when they had met in Metz – to find out why she had become the target of an assassin.

He responded with a Cheshire Cat grin. "That's good because I have a front seat ticket to the first annual Vaduz Backgammon Tournament. I wouldn't want to have to apply for a refund from the event organizers." With greater concern in his voice, he added, "Take care of yourself and keep in contact. I have no doubt Lucas will be bugging me for updates at least hourly."

She interpreted his request to include himself in the request for regular updates. If Moscow had been behind the explosion of both her house and Jane's, not Elana, the threat remained imminent.

CHAPTER 45

Their connecting flight from Vancouver International Airport to Victoria was about to board. Alexandra texted Tatyana and Yusuf with the description of two individuals who appeared to be following Alicia. One was an Asian whom she described as having no distinguishable features apart from being Asian. The second was a Caucasian with the rugged physique of a Mongolian woodsman. Alexandra would point out both when they arrived.

As the passengers on the Victoria flight left the secure area and congregated around the luggage carousel, Yusuf tailed the Asian while Tatyana sauntered alongside the Mongolian as if waiting for her own luggage to appear through the luggage doors that swung like those in a saloon in a Hollywood black and white western movie, less the miniature dust bowls and sage brush swirling at the entrance. She nonchalantly gazed at his cellphone. The text was in Cyrillic script. She met Yusuf's gaze and acknowledged his subtle nod with one of her own. *A Russian in addition to an Asian following Alicia*, she mused. Neither seemed to be aware of the other tracking the same target. *Sloppy*, she grumbled to herself. *This would never have happened in my day with the KGB. The quality of recruits and the training for the FSB has become reduced to an unacceptable level. Perhaps she and Yusuf could start a finishing school for spies of any stripe.* She was certain there would be no shortage of applicants wanting to improve their skill set and size up the opposition.

As Alicia hailed a taxi, her tailing duo jostled for the next cabs in line. Tatyana and Yusuf jumped the queue in front of the disconnected surveilling duo, causing a minor commotion with an exchange of cross words and shoving. They stepped back away from the line after apologizing. In the interim, Alicia's taxi had sped away, free of her surveillance tails. Tatyana and Yusuf crossed the road quickly and stepped into another vehicle momentarily stopped opposite the congested taxi line.

Forty minutes later Alicia entered a private business club with upscale accommodation for members and guests of members. As she was receiving her security pass cards from the receptionist, Alexandra and Paul were being greeted as guests under the same member policy.

"I trust that you had a good flight?" Yusuf asked. "Once you are settled, please join Tatyana and me in the lounge. We have made arrangements to have your room and all other expenses put on our member account."

Minutes later, as they strolled into the lounge, Tatyana enquired, "Your accommodations are acceptable?"

"Wonderful," all three replied in unison.

"Cognac is served." Yusuf joined his guests.

"Thanks for the update on the investigation," Tatyana said. "If the truant MI6 file is what I think it is, I can understand why both Moscow and Beijing are closing in on Alicia. Its disclosure would result in horrific consequences the likes of which the world has never experienced. I first became aware of it when I transferred from the KGB to the FSB. Its existence was highly suspected but its whereabouts remained curiously elusive. There was a great deal of wringing of hands and grinding of teeth by the most senior members of the Kremlin's inner circle. There were strong rumours that MI6 was aware, mostly because we knew that there was at least one additional actor beyond Kim Philby and the Cambridge Five who had access to files held in private secure cabinets accessed only by a very few senior MI6 administrators."

Yusuf sat quietly, observing the reaction of his guests to Tatyana's revelation. His gaze rested primarily on Alicia who seemed to react with cautious confidence. Her expression neither faded nor faltered. Continuing to monitor Alicia over the rim of his cognac snifter, he directed his question at her. "What were the circumstances surrounding your contact with the occupant of Consort House in Brighton?"

Alicia stared back questioningly. *How would he have known about her visit? The only others to have been aware beyond Lucas were Daan and Yolina,* she pondered. Either she and Lucas were under surveillance the entire trip or Philippa was not the naïve innocent school girl she had presented herself to be. Or were surveillance cameras from other sources following their every move with monitors in foreign third-party offices.

Yusuf elaborated, "Daan passed this information along to us because he believed that its relevance was beyond rumour. Tatyana and I agree, given the direction this case has taken and the attention it has drawn from Moscow and Beijing. Consort House may be central to understanding the implications. Unbeknown to most, the occupant of Consort House with whom you met and briefly spoke was a senior member of MI6, supposedly retired like John le Carré's fictitious character, George Smiley."

Alicia lingered on the outcome of her analysis as she connected not just the fog banks but the dots which were being revealed for the first time. An unknown was now known. She recalled mentioning to Daan when they first met in Metz, once she found out why she had become a target for assassination, other unknowns would be exposed. Where was Lucas when she needed him? Slacking off again. He would owe her, big time. She was surprised at how much she missed his enquiring presence, his prompts. And….

With an encouraging smile, Alexandra nodded.

Alicia replied, "I wasn't aware she was a senior MI6 operative. Now I think, it makes perfect sense. Daan had asked the two of you to search the tunnel between my house and the garden shed because my father had mentioned a tunnel. I went to Consort House because my father had met with Philippa's father a few times, at least once when I was with him. Their conversation was lengthy and private. I surmised he might have used the tunnel between Consort House and the beach to hide the document. The owner explained she had completely refurbished the tunnel. So, if it had once been there, there was a high probability it wouldn't be anymore. She must have recognized that fact. I wasn't aware anyone had me under surveillance when I arrived at her doorstep. I can only conclude she must have done something to get a lot of people out of bed, so to speak – perhaps a mole whose loyalty was not wholly devoted to Her Majesty's Secret Service."

It was Yusuf's turn to ponder in silence. He and Tatyana exchanged solemn glances. "Thank you for sharing that. It explains a great deal." He rested his chin on his steepled fingers as he thought. A smile came to his eyes. "Not to worry," he announced with an assuring tone. "Not to worry," he repeated. He reclined in the high-backed padded leather chair. "I will take care of everything." He and Tatyana again exchanged glances. She smiled ever so slightly.

"What are your plans for tomorrow?" Tatyana asked. "We need to coordinate our surveillance and security team for you, Alicia. As Yusuf said, you will have nothing to worry about."

Alicia listed her priorities all of which had to do with the assessment and repair of the damage caused by the explosion including the removal of her burned out SUV from the driveway. She failed to mention plans to search for the elusive MI6 file which had crossed her mind when rescuing Lucas. She reflected on his words: I still have to beat you at backgammon, and her reply: you are brilliant Dr. Peeters, absolutely brilliant. Two minds working in unison were better than one.

CHAPTER 46

Alicia stood in the front yard of her quiet, secluded Pemberton Estate home. The damage was more severe than she had imagined. But she had never stopped to assess the impact of the explosion on the structure from the front yard or from the side of the driveway. The image of black acrid smoke billowing beyond the roof was her final memory of what had been her house before she exited the garden shed at a speedy pace hugging the hedgerow as she made her way to the safehouse with satchel in hand. The scene seemed surreal as did her thoughts.

Today, she was warmed by the presence of her colleagues posing as gardeners parked on the street at the property line in between her neighbour's property and her own. Tatyana and Yusuf, her new acquaintances, were partially hidden by the garden shed in the back yard where they stood sentinel. She still wasn't sure she was safe from harm's way. Her intuition was never wrong. Only her misinterpretation or complete disregard of her intuition would result in her taking the wrong path.

She felt disoriented in the rubble of her kitchen. At first glance, nothing appeared to have been removed from the disarray. She would check more closely later and go in the girls' bedrooms as a final task. But first she made her way to her father's study. It too was in disarray although the structure seemed sound having escaped the direct impact of the explosion. There was an assortment of framed photographs on the wall, hanging at awkward angles. Others lay on the floor below where they had once hung, broken glass from the frames now askew amidst other debris.

The bookshelf that held her father's antiquarian collection was intact. The books, although layered in dust, were protected by their plastic fitted covers. He had been fastidious about preserving his collection of all fourteen mint first edition, first print original signed Ian Fleming novels from Casino Royale to Octopussy, all published by Jonathan Cape. He believed the author had taken some licence in describing the daring exploits of his often impetuous 007 character, James Bond. It was from such exacting care that Alicia had learned to pay close attention to detail and to appreciate perfection.

On the far side of the display case that once held Uncle George's military medals and Egyptian artifacts was her own mahogany chess board with its ivory and ebony players. Her father had presented it to her as a graduation gift from Oxford. She had mastered the competencies of the game after innumerable hours of his one-on-one instruction.

Directly in front was her father's backgammon board with all twenty-four points meticulously inlaid with silver. He had acquired it in Morocco. It too was covered in dust and debris. She recalled her father shrewdly providing advice on gamesmanship while they played more games than she could accurately remember unlike all the lessons she had committed to memory. She recalled scrutinizing his every move as he emerged victorious from the European Backgammon Tournament exclaiming, "Obviously obvious." She acknowledged but had not fully comprehended his sage utterances, cloaked in the wisdom and intuitiveness of Yoda, the Star Wars Jedi Master. From this acquired knowledge and patient mentorship, she had risen to become the British backgammon champion, a distinguished accomplishment in its own right, especially for a woman. There were more females today amongst the ranks of the champions whose photos adorned the walls of the backgammon pantheon much to the chagrin of their male counterparts many of whom were cut from the same arrogant old-boys dinosaurian cloth.

With a sense of confidence accompanied with a tinge of anticipation, she delicately pressed the mother of pearl button along the carved frame of the case below the playing surface. The drawer silently emerged. Reaching inside, she deftly slid her fingers along the upper surface of the tunnel, the term her father had used on a few occasions. She further recalled that on each occasion he had stared at her yet said nothing, obviously obvious. There she felt the outline of an envelope wedged into the moulding of the drawer tunnel. Pressing her fingers firmly against the surface she gently pulled her hand toward her, guiding the envelope into view. The upper left-hand corner was torn. The slightly faded letters MS appeared. "You are brilliant, Dr. Peeters," she reminisced as the image of Lucas slumped in the back seat with blood oozing from his shoulder appeared on the monitor of her mind.

"Obviously obvious," she muttered as a satisfying smile embraced her lips, then rose to encompass first her eyes and finally her entire face. She leaned back. The well-worn curves of her father's posture embedded into the padded folds of the Edwardian armchair hugged her as he had done when she was a less confident child seeking reassurance and conviction. She laid her head against the headrest, confidently closed her eyes, and inhaled a series of relaxed breaths as never before. Tears rolled down her cheeks as a lifetime of stress resulting from ever present doubt dissolved. It was replaced with a feeling of freshness like the atmosphere after thunderstorm clouds emptied their droplets, thus providing nourishment for nature's flora and fauna.

After a moment, she opened her eyes and scanned in detail the onionskin pages of typed notes of the elusive MI6 file. The elimination of the Cambridge Five – Kim Philby, Donald Maclean, Guy Burgess, Anthony Blunt and John Cairncross, had not been complete. There was a sixth. The five were all similar in pedigreed background, manicured culture and privileged education yet different from the sixth. One had survived the purge because of the difference. Her immediate reaction was not one of mounting tension but of focused analysis. Her emotions teetered between shock and disbelief. Was her father's revelation for her eyes only? Her Yoda had known about the sixth yet had kept his awareness a secret known only unto himself. Yoda had a murky history. Could she ever completely trust anyone, any organization again? What good could be gained by posthumously exposing the name, the details, the circumstances without context?

The Four Horsemen of the Apocalypse – Death, Famine, War and Conquest were being led from behind by another image barren of a horse and rider. Although known to her father and potentially one other now also deceased, the consequences of its elimination could be vastly more devastating. She recalled in greater detail the Consort House tunnel. Her father had made a marginal reference to Brighton on the south coast of England and another to Donostia-San Sebastián on the north coast of Spain with an additional reference to Valencia on the Spanish Riviera. There was a Basque connection after all with a Russian affiliation. Alicia reflected longer than she ever had on any other decision point. Like her father, she would be damned if she did anything and damned if she didn't, and double-damned if she failed to decide at all, to entomb the truth like her father had done but without a trail to a tunnel. She now knew why he had kept the file, but the justification for that decision no longer mattered.

Alicia was as horrified by the content as she had been when she first heard the news from Daan – she had shared her bed with a bigamist and the murderer of her fiancé, deceitful in his own intentions. Jacques' remains had been buried in an unmarked Iberian grave, and Marc's in an equally anonymous Basque crypt. Now, the MI6 documents needed to be condemned to the flames of Dante's inferno, cremated unceremoniously and entombed in the open casket of the fireplace, so to speak, in the Pemberton Estate house. It was her decision and only hers. Her father would approve.

CHAPTER 47

Alicia clicked the fireplace lighter once, and again. There was fuel and a spark, yet no flame. "A lesson in persistence," her father had repeated many times when she started to become frustrated with automation supposedly created to make lives easier, like some aspects of computer technology. She wiped the tip and clicked once more. The flame lit the corner of the pages. As if penitence, she held the documents until the tips of her fingers burned. Her faint smile faded as the flames then died down. She carefully crushed the incendiary remnants of each page into a shallow indistinguishable trace of ashes in the cauldron mixed with the existing dust and debris from previous fires which had brought warmth to the hearth. She relished the comfort one last time.

She folded the empty envelope and slid it back into the tunnel as a final reminder of her father and all his lessons. Some knowledge he had taught her, other knowledge she had learned on her own through observation and reflection, such as how to become a champion backgammon player. Understanding your own strengths and weakness and those of your opponent were critical to success. Many of the competencies needed were related to layered pattern recognition. On occasion, she would baulk at his most challenging puzzles by uttering: "There is no pattern." His response was consistent: "There is always a pattern, you just haven't found it."

And there it was, a pattern, not as meticulously consistent as it could have been but revealing an inconsistency where a pattern should have been. A lesson that had been taught by the master and learned by the protégé. She took a slow deep breath. Had anyone else found the envelope and enclosed documents – Jane? Tatyana and Yusuf? Someone else? They were not painstakingly thorough whoever they were. The documents once removed had been reinserted into the envelope upside-down. Likewise, the envelope had been re-inserted into the smooth felt tunnel back to front. *Slipshod*, she ruminated. Whoever they were, they had not been privately tutored by the best in an era when excellence meant survival. Jacques, Marc, Elana, and Jane were among the deceased. They were not graduates of excellence *cum laude*.

Alicia stood at the entrance of the girls' bedrooms. Each had their own name plate fixed to their door. Camilla's was plain except for delicate flowers around the perimeter. Sophia had decorated hers with a profusion of colours and no set design. Alicia had looked at them each time she had entered their rooms but had not seen them, really taken notice of their individuality until now. Camilla's medication was on the dresser. How had Marc overlooked the container? He had said on numerous occasions he loved them more than anything. If he had, how could he have walked away without packing the pills? They should have been the first items he placed in her carry-on hand luggage for immediate access. Can you look without really seeing? She had looked at their name plates countless times without seeing. She had looked at Marc more times than she could count without seeing him for what he was.

A Pemberton Property Management representative met her at the front door of the house as previously arranged. They surveyed the damage and agreed on a reconstruction plan. What she saw was objective. What needed to be done was pragmatic. She was divorced from emotion. It had been a house, never a home. Not even when she lived there with her parents was it a home because each loved in their own way, going through the motions of a family but devoid of endearing affection. She shook hands with the representative on the front lawn, and gave a polite terse nod.

Alicia met her three colleagues; Yusuf was notably absent. Unlike her arrival at the house, she had no sense of being tracked by anonymous menacing eyes. Tatyana again assured her there was nothing to worry about. Yusuf had "taken care of everything." She was acutely aware of the connotation. The veiled language of the tradecraft was certainly not new to her. Yusuf would join them for dinner at the private business club. Celebratory drinks would be served in the relaxed atmosphere of the stately lounge.

 That evening, Alicia watched Alexandra and Paul as they interacted with Tatyana and Yusuf like life-long friends. Each couple was a loving pair, two peas in a single pod. She was envious of what they had in addition to the experiences which bonded them, comrades. Their expressions were not contrived but sincere. She had sought such a relationship. Alas, it had escaped her. Perhaps, it was not to be. She was resigned to accept that.

 She observed the interaction between other couples, a special relationship. Although she was a colleague, she was not one of them, two couples plus one, four friends plus one, relationships forged under fire plus one. After she had interrogated the captain, she had asked Alexandra about Tatyana and Yusuf. Alexandra had replied with a question of her own, "Are you asking whether I trust them?" Alicia had replied, "I'm asking if I can trust them." Alexandra's final comment was imprecise yet concise. Alicia would have to decide for herself.

 It wasn't that she didn't trust Tatyana and Yusuf, but she trusted Lucas more. And it wasn't that she didn't trust Alexandra and Paul, but she trusted Daan more. Although trust was an emotion, it was an impartial, detached emotion for her, built on experience and intuition. In the same way, the content of intelligence in the hidden MI6 file was precarious in the context of espionage where there were truths, partial truths and make-believe truths. It was all relative.

 Then there was the discovery of her father's documents in the torn OH / MS envelope hidden in the backgammon board tunnel as her father had called the drawers. Each one contained fifteen pieces. Sharing was about trusting. She would share her revelation about the tunnel with Lucas and Daan. She would not share her assessment – it might have been previously accessed by someone else. She had no proof, just suspicion, intelligence, not evidence, at best. Jane was out of the picture. Tatyana and Yusuf remained in the frame. She would, no doubt, be working with them again if she kept her word with Daan and Yolina to remain in the fold of the European Union Intelligence Unit.

She had one final task to complete before returning by the all-too-familiar flights to Vancouver, Toronto, and Paris. Then she would connect via highspeed Eurorail to Metz and then on to Zürich, before the final leg to Vaduz in the fairy-tale principality of Liechtenstein. The journey involved brief stops at safehouses for the obligatory change in identity and exchange of passports. There were truths, partial truths and make-believe truths like her myriad of interchangeable identities. Any partner she had would have to accept that eccentricity, even Lucas. She was comfortable with that. She was her father's daughter after all, but no longer walking lightly in his enigmatic MI6 footsteps.

Before departing, she spent quiet time alone visiting the marked gravesite of her father and mother under the watchful eyes of her colleagues. A sensation ran the length of her spine, causing her to stand more erect. She paused. She gazed up as if in reverent contemplation. Her eyes then scanned other markers in the cemetery as she had done when she looked at the headstones of Uncle George and her father in Warwick. Only she knew which held her father's remains and why there were two headstones. Her father had purchased a double lot and a double headstone in the Ross Bay cemetery for his wife and himself. Both of their names had been etched on the façade of the polished black granite surface. Only his date of death would have to be added. She had taken care of that final task. In this instance, she was still her father's daughter. She was acutely aware that others held suspicions regarding the circumstances surrounding his retirement from MI6, and her own through association. Prudence, if not continued caution, was in order.

She had always referred to them as her father and mother, not as her parents. The distinction was subtle but a reality. The term "parents" suggested a family. She had accepted that fact. It was what it was and she could not alter the reality. Although she was emotionally attached to Camilla and Sophia, they were not her children. The term "stepchildren" had a negative crass connotation as in the storied existence of Cinderella. Her relationship with each of the girls was warm as it had been with her father and mother. She would always remember Camilla and Sophia as she would always remember her father and mother, and Uncle George – all part of an extended family. She accepted the fact that without the details of the family encoded in the DNA, and recorded in photographs amassed in boxes of memorabilia in attics and basements, we are just left to accept the crumbs.

CHAPTER 48

"It is good to be back in the fairy-tale Principality of Liechtenstein," Alicia whispered. "How is the patient?"

Daan wore his customary smile. "He is doing well and has been asking about you. I think he was worried you would not have been able to function without him. For your information, Yolina has signed your full-time employment contract. The EU Council approved funding without blinking an eye, a fait accompli. You and Lucas are in their best books and for good reason. Once Lucas has recovered sufficiently, you will both be quietly commended in Brussels for your exemplary conduct. The large seizure of surface-to-air and surface-to-surface missiles, rocket-propelled grenades and Russkiy Sokol mini drones from the compound effectively negated the threat to the European Union. The seizure of the small arms, the semi-automatic rifles and explosives, all but eliminated any serious threat in the Pyrénées region. Most significant was the identification and arrest of foreign insurgents and the subsequent intelligence they provided while detained. Don't let it go to your head."

"Tatyana and Yusuf are interesting colleagues with great strategic, operational and tactical talents," Alicia noted with a pragmatic expression. "We talked about their unsuccessful search for the truant MI6 file in the tunnel between the house and the garden shed." She stopped short of sharing her intuitive suspicion that Tatyana and Yusuf might have found the file in the backgammon board tunnel. "The MI6 file notes had been enclosed in one of my father's old envelopes with the OHMS initials in the upper left corner. After reviewing the contents, I concluded they revealed nothing of consequence. So, I condemned them to the flames of purgatory as the only viable option. Tatyana and Yusuf let it be known in their network that the elusive file never existed in the first place. It was all a ruse by MI6 to consume scarce Russian intelligence resources and perhaps those from other foreign agencies." She reflected on the image of the smouldering ashes in the fireplace. She had learned well from her Yoda.

Daan's smile broadened. "Sometimes a quiet individual decision is the best choice. I have been known to have taken similar action and slept considerably better as a result. The existence of the file was known only in our EUI Unit and only at a senior level. If asked, we will confirm it was an intelligence ploy like many others created as a distraction at the zenith of the Cold War version one. The realm of espionage was always rife with such schemes. Always is a very long time and I have consistently encouraged people to refrain from using similar superlatives. I can only say the probability of *not* employing ruses as a strategy in future espionage exchanges is so infinitely small it might be best to commit to never. So, no one should be the wiser except those with egg on their face who were adamant as to its existence."

Alicia looked up as the hotel proprietors approached. She thanked them for their support and surveillance.

"All part of the family," Paul replied breezily.

"Do you have a moment?" Alicia asked Alexandra.

Paul sensed the unspoken request for a private chat. He turned his attention to Daan and others assembling in the lounge.

"Regarding Tatyana, I asked you if you trusted her, if I could trust her. You replied that I would have to make my own decision. Having worked briefly with Tatyana and Yusuf, I can say without a doubt I have confidence in her, in both." Alicia was terribly charming when speaking as her father had taught her to do on such occasions. She acknowledged she was a poor judge of men with amorous intentions but an excellent judge of friend and foe.

"I'm pleased. I was confident you would," Alexandra replied with a warming smile and a gracious bow of her head.

The images of Camilla and Sophia appeared on the monitor of Alicia's mind, which prompted her to ask: "You mentioned you had a new granddaughter. Perhaps, I might meet her when next we are in Paris."

"My daughter, Collette, and her husband, Jean, will be visiting here next month. Vanessa, my granddaughter, will rarely be out of my arms," Alexandra replied, her face glowing in pride and anticipation. "For your information, Jean is Paul's son from his first marriage. Collette is my daughter from my first marriage."

Alicia's expression was one of inquisitive astonishment and gracious kindness for sharing such personal information.

"It's a long story," Alexandra replied. "There are tentacles reaching into a previous EUI Unit case. I'll tell you about it sometime."

Genuine banter flowed. Their relationship matured.

Alicia reflected on her concluding conversation with Daan regarding the cremation of the contents of the MI6 file. She surmised that Daan's comment regarding the employment of ruses was made in jest. Both would employ distracting strategies as circumstances dictated. She was, after all, the daughter of a master spy of MI6.

CHAPTER 49

Alicia placed her father's backgammon board on its hand-carved mahogany stand in front of Lucas's chair by the expansive Victorian bay window in the hotel lounge where they had first discussed their partnership. It was highly unlikely it was the only time they would meet to strategize or simply enjoy the view of the awe-inspiring Swiss Alps. She remembered with a chuckle his light-hearted welcoming invitation: "Come into my office." She had recalled the opening lines from Mary Howett's poem by the same title, "'Will you walk into my parlour,' said the spider to the fly.' Alicia had been the spider inviting the fly to a friendly game of backgammon which she knew would become a never-ending tournament.

"Press the mother of pearl button on the side of your home board," Alicia instructed. "It will give you access to the tunnel where your pieces are safely secured. Obviously obvious," Alicia commented, lingering long enough to allow Lucas to work out the connection. She had the intuitive sense to use silence as an emphasis as had her father. She gazed at Lucas over the rim of her glass of Côtes du Rhône Pinot Noir while waiting for his response.

With his index finger gingerly tracing the hidden edge of his inner board, Lucas looked at her with surprise. He pressed the mother-of-pearl button. An emerald green felt-lined drawer silently slid toward him revealing fifteen dark-brown ebony pieces, in contrast to her cream ivory pieces. "The tunnel," he smiled. "Obviously obvious."

"Gently reach in the tunnel while running your finger along the top. You will find a sleeve. Gently pull out the envelope." She watched his expression transform form obediently inquisitive to gratifyingly curious.

He followed her instructions. On the upper left-hand corner were the initials OMHS similar to the partial letters, OH, on the torn envelope she had retrieved from under the choir pew in St. Nicholas Parish Church in Warwickshire. "You are good, partner. No, you are damn good," he emphasized. "You need to teach me how to listen and respond to my intuition."

"My father described the hidden drawer as the tunnel. Like the game itself, the outcome is governed by knowledge of the odds and mathematical precepts melded into thought processes and stratagems. It's obviously obvious."

Drawers, her father had cautioned her as a child – some drawers you may decide to open but others you do not access under any circumstances. There are some things that you need to be aware of but they need to remain locked in their respective tunnels. It is just safer that way.

"Yes, obviously obvious," Lucas repeated glibly as if common knowledge, "like Alice's interpretation of Lewis Carroll's White Rabbit hole at Consort House. Only in this case, it's Alicia's reading and appreciation, not Alice's Wonderland."

Their banter went unnoticed by the select spectators assembling with Swarovski crystal snifters of cognac to witness history in the making.

"The rules of backgammon allow the elder player first choice of ebony or ivory," Alicia mentioned in respect to the senior senator. "Keeping with tradition and European competition rules, the senior players select ebony. What is your preference?"

Lucas acknowledged her choice. "And as a British backgammon champion, tutored by a European backgammon champion. I'm at a disadvantage," he gestured in a courtly manner.

"You of all people should know to do your research before you accept an assignment, Professor Peeters," Alicia admonished. "Would you not remind your students to do just that?" She held his gaze as she took another sip of wine. "How's the shoulder? I don't want to take unfair advantage of your weakened condition."

"Touché. I'm well enough to trounce you."

"Shall we say best five out of nine for this initial tournament?" She stopped momentarily and reflected on the final conversation with the Moroccan: *"I miss playing backgammon with Friar Tuck. I trust he taught you the intricacies of the game."* And her whispered reply: *"That he did."* Perhaps one day, she would play a few games with the Moroccan. She would learn more about her father as an MI6 agent. The Moroccan might even tell her stories about the content of the MI6 file. Although a young lad at that time, he was now the last man standing from that era as far as Alicia could presume.

Her Yoda had reminded her repeatedly she could best judge the character of her opponent, be they friend and foe, by the way they approached and played the game, and especially by the banter exchanged as the dice rattled. The opponent's eyes were a tunnel into their personality, illuminating each trait along the way to be assessed by those who did not just look but took the time to see, to evaluate as intelligence or evidence, each with a different end state in mind.

Each piece on the backgammon board took on a different personality depending on where it was located and the evolving congestion, like a chameleon adjusting its colour to the flora in the environment. Although she played both, she preferred backgammon to chess because it was a faster game requiring greater cognitive agility. In the final analysis, it was all a game, played with a combination of luck and skill. She enjoyed learning from each game. She looked forward to learning from Lucas whom she assessed as being a worthy opponent, a thinker, a strategist, a player, an equal and above all, a partner she could depend on. They would learn the fine art of reading each other as the tournaments progressed.

CHAPTER 50

"Final debrief on the Basque file," Daan announced. "There are four outstanding issues. First, we are in the process of identifying the ninth tentacle, the mole whom Liu warned had infiltrated the EU intelligence community. Although we have our own intelligence agents and, in addition, have firewalls between us and all other EU intelligence agencies, we remain constantly vigilant. Occasionally, one slips through." He glanced over at Alicia. They had had an earlier conversation regarding the old black and white photograph of the person in the fedora standing next to the Sphinx at Giza.

She validated his observation with a slow nod. Jacques had evaded her naïve radar. Today, she was no longer her father's daughter merely following in his footsteps in this arcane arena but her own person forging her own sword of Gideon in the truest sense. She would be an operative within the European Union Intelligence Unit like the Gideon Force, a small elite British military organization, had been in the East Africa Campaign during the Second World War. She knew of its existence because her Uncle George had served with that specialist Unit with its unique mandate.

She very much appreciated Lucas's prompt and his constant reminder to scrutinize the room for elephants. She had never had a professional partner on whom she could depend. He might even knuckle down and adopt a few of her modified Maslow interrogation techniques.

"Second point," Daan continued, "Marc Bolibar alias Santiago López wanted Basque Country independence but initially not at the expense of World War III. He succumbed to the spells and incantations of the birthmother of his daughters, and her Russian trainer in the art and science of espionage hypnosis. If you ever have any doubt about the extent to which some individuals will go to undermine the European Union, just think about Camilla and Sophia who paid the ultimate price." He again glanced over at Alicia with a slight smile. Others followed his lead in silent yet stalwart support. The memory of the girls was a somber reminder.

"Third, Jacques Bernard was a Basque separatist negotiating with Beijing to import armaments. Marc a.k.a. Santiago did shoot him. It is unclear whether he acted to prevent the importation of missiles and other weapons of war in order to stem the possibility of horrific violence, or whether he was under the hypnotic influence of Elana. We may never know. Santiago became Marc and fled to Victoria with the girls to protect them. Elana in her transformed persona as Sapphire was able to manipulate him with the threat of kidnapping Camilla and Sophia and taking them to Moscow."

"Fourth and final point, the missing weapons. From the few Basque contacts that Liu identified, other smaller caches of weapons have been recovered since his death. But not all. The good news is all the surface-to-surface and surface-to air missiles, Russkiy Sokol mini drones and rocket launchers have been accounted for."

Daan turned to Yolina. "Final thoughts?"

"I reiterate Daan's comment regarding our mandate. We are here to protect the European Union from all threats. We take direct action to eliminate all internal threats and liaise with other jurisdictions to handle external threats. If you ever have any doubt about the extent to which some individuals will go to undermine the European Union, I repeat Daan's comment: just remember Camilla and Sophia who paid the ultimate price. Bravo Zulu to all." She knew in her own mind that Alicia would grow into the role when she had first agreed with Daan's request to re-hire her.

That confidence was solidified after their conversation at Fort de Queuleu regarding the violent fate of their respective family members.

"One tangential benefit from this file," Daan added, "we have cultivated a Russian détente diplomat who believes there is greater benefit in warming East/West relations than maintaining the century-old Stalinist deep freeze."

Daan whispered to Alicia as the meeting adjourned. "I have mulled over the intelligence from our new Moscow détente contact regarding Jane's loyalty." He paused with a pensive frown. "I share your apprehension. I just don't know, and that causes me considerable grief."

Alicia held his wary gaze. "Thanks for your candid support of my suspicions." She knew Jane had played backgammon with her father in the study of the Pemberton Estate. Out of tradition, he had always selected the dark brown ebony pieces. It was in that tunnel the envelope had been hidden. Had her father suspected Jane and played games with her, while knowing the documents were hidden within her reach? Had Jane ever discovered the cache? If so, had she passed on the alarming details and implications of its content to colleagues of other political persuasions or, like Liu, been an intelligence entrepreneur and sold them for profit to the highest bidder?

In retrospect, Alicia had always held back on trusting anyone completely. Even her best school chums she never did fully trust. It was just the way she was, raised to question. Not surprisingly, she always held reservations about Jane. She was her father's acquaintance and colleague, not her own. She felt a similar reservation about Tatyana, and Yusuf to a lesser degree. They were acquaintances and colleagues of Alexandra and Paul and Daan, not her own. She would make extra efforts to get to know Tatyana and Yusuf better. That was her motivation to rent the refurbished Pemberton Estate house to them. It would be a cover to engage in conversations that mattered under the guise of a landlord-tenant relationship. Most importantly what they might reveal in those casual discussions would be more telling. Statistically, research could only purport 99.98 percent, never 100 percent confidence.

"Always assume that the other side knows. It's safer that way," her father's sage words resonated in her mind. She missed those conversations with her Yoda but knew he would have been pleased with her deductive reasoning. Perhaps that was his final test for her to accomplish before graduation *cum laude*, as an agent of the tradecraft. It certainly required that she exercise all the physical, mental, spiritual, emotional, cultural and intellectual skills he had passed along. "Do or do not, there is no try," Yoda, the Star Wars Jedi master, had said to Luke Skywalker.

Daan pondered: *Were we dealing with one case that involved armaments and high explosives being supplied to a select group of individuals who were pretending to be Basque separatists but who were somehow connected to a furtive MI6 file hidden in a tunnel? Or were these two cases connected only through coincidence, yet linked to Alicia via her father? A moot point for now.*

Alicia gazed in silence at his absent expression, replete with knowledge gained from experience that cannot be taught in a classroom. Words unsaid had more power at that moment. Like Daan, she would file it under the category of outstanding unresolved but not forgotten.

"Looking for a long-term residence in the EU?" Daan enquired as they sauntered away. He remained occupied with questions not yet asked and answers not yet heard.

"I've had my house in Victoria refurbished and rented to two of our semi-retired colleagues. So, in response to your question, yes, I am looking for accommodation, perhaps the Benelux region. Once I get settled, I'll decide what to do with the cremated remains of Camilla and Sophia."

Daan smiled and held her gaze in support of the wisdom of Zeus. Time does help in the healing process, in addition to support from close friends.

In her mind's eye, the images of their faces appeared as the voice of Joan Baez resonated: *"May you stay forever young, may you stay forever young."* Music is the most cursive form of language and language the most expressive form of culture.

Sophia would dance as a flower child of the sixties would have done when Alicia played her Joan Baez tunes. Camilla would watch from a distance, bobbing her head to the beat of that culture, her anxiety mitigated by both the melody and the lyrics.

"As always, your thoughts are welcome as to where I should start my search for suitable accommodation, preferably close to everywhere and distant from nowhere," Alicia replied to Daan.

She remained acutely aware of the duplicitous currency of security and intelligence; nothing exists without context. More importantly, intelligence and context were askew on the periphery of espionage where there were truths, partial truths and make-believe truths. Such were the defining characteristics of the arcane game with its intoxicating charm and deceptive addiction.

– F I N –

Manufactured by Amazon.ca
Acheson, AB

10409575R00164